I0645687

Darke Paranormal Investigations

DARKE MUSIC

ROSANNA LEO

Darke Music
ISBN # 978-1-80250-535-1
©Copyright Rosanna Leo 2023
Cover Art by Kelly Martin ©Copyright May 2023
Interior text design by Claire Siemaszkiewicz
Totally Bound Publishing

DARKE MUSIC

Dedication

For my sons, Daniel and Andrew. You continue to inspire me and I couldn't be prouder of you.

Acknowledgements

I am so grateful for the team at Totally Bound Publishing, not only for bringing my stories to readers but for constantly seeking ways to innovate and for finding new reader platforms. I love working with you all.

Thank you so much to my editor, Rebecca Baker. Rebecca, I appreciate that your door is always open and that you've always been willing to flesh out ideas and share your enthusiasm. I'm so lucky I get to work with you!

I'd like to offer huge thanks to artist Kelly Martin for creating another beautiful cover. Your art leaves me in awe every single time. Once again, you have brought my characters and setting to life.

I was fortunate to have several author friends read an early version of *Darke Music*, and I am grateful for their input and their kindness. I urge you all to read their excellent books. Thank you, Ellen Mint, Karla Kratovil, Jemi Fraser and Sara Ohlin. I appreciate you all very much.

Author's Note

As in *Darke Passion*, book one of this series, *Darke Music* is a blend of real history, real locations and imagination. The Asch Institute of Opera is inspired by a building that sits in Toronto's downtown, at 273 Bloor Street West. It is the Royal Conservatory of Music. Not only does it represent over a century of Toronto history, it has played a part in my own history.

Many years ago, I first entered the Royal Conservatory of Music for a piano exam. I remember feeling very small in the grand old building and having a sense that many others had come before me. I had the opportunity to revisit the RCM years later when I embarked on my classical singing education and it still left me awestruck.

Just like my fictional school, the RCM building dates from 1881 and eventually became a part of the University of Toronto. The RCM occupied the building in 1936 and remains there. It has played a huge role in educating Toronto's young people in the wonders of music.

My own Asch Institute is actually an amalgamation of the current RCM and its predecessor, the Toronto Conservatory of Music. The conservatory was founded in 1886 in a different location at Dundas and Yonge Streets, and it addressed the growing city's need for music education. It was founded by conductor and musician Edward Fisher, on whom my character Victor Asch is loosely based.

My character Melba Flanagan was also inspired by a real person. The extraordinary Marion Ferguson was the first registrar of the Toronto Conservatory of Music and she worked closely with Fisher. Author Ezra Schabas has written an excellent history of the RCM. According to him, Marion had come to Toronto to study music but after meeting Fisher and his wife, was persuaded to take on the role of registrar/secretary. Schabas detailed that Marion was a tremendous asset to the school, serving under three directors. She worked there for fifty years and was beloved by students and staff alike. After reading about this incredible woman, I knew I had to give her a role in my story.

They say the RCM building is haunted. Voices have been heard telling people to get out. There is apparently a spirit man who will appear to staff on occasion and he can sometimes be seen looking out a particular window. However, most of the ghost stories take place near the central staircase, where the ghost of a Victorian man in top hat and tails can sometimes be seen rushing around.

The basement practice rooms were based on a feature of another building. I attended the University of Toronto's Faculty of Music for classical singing. In the Edward Johnson Building, where the faculty is housed, there is a basement hallway lined with rooms that the students use for practice and warmup before classes. Every single time I descended to those rooms, I felt eyes at my back. Although I'm not aware of any ghost stories connected to the area, I wouldn't be surprised if someone discovered one.

While at the Faculty of Music, I had a wonderful teacher named Henriette Asch. A former opera singer, she taught singing for many years at the university, and her kindness to me cannot be overstated. Working with her at the time was Victor McCorry, a musical coach who always made me laugh and who taught me not to take myself too seriously. Because of the impact they had on my life, I named Victor Asch in their honor.

Prologue

Toronto, 2002

As the subway pulled into St. George station, Luca Brizzi's shoulders began to tense under his backpack straps. He gripped the rail, staring straight ahead at the ugly green tiles on the wall until his vision started to blur. The train stopped with a lurch. On a sigh, he piled out of the car with the other commuters and headed toward the stairs. He kept to the right on the staircase, making room for the suits who wanted to sprint to work.

Even though Luca knew he should be in a hurry, he couldn't seem to make his feet move any faster. Bracing himself, he trudged up the last few steps and exited onto St. George Street. The bright sun hit him in the face. He squinted, imagining himself on a hot beach, anywhere but here.

The Asch Institute of Opera loomed, a city block away. Despite how hard Luca had worked to get into the esteemed opera school, he'd always hated the building itself. The massive red brick and stone structure reminded him of a stern Victorian schoolteacher just waiting to rap its next pupil on the knuckles. It was the Ebenezer Scrooge of architecture.

He had to perform for Professor Kraus today, and he would suck. He already knew it, as well as he knew his own voice.

He *used* to know his own voice, the gift that had allowed him to enter the school this past September on a full scholarship. His mom had always told him his voice would take him places. "A beautiful tenor like yours, Luca," she would say, "only comes around once in a generation. You're destined for the opera."

It was the kind of voice that used to solicit hushed accolades from astounded professors. A warm, mellow tone that had caused other students at the school to make way for Luca as he walked down the halls. A true gift, his vocal coach had told him again and again, and one not to be wasted.

But Luca had quickly discovered it was the kind of gift that could isolate its owner too. He'd felt the jealous stares of other students boring into his back and had already lost a couple of friends.

At least he still had Noah and Blake.

Noah Bellamy and Blake Campbell were the only ones who ever wanted to hang out with him anymore. Fellow tenors, both really talented, they understood the pressure. In fact, they had also been identified as potential stars of the opera program. They were Luca's best friends and they'd had his back several times when others had made catty comments. The three guys often joked that one day they'd create their own tenor supergroup and have millions of fans around the world.

But lately, Luca had been struggling. Vocally, he just couldn't seem to make things click. His grades had begun to suffer too. He'd barely passed his last written assignment. To top it all off, he just hadn't been feeling very good.

Luca's professors, the ones who'd been so quick to label him a future star early in the school year, kept pushing him and pushing him. Every time he walked into the Asch now, he was hit with this enormous pressure. It came out of nowhere and overwhelmed him. It had definitely taken a toll on his singing. Over the last few weeks, he'd seen his own spark, his own enjoyment of the craft, disappear, and he didn't know how to recapture it. Life at school was slowly draining him.

Luca reached the entrance of the Asch Institute. The imposing entrance archway beckoned—a gaping mouth ready to swallow him whole. As he glanced up at the numerous front-facing windows, he could imagine the faces of students from long ago, warning him away.

Run, Luca. Don't ever come back.

He brought a trembling hand to his moist brow. This place, it was stressing him out. Even now, his heart tripped into an uncomfortable rhythm.

Just get it together. You're Luca Brizzi, for fuck's sake. You're going to be the greatest tenor Canada has ever known, maybe even the world. People will remember your name long after you're gone.

He was just going through a rough patch. He could do this.

In thirty minutes, he would stand in one of the building's classrooms and perform for Kraus and the rest of his German diction class. That meant he still had some time to warm up and practice.

Seizing a deep breath, Luca walked up the entrance steps, and opened the door. Once inside the foyer, he turned automatically to rub the bronze statue of Victor Asch, the school's first director. Standing just inside the door, the statue faced the main stairway. Luca had always liked the look of Dr. Asch. With his jaunty top hat and cane, the old Victorian man seemed friendlier, somehow, than the building that now carried his name. Every student that had come through those doors had rubbed the hand holding the cane, and now Asch's knuckles gleamed from decades of superstitious polishing.

"I could use your help today, sir," Luca whispered.

They said that Victor Asch haunted the building. People had seen an elderly man wearing Victorian clothes and a top hat, one who would disappear immediately afterward. Some even heard the *click click click* of his cane on the hardwood floors when the conservatory was quiet and still. The stories had always freaked Luca out, but old man Asch was supposed to be a friendly ghost.

During their orientation the first week of school, someone had said Asch's wife haunted the building too. They called her the Gray Lady because her long gray skirt trailed on the hardwood floors. Luca was sure there were other ghosts too. There were too many stories of whispers in empty halls and doors slamming when no one was around. Students had been locked in rooms over the years. Hell, Luca had been locked in rooms a couple of times. The whole place had a creepy vibe about it, and Luca was always relieved to leave at the end of the day.

He hurried downstairs to the basement warren of practice rooms. This part of the building was cramped and dreary as shit, but it served a purpose. About twenty small practice rooms lined the long hallway. Students could reserve the rooms for private practice. It wasn't unusual to walk that corridor and hear numerous voices coming from behind the closed doors as students rehearsed.

Today, for some reason, it was silent.

Strange. It's normally busy at this time of day.

Luca had reserved the room at the far end. His footsteps echoed as he walked down the hall, giving the impression someone was following just behind. A quick glance over his shoulder confirmed he was alone.

The lights flickered, making him jump. "Stupid old building. Would it kill them to fix the lights?"

He got to his practice room, shut the door behind him with a bit too much force and tossed his backpack to the floor. An old upright piano sat against the wall. He flipped up the fallboard, exposing the keys.

All alone in that little room, the pressure upon Luca mounted. His mom said it was "just a bit of anxiety." A bit. Right. Then why did it always feel as if the school itself was closing in on him, trying to tell him he wasn't good enough? And why did it always seem worse whenever he walked into the goddamn practice rooms?

Maybe he wasn't cut out for the stage at all. If he couldn't get through his schoolwork without freaking out regularly, how would he ever get through grueling opera auditions, never mind actual performances? Maybe he should stick to something that wasn't in the public eye—a nice nine-to-five job behind a desk. He could still sing in the shower.

To rouse him out of his funk, he hit middle C on the keyboard. With the note in mind, he faced the small mirror on the wall. Each room had a mirror to help the students keep an eye on their posture and facial tension.

Luca sent a silent prayer into the universe. *Please help me. I need to be perfect.*

In the mirror, a stranger's face appeared over his right shoulder. Luca's body temperature plummeted, chilling him through. Even though he was seized by fear, he couldn't look away.

Two penetrating eyes claimed his attention. The man smiled. *"Of course, I'll help you, dear boy. I've been waiting for you."*

Chapter One

Toronto, present day

Noah: *Hey. I know it's last minute, but are you free for dinner tonight? My treat. There's something really important that I need to discuss with you.*

Susannah Darke sat at the Italian restaurant bar and read the text for the umpteenth time that day. It wasn't unusual for her to get texts from Noah Bellamy, her favorite hookup. It was just that most of them consisted of raunchy invitations to, well, hook up.

She wasn't opposed to the messages being raunchy either. God only knew she'd sent her share of eggplant emojis to Noah. It was their thing.

They'd met about a year ago at a soul-sucking group dating event. After ingesting a couple of limp spring rolls and some very cheap wine while dodging guys who wanted to regale her with their thoughts on cryptocurrency, she'd spotted Noah across the room. He was handsome and looked bored, and she'd recognized a kindred spirit of sorts in the way he'd clutched his wineglass as if it were a life preserver. Feeling in need of her own lifeline just then, she'd cut through the crowd toward him.

A pleasant conversation had ensued, one in which they'd realized neither of them actually wanted to be there. Susannah had only agreed to attend the event because her sisters had egged her on, saying she worked too much and had no social life. Completely true, of course, but it didn't dispel her loathing of awkward group events. As for Noah, he'd attended with a friend who didn't want to be on his own.

She'd gone home with Noah for the first time that night, and they'd discovered they were really good in the sack together. Devastatingly good, in fact. Equally beneficial was the fact that neither of them wanted anything more than that.

As a result, their text conversations tended to be short, succinct and peppered with rude depictions of fruit, vegetables and little devil faces. She got a thrill every time she received one.

But this felt different.

She and Noah didn't "go out to dinner." They didn't "discuss important things." Heck, sometimes they barely had any conversation at all. They met when they had a particular need, one that involved an hour or two of mindless fornication.

What on earth could he want?

What if, after a year of happily messing up her sheets and ruining her best panties, he was no longer happy with their arrangement? She would hate to lose what they had. It worked so well.

Had he met someone else? It wasn't out of the realm of possibility that Noah might fall in love and want to settle down. He was a great catch. Although he'd always made it clear he was on the same page she was, and that he guarded his single status.

Or was it the alternative? For a fleeting moment, Susannah teased herself into thinking Noah might want something more...with her. A tingle shot up her spine. What if Noah Bellamy, her hot hookup buddy, wanted her, *all* of her?

Surely not.

Would she even want that?

Surely not.

The bartender approached and took her order, returning shortly with a white wine. As he handed it to her, his fingers brushed against hers and he smiled. He was cute, and his attentions weren't unwelcome, but Noah would be there shortly. Even though Susannah was nowhere near being exclusive with Noah, she wasn't in the mood to encourage anyone else. She thanked the bartender and concentrated on her phone.

Within minutes, Noah arrived. He stepped into her space, resting a hand on her lower back. Again, not unwelcome at all. "Hey, you." He leaned over and dropped a kiss on her cheek. Lingering there, he whispered, "Thanks for coming."

Susannah sucked in a breath. A flutter of delight rippled under her ribs. "Hey. I was surprised to get your message."

One side of his mouth quirked up. "I know, right? Not a single eggplant emoji in sight." His gaze dipped to take in her outfit, an intimate acknowledgment of all the sexy times they'd had together. "You look gorgeous, as always."

"Thank you." Confused and curious about his invitation, she'd made an effort to look nice, and had changed from her jeans and T-shirt into a slinky black dress that cinched at the waist. She checked out his perfectly tailored navy suit and impeccable dress shoes. Every time she saw him, he seemed to have a new pair. These ones, gray Oxfords, shone as if a butler had spent half a day polishing them. Noah liked fancy shoes even more than she did. His style sense, combined with his short black curls and strong jaw, made for a devastating combination. "You're looking pretty good yourself."

"Thanks." He picked up her wineglass and grabbed her hand. "Come on. I've got a table."

As he led her through the restaurant, several heads turned his way. She understood his allure. It wasn't even that he was handsome in a high fashion model kind of way. He had what some might consider imperfections. His nose was crooked enough to make one think he liked a bit of mischief. He had some mild scarring on his cheeks — probably old acne scars — and his thick eyebrows tended to give him an air of severity, even anger sometimes.

But Susannah had seen him break into huge smiles, and she knew a cheeky sense of humor hid beneath his intimidating exterior. She'd seen him cursing at the arrival of a shattering orgasm and had witnessed the transformative beauty of that moment. She'd heard him talk about the students at his school with pride and awe, and nothing would ever convince her he was less than stunning.

Uh, Susannah. Remember your boundaries? He's your fuck buddy, not your soulmate.

Besides, she still didn't know the reason behind this unusual social call.

If only she'd gathered her thoughts a bit better. If Noah did indeed want to take their relationship to the next level, she would have to let him down gently but firmly. She wasn't interested in having a partner or a husband, or even a boyfriend. She was happy on her own. At thirty-four, she'd seen enough of the dating scene and its miseries to know it wasn't for her.

As for the marriage scene…well, she only needed to look at her circle of friends for a stark reminder of how badly that could go.

All Susannah needed was for someone to help her with her sexual needs every so often. If Noah was no longer up for the job, she'd find someone else. Although it would make her sad to lose him.

Really sad, come to think of it.

When they got to the table, a booth tucked into the far corner of the restaurant, he set down her wineglass and they sat across from one another. A server arrived, told them about the specials, and took Noah's drink order. As soon as the server was gone, Susannah turned to Noah in anticipation. "My curiosity is killing me."

"That's what I love about you, Susannah. You hate small talk as much as I do."

"It's not that I hate it." If anyone else were currently sitting across from her, she'd have no problem indulging in some chatter about the weather or what she'd had for lunch that day. But this was Noah, and they usually got straight to the point. "I don't want you to think I don't care about how your day went. I guess that's just never been our style."

He paused, mysteries swimming in his dark eyes. "I care too. I hope you know that." He reached for her hand. A hint of a smile tickled his lips again, and her heart swelled in response. "That being said, how was your day?"

"Fine, thanks. I'm about to finish writing a new article for *Ontario's History*. It's about the role of the rebel Canadian Volunteers during the War of 1812, and the impact their traitorous actions had on their communities."

"Sounds fascinating."

"I hope so. I was inspired to dig a little deeper when we had that case in Niagara." Susannah liked the eclectic nature of her work. She was a regular contributor to a couple of historical periodicals on Canadian history, which kept things fresh and exciting. She supplemented that work with some lecturing at centers for adult learning and even at different universities from time to time. "And, of course, things are busy as usual on the DPI front. My sisters and I are getting ready to debrief a couple of clients, and we're in the midst of scheduling the next ones."

As much as she loved her writing and teaching work, Darke Paranormal Investigations had become her true passion. Along with her sisters Edwina and Adelaide, Susannah investigated sites that were reputed to be haunted, and the three of them had made a name for themselves on their YouTube channel. Each investigation was the basis for a new episode. Their subscriptions had exploded about a year ago when they'd uploaded the footage from the King Street Bed and Breakfast in Niagara-on-the-Lake. Not only had they discovered the source of the paranormal activity, they'd unearthed the remains of an early Canadian military hero. Since then, the Darke sisters had been fielding calls from TV producers and people who wanted to take them to haunted locations around the world, but the sisters weren't interested in relinquishing control over their investigations. They agreed they wanted to retain the focus on Canadian sites and Canadian history.

"Actually," said Noah, "DPI is the reason I reached out to you today. Do you think you could squeeze me into your busy schedule? I need your help."

Icy shivers raced down her spine. Susannah leaned in. Knowing what Noah did for a living, she'd been wondering if this day might come.

Noah was the dean of the Asch Institute of Opera, a prestigious school that coached young singers who were destined for careers in operatic performance. Some of them had already attended the nearby University of Toronto's Faculty of Music, and they went on to do an intensive performance-driven program at the Asch. It had nurtured many young stars, and its list of alumni was impressive.

Susannah had been inside the building before, but not for many years. The place had made an indelible impression on her, and not necessarily in a good way. Even though a part of her never wanted to revisit the Asch Institute, a more significant part of her wanted to investigate it and debunk its stories. Debunking her own experiences there would be even better. "Tell me everything."

The server returned to the table with Noah's beer and asked to take their orders. They both realized neither of them had even looked at the menu yet, so they just ordered two of the pasta specials.

Once they were alone again, Susannah pulled a small notebook and a pen out of her bag. "Do you mind if I take notes?"

"I figured you would. Things have been…unsettled at the Asch for a long time now. But lately, I've seen it affect my students in a big way."

"To be clear, you believe the Asch Institute of Opera is haunted?"

"I was a student there. I know it's haunted, but it feels like it's escalated. In the past, I wasn't in a position to do anything about it. Now I am."

"What kind of phenomena are we talking about?"

23

Darke Music

"Items are thrown around the classrooms, things like chalk and sheet music. Music stands are knocked over when no one is nearby. There are footsteps in empty hallways, disembodied voices, doors slamming, that kind of thing. Worst of all, some students claim they've been locked in rooms from the outside."

"Any apparitions?"

"I've never seen any, but there are plenty of accounts. People have seen a man in a top hat and cane. Dr. Victor Asch, presumably. There have been lots of shadow figures too. Oh, and there's one everyone calls the Gray Lady."

"Right." Susannah scrawled those details down as quickly as she could. "I'm familiar with the story of Dr. Asch. His wife died on the school property. I understand she fell down the stairs. I always used to hear that he haunted the building, searching for his lost love."

"Well, if that's the case, it's not as romantic as it sounds. It's become very distracting. I'm worried about one of our students, actually. She's our star mezzo-soprano. Her name's Ava Choi. When you look into her eyes lately, she's just not there. She began the school year with so much promise, and now she seems to be wasting away."

"I don't like the sound of that."

"No. I've talked to her several times, to see if she's having problems in other areas of her life, but she swears she isn't. She has lots of friends, but I haven't seen her with them for some time. She spends hours in the basement practice rooms. We can't seem to pry her away from them. She's even missed a few classes. I just can't shake the sensation that something is wrong, and it's something I can't see."

24

"My sister Edwina would say we should look at the most reasonable conclusion first. Ava could be dealing with stress. She's chosen a demanding career. Maybe she's not cut out for the opera."

Noah shook his head. "You should see her perform. She was born for this. Besides, it doesn't change the fact that the other students are freaked out too. These aren't little kids, either. They're young adults. The conversations in the hallways are wild. All they do is talk about the haunting."

"It is one of Toronto's famous urban legends."

"I get it, and I'm sure every creaky Victorian building has its stories. But this is my old school, and these are my students. I want them to be safe."

The server returned with two steaming pasta specials. Susannah and Noah tucked in, and he shared a couple of the accounts of students getting locked in the practice rooms, despite the fact that there were no locks on the doors. Because those rooms were located in the basement of the Asch Institute, it had to have been a scary experience for them. Whether or not the phenomenon was truly paranormal, Susannah didn't like the idea that Noah's students felt uncomfortable in their place of learning.

She understood that feeling, and all too well. When Susannah had been about ten years old, she'd taken some private piano lessons at the Asch. At the time, it had housed a different music school that offered Saturday lessons for beginners. She'd studied there for about a year, until she'd had her own brush with the paranormal within its walls. The experience had changed her, and in ways that still haunted her.

"What do you think?" Noah twirled a length of fettuccine around his fork. "Does it sound like the kind of case that might interest you and your sisters?"

Susannah didn't even need to consult with Edwina and Adelaide to know they'd be interested. In fact, ever since she'd spilled the beans about sleeping with Noah, they'd been asking her to finagle an invitation to investigate the Asch Institute.

What she really needed to decide was whether or not *she* could take on this case. As a kid, she'd tucked her frightening moments at the Asch into a deep pocket of her soul. Even now, she didn't like thinking about them.

Perhaps it was time to face the beast. If she took the case, there would hardly be a choice. She knew how these things worked. If she started exploring the building, even for someone else, those disturbing memories would resurface whether she wanted them to or not.

Could she turn Noah down? Sure. They had plenty of cases awaiting their attention.

It just didn't feel right, though. She considered his students, in particular his star mezzo-soprano. It sounded as if Ava had a bright future in opera. She didn't deserve to lose it because some faded wraiths insisted on clinging to a structure they knew in life.

If anything, Susannah and her sisters were in the best position to help. "I can speak for my sisters. We'll take the case."

"Great. How soon can you come?"

"Oh gosh. That bad, huh?"

He nodded.

"Noah, I haven't done any prep. I mean, I know a bit about the history, but not enough for the purposes of a full-scale investigation. I don't like going in unarmed."

"We have a library at the school. I can get you access to whatever you need. Would that help?"

His eager expression caused a wibble-wobble in her stomach. She couldn't disappoint him. "Tell you what. I'll book a time for a walk-through so we can get the lay of the land. I just need to check with Edwina. She's the one with the theater job in Niagara-on-the-Lake, so we have to work around her schedule. In the meantime, I'll start gathering some information."

"That would be awesome."

"Of course." Susannah's face heated upon seeing him brighten. "I don't want to leave you in the lurch. Paranormal activity can be upsetting, even at the best of times."

"You're the greatest, Susannah. Thank you." He glanced down the hallway leading toward the restrooms. "Excuse me. I'll be right back."

While Noah visited the restroom, Susannah called her sister Edwina.

Edwina picked up right away. "Hey, Suz."

"Hey. You won't believe the case I just snagged for us. Noah wants us to come to the Asch Institute."

"Get out!" A muffled shriek of excitement accompanied Edwina's exclamation. "We finally get to dig through the scary place where you took piano lessons as a kid?"

"Yup."

"Wait. Are you okay to go back there?"

"Sure. The place always creeped me out, but this is a paranormal investigator's dream. It's an iconic example of old Toronto architecture, and it's bound to have all sorts of dark corners and secrets." Another series of shivers assaulted her backbone, but she rolled her shoulders to ease them. If only a good stretch could eliminate the sudden ache in her stomach. "This is a chance to uncover the truth behind the Asch. I'd be foolish not to take it."

"As long as you're sure. Wow. I have to tell Addy right away."

"Addy's there with you?"

"Yeah. I had some questions about the whole mediumship thing, so she came out to Niagara-on-the-Lake to have dinner with Simon and me."

"Oh." The tenderness in her stomach turned into full-on cramps.

"She's just the only one I can talk to about this stuff. Hang on. I'll be a sec."

Stricken by a sudden case of FOMO, Susannah cleared her throat. She knew her sisters wouldn't purposely try to exclude her. They just had things to talk about, things to which she couldn't relate.

A couple of important developments had happened during their investigation at the King Street Bed and Breakfast. Firstly, Edwina had fallen in love with Simon, one of the property owners. Secondly, Edwina had learned she was a medium, a gift she shared with their younger sister, Adelaide. Because Adelaide had been talking to dead people all her life, she was able to help Edwina with the strange transition.

Susannah didn't have any unusual gifts, unless one counted the ability to talk for hours on end about early Canadian social history. Now, after months of conversations to which she couldn't really contribute, she was feeling left out. Suddenly, after a lifetime of being especially close to her sisters, it seemed she had less in common with them. Twinges of jealousy tore through her whenever one of them brought up their unique bond.

Susannah listened as Edwina shared the news with Adelaide. When Edwina got back on the phone, Susannah didn't really feel like chatting anymore. "Listen, Noah's on his way back. Could you just text me your availability for the next few weeks? I'll talk to you later."

"Okay." She could almost hear Edwina leering over the phone. "Have fun with Noah." She made a bunch of kissy noises.

Susannah disconnected the call. *See? You're being silly. It's not as if they set out to exclude you.*

And yet, this wasn't the first time they'd hung out without her. It had been happening a lot, and despite her best efforts to let it go, the knowledge triggered the worst of her insecurities.

Noah returned and sat down. "Feel like some dessert? They have amazing cannoli here."

A conversation from Susannah's childhood suddenly popped into her head. When she and her sisters were little, they'd all had to grapple with Adelaide's strange talent. Whenever she would communicate with dead people, Susannah and Edwina had had to deal with the comments and the stares. One of their aunts had tried to console them by saying, *People just don't understand that Addy's special.*

Of course, that hadn't been any consolation at all. And now Edwina was "special" too.

What did that make Susannah?

Don't be childish.

"Did I lose you," asked Noah, "or are you just distracted by the idea of those cannoli?"

"Dessert, right." Feeling untethered after her quick conversation with Edwina and the news that the Asch Institute was still a source of concern, Susannah was consumed by the need to hold on to something.

Someone.

"Hmm." She grabbed Noah's hand and pulled it toward her. Leaning forward on the table, she pressed her breast against his knuckles. "What if I told you I don't want dessert tonight?"

"Oh, yeah?"

"Yeah. I just want you."

Their corner of the restaurant was dimly lit, and no one was looking their way. Noah discreetly brushed his thumbnail across her nipple, over her dress bodice. When he spoke, his voice was hoarse. "That can be arranged." He sat back, hailed the server and quickly paid for their meals. He stood and held out his hand. "Your place or mine?"

They both lived downtown, but Susannah's condo was only a block away. "Mine."

They exited the restaurant and marched down Bloor Street West. Neither of them said a word as they walked north on Bedford Road, toward Prince Arthur Avenue. They remained silent as they entered Susannah's condo building. When they got on the elevator, they had to ride up with a couple of other residents, so they didn't say anything then either.

They arrived on her floor and hurried down the hall to her unit. It was only as she stuck her key into the lock that she noticed the tension in Noah's jaw and the heat in his eyes.

Good. That was how she liked him. Focused, hard and hot. As they shoved her unit door open, his thick eyebrows became a slash of concentrated desire.

Noah closed and locked the unit door for her, then moved her up against her foyer wall. "You're a naughty girl, aren't you?"

In response, Susannah reached under her dress and tugged on her panties. Still in her heels, she slid the silky scrap of fabric down her legs and over her shoes. "I have my moments."

She was about to toss the panties on the floor, but he took them from her hand. His gaze never leaving hers, he shoved the panties in his suit jacket pocket.

"I happen to like those, you know," murmured Susannah, even though she didn't mind him taking them in the slightest.

"You'll get them back. Eventually."

"Looks like you're the one being naughty now."

"Oh, yeah? My behavior's about to get much, much worse." His breath coming hard, Noah dropped to his knees and pushed the bottom half of her dress up toward her waist. With one hand, he urged her thighs apart then slid his fingers between them. "Already wet, huh?" He brought a finger to his mouth and sucked. "Delicious."

He moved one of her legs over his shoulder, buried his face between her legs and licked.

Susannah closed her eyes and dug her fingers into his thick curls. *Yes, this.*

She was already out of sorts after hearing about the phenomena at the Asch Institute, and the weird situation with her sisters just amplified it. This was all she needed. A sexual recalibration. When Noah was between her legs, she forgot everything else. He was her perfect distraction.

They would have a lovely fuck, hopefully up against this very wall, and her emotional slate would be wiped clean.

Perfection.

Only, as her orgasm began to build with wave after wave of heady sensation, Susannah remembered her earlier questions. At the start of the evening, she'd wondered if Noah might ask to take their relationship to the next level, but he hadn't.

He didn't want her, after all.

When the first noises ripped from her throat, they sounded like her usual cries of ecstasy. But something else propelled them, something unsettling and mysterious.

Something that felt an awful lot like disappointment.

Chapter Two

Noah headed home just before midnight. He exited Susannah's building and strolled toward Bloor Street West, not really in any hurry to get home. One of the great things about being in a sexual relationship with Susannah was the fact that they lived so close to each other. His own condo was just a few city blocks away, at the corner of Bloor and Sherbourne Street. It was easy to stumble home after a night out — or a night in, as was their custom.

He always went home afterward, of course, but at one point tonight he'd been tempted to stay. They'd had the light on, and Susannah had been curled up in his arms as they caught their breath. He had stroked his fingers through her blond waves, memorizing the position of each highlight. She'd stirred and yawned, and he'd taken the hint. But for some reason, rolling out of bed to collect his clothes from the floor had felt like an insult.

Sounds like love, big boy. How long are you going to try to deny it?

Noah had a nasty gremlin that lived inside his head, one that loved taunting him about Susannah. He hated that fucking gremlin with all his might.

He wasn't in love with Susannah. He'd just gotten a bit sentimental, that was all.

Pensive, he decided to head south on Philosopher's Walk, the picturesque green space that stretched between the Asch Institute, the Royal Ontario Museum and various buildings connected to the University of Toronto. It was out of his way, and he didn't normally walk along the scenic footpath in the dark, but something drew him there.

Maybe it was because he needed to clear his head. His senses pinged with memories of Susannah. When he breathed in, he still smelled her flowery perfume. When he licked his lips, he tasted her. He couldn't seem to shake the image of her coming apart in his arms. With her long hair draped over a pillow, she took his breath away. And to see her brown eyes lit with an almost feral delight was the most incredible thing in the world. Even a year later, he couldn't get enough of her.

He cursed under his breath.

What was he thinking?

The reason he and Susannah worked was because they didn't get caught up in romantic bullshit. It wasn't that he didn't believe in love, but he had always known marriage and kids weren't in the cards for him, and that was a dealbreaker for a lot of people. His career was his life, and he'd had to explain that to several sexual partners who'd wanted more. Susannah, on the other hand, had been clear from the start that she wasn't interested in anything more than fucking. Frankly, he was at a point in his life where that suited him just fine.

He was lucky to have Susannah because they clicked on every level. They were on the same page, and it would be a terrible idea to allow himself to entertain the thought of something more.

Only he had been, and he hadn't been able to shake this restless yearning.

He wasn't the type to pine for someone the minute he left their presence.

Was he pining? No, he'd know if he were pining. He'd been in that situation before, and it wasn't pretty. Like anyone else, he'd had his heart broken in the past, and he still bore the scars. He had no desire to revisit that shitshow.

This was just...something different.

Annoyed, Noah marched through the Alexandra Gates, the decorative entrance to Philosopher's Walk, and plowed down the dark path. He shoved his hands in his jacket pocket and met with something silky.

Right. He'd taken her panties.

That was something else he'd never done before. He wasn't the sort of person to need a souvenir.

And yet, in that insanely hot moment when she'd slid them down her legs, he'd already known he would pilfer the garment. Even now, he fingered it inside his pocket, and allowed himself to remember how it felt to finger her, and to have her melt on his tongue just moments later.

Imagine how amazing it would be to have that feeling every day.

He huffed, scoffing at his inner voice. The gremlin seemed to love the idea of taunting him with commitment, and with Susannah specifically. It had been planting all kinds of ideas in his head.

It's just sex, he countered. *That's all it's ever been.* Really good sex with a person he liked.

Nonetheless, if he were being honest with himself, he'd admit he'd been thinking of her in ways that weren't even sexual recently. In fact, the other day, he'd woken up from an amazing dream in which they'd had a fun picnic in a park then gone for a walk along the waterfront. They'd laughed and held hands and talked about the future.

Picnics and a waterfront stroll. What was all that about?

It must be the situation at the school stressing me out.

Just then, he walked past the east side of the Asch building. He glanced up at the institution that had become such an important part of his life.

Even though the school was closed at this time of night, one of the third-floor rooms was lit up.

Noah checked his watch. It was ten past twelve. The nighttime cleaning staff would have been long gone by now.

A figure appeared at one of the illuminated windows, its form blacked out because of the light behind it. It stood in profile and he was able to make out a nose, hair and a man's chest. As he peered at the figure, it turned in his direction. Even though Noah couldn't make out any of its facial details, he knew the person was staring at him.

"What the hell?"

Without thinking, spurred onward by his need to keep the school a safe place, Noah raced toward the side entrance of the building. There was an alarm system, and the little red light indicated it was still armed. How was that possible?

Noah was one of the few people who knew the code, of course. He stuck his key in the lock, disarmed the security panel and flicked on the hallway lights.

Taking the stairs two at a time, he headed toward the third floor, turning on other lights as he went. His footsteps echoed in the hallways, making it sound as if someone was running behind him.

He arrived on the third floor, panting from his run. Noah stared down the corridor toward the spot where he'd seen the figure.

At the end of the hall, a dark shadow appeared and walked into the last classroom.

Noah clenched his fists, bracing himself. "Hey! Who's there?"

There was no response.

He looked around for something to use as a weapon, but there was nothing. All he had were his keys, which he held in his fist so that one of them protruded. It might not be much, but if he could get a good swing in, he might be able to knock the guy out.

Slowly, he headed toward the classroom at the end of the hall. There was nowhere the person could have run without Noah seeing. They had to be in that classroom.

As Noah approached, he gave thanks that the light was already turned on. He didn't relish having to stick his arm into a dark room to turn it on. He inhaled sharply, and jumped into the room, shouting his best war cry.

But there was no one there.

No person, no shadows, nothing. Noah was completely alone in the school, as far as he could tell.

His mind raced as he contemplated how he might have gotten things wrong, but he knew he hadn't. Someone had gotten past the security system, had turned on the third-floor lights, and someone had appeared in that window.

He stood still for a moment, listening for retreating footsteps, but heard no such sound.

His stomach turned over as he considered the implications, and the taste of old pasta replaced Susannah's sweet flavor.

"Okay." He took a deep breath. "It's been a long day. You're tired. Go home."

As Noah walked back down the hallway, turning out all the lights, he moved quickly and didn't look back. Swiping at the perspiration on his upper lip, he hurried downstairs. He set the alarm and secured the door, giving it an extra yank to be sure it was locked.

He didn't finish his moonlit stroll through Philosopher's Walk. Instead, he headed back toward the lights of Bloor Street, silently giving thanks for each bright bulb.

"It was an optical illusion," he muttered. "A trick for tired eyes."

No matter how many times he tried to console himself with that thought, he didn't believe it.

Chapter Three

Oh! I remember my time at the Asch Institute of Opera with great fondness. Everyone there was passionate about making beautiful music. You would walk in every morning and be met with such a wonderful clamor. I confess, I never liked being there after the sun went down, though. I always felt as if I was being watched, you know? A friend of mine, a very no-nonsense baritone, once swore up and down that he ran into the famous Gray Lady. Did I ever see her? No, but I will go to my grave insisting that there is a presence at the Asch. There were times when I sensed a sort of darkness, like something was clinging to the shadows. Probably just the ghosts of divas past. Whatever it is, I think it must be drawn to artists. We feel things differently, and maybe on some level, we're more receptive.

1992 Interview with Grace Jackson, soprano with the Canadian Opera Company

"That is one scary-ass building." Edwina readjusted her auburn ponytail and secured it with an elastic.

"I think it's beautiful," said Adelaide, "but it has a strange atmosphere. The closer I get, the more I feel eyes on me. Like, lots of eyes."

Susannah held her tongue as she stood with her sisters on Bloor Street West outside the Asch Institute, the Thursday after her dinner with Noah. They stared up at the imposing edifice, each of them soaking it up in their own way. She was inclined to agree with Edwina. Although it was a magnificent building, it made her skin crawl. Maybe it had something to do with the many front-facing windows. It was hard to shake the sensation of being appraised.

Don't be silly. It was easy to get lost in daydreams about this place, but she had to stick to the facts.

It had been a week of furious activity. Not only had Susannah managed to finish and submit her article, they'd also debriefed their other clients and she'd begun her research on the Asch Institute of Opera.

Built in 1881, it had been designed by the well-known Toronto architecture firm, Berry, Berry & Horne. In its early days, it was known as the Toronto Conservatory of Music. Back then, it had been one of the growing city's largest and most impressive buildings. The four stories were richly ornamented with decorative brickwork, rock-faced masonry and projecting bays. The oldest part of the structure faced Bloor Street West, with a couple of newer additions tucked behind it. Despite its symmetry, there was something eclectic and rambling about it. Susannah had always felt as if it was the sort of building one could disappear into, and she'd always wondered if the Messrs. Berry, Berry and Horne had tucked a few secret rooms into their creation.

Just walking up to the entrance caused goosepimples to erupt all over her skin.

It doesn't have to be scary. It's just a pile of stone and bricks.

Whatever you're feeling, put it away.

Normally, when they embarked on a new case, Susannah and Edwina would scope out the location first and gather any preliminary tidbits of information that they could. Because Adelaide was a professional medium, she typically joined them after the fact. She went in cold, with no previous knowledge of the property, so that her observations could be validated for their YouTube audience.

In truth, now that Edwina had come into her own abilities, they had two mediums on the job. Nevertheless, Adelaide still took the lead in matters spiritual. Edwina was in charge of their tech, and Susannah was the resident history geek.

This investigation wouldn't take the same shape as the others. They weren't concerned about capturing ghosts on film, although none of them would refuse the opportunity. In this case, the plan was to quickly debunk the phenomena, or clear the building of any unwanted spirits. The Asch was a busy school and they had to be mindful of the students and staff.

"What do you think?" asked Adelaide as they walked up the steps to the main door.

Edwina cracked a smile. "What I think is I really want to meet the famous Noah Bellamy. He's been sleeping with Susannah for a year now, but neither of them thinks they're in a relationship."

"Right. Not in a relationship." Adelaide's beatific grin twinkled with mischief. "That's why whenever Suz gets a message from him, her face turns ten orgasmic shades of red."

"Must we have this discussion again?" asked Susannah. "I feel like we have it a lot."

"That's because I find this scenario intriguing." Edwina eyed her like an entomologist sizing up a strange new insect. "I'm so excited to meet your fuck buddy."

Susannah shushed her. "We're about to enter a school where Noah happens to be the dean. No fuck buddy talk. Besides, there's nothing wrong with two consenting adults having sex on their own terms, with no other expectations."

"Of course not," agreed Edwina. "More power to you. I just think you really like Noah."

"You haven't even seen us together."

"No, but I've heard you talk about him...at length. I've also heard you talk about *his* length." Edwina elbowed her. "You've never talked about any of your other fuck buddies. Sorry. *Bedtime pals.*"

Susannah didn't have a response to that. Well, she did, but it shouldn't be said on a school campus either.

"She wants to marry him and have his babies," teased Adelaide.

"Ew." Susannah snorted. "As if."

"Do you have something against the holy state of matrimony?" Adelaide persisted.

"Uh, yeah. Remember my friend Paula? Divorced, after four years of wedded bliss. Her husband decided, after impregnating her twice, that his family was 'holding him back from living his life.' Oh, and then there's Rosalind. Her marriage only took a year to crumble. And they're just the most recent ones in my friend group. They're all divorced. Every last one."

"How is Rosalind holding up?" asked Edwina.

"Fine, I think." Susannah frowned as guilt lashed through her. "I haven't been able to catch up with her for a while." She knew she should reach out to

Rosalind, but the last time she had, her friend's pain had literally made her feel sick.

From a young age, Susannah had been labeled as highly sensitive. She felt things keenly, too keenly sometimes. She'd always been hyperaware of changes in her environment and she became stressed in emotional situations. Even evocative smells could set her off, to say nothing of sad movies or beloved books. As a result, she tended to hide her feelings or retreat from circumstances that made her uncomfortable.

It wasn't that she didn't care. She just had to create boundaries and had learned to maintain them for her mental health.

"Look, sometimes it doesn't work out for people," said Edwina, "but it's not as if you don't know of other successful relationships. They do exist. You seem to have a powerful connection to Noah. I know you, and I'd be willing to bet you might regret not exploring that."

"Guess who knows me even better than you do." Susannah pointed at herself. "Me! Now, any other thoughts on my innermost feelings before we do this walk-through? Addy? Anything you'd like to contribute about my hopes, my dreams or my sex life?"

Adelaide bit back a smile and tucked her bobbed brown hair behind her ear.

"Excellent. Let's go." Susannah opened the door to the school. Sometimes she regretted having such an open, honest relationship with her sisters. "Noah said his office is down the hall to the left."

It turned out they didn't need to go any further than the entrance foyer. Noah stood before the main staircase, talking to a student.

Susannah was hit with déjà vu. How many times had she raced up that staircase as a kid, her palms sweating with excitement for her piano lesson? Attending those Saturday morning lessons had been her perfect little escape, something just for her. The old hardwood floor looked the same. It probably still creaked in the same spots.

Noah looked over, noticed the sisters and motioned that he'd be a moment. When his gaze met Susannah's, he broke into a breath-stealing smile.

That smile had been doing things to her lately, puzzling things. Fighting the urge to beam like a delighted child with a lollipop, fresh out of its wrapper, Susannah settled for a demure nod of the head.

Edwina leaned over. "I've seen you with him now, and you're blushing."

"Ed, please."

"There's no shame in it. That is one attractive man."

"Ooh." Adelaide gurgled in her Yoda voice. "His shoes, I like. Pretty, they are."

Susannah quickly checked him out. He wore one of his great suits, a tan one this time. Underneath it, he wore a crisp white T-shirt, instead of a dress shirt. And his shoes were indeed pretty, two-tone Oxfords in a burnished brown leather.

The man knew how to dress.

He knew how to undress too, but that was beside the point.

Susannah couldn't hear what he was saying to the student, but the young man seemed down and was shaking his head. Noah leaned over to look him in the eye and said a few more words. Whatever they were, the student perked up on hearing them. He took a deep breath, nodded and grinned. The student then hurried down the hallway, clutching his backpack. "Thanks, Dean Bellamy."

"You've got this, Zaid." Noah gave him a thumbs-up. "Let me know how the audition goes."

Susannah had heard Noah talk about his students a few times, but she'd never seen him in action. He had a natural warmth that just emanated from him, and he'd really made an impression on Zaid. Even as he headed over to greet the Darke sisters, a couple of girls passed him in the hallway and stopped to offer him an enthusiastic hello.

He was clearly well loved at the Asch, and for some reason, the knowledge made Susannah's throat constrict.

"Susannah, thanks for coming." Noah reached for both of her hands and gave them a quick squeeze, but didn't pull her in for a kiss as he usually did.

Of course, he's not going to kiss you here. He's at work. Calm your tits. "We're happy to be here. Let me introduce you to my sisters. This is Edwina, and this is Adelaide."

"Call me Ed." Edwina shook his hand.

Adelaide did the same. "And I'm Addy."

"It's great to meet you both. I've heard so much about you."

Had he? Susannah couldn't remember if she'd ever told him very much about her sisters. Whenever she met up with Noah, their mouths were usually too busy to talk about family. Still, she must have spat out a couple of tidbits along the way, between frenzied gropes.

"So, this is the famous Asch Institute of Opera." Edwina turned to Susannah. "Does it still look the same as when you had your lessons?"

"Wait." Noah's eyes lit up. "You studied here? You sing?"

Pinpricks of heat burst across Susannah's cheeks. "No, I play the piano. Or, at least, I did when I was younger. I took lessons here, but that was back when the Royal Conservatory of Music was using the building on Saturdays."

"Right. They've rented out the building from time to time." Noah peered at her. "Fascinating. You'll have to play for me some time."

"I don't play anymore. I'd be pretty rusty if I tried."

"Don't let her fool you," Adelaide said. "Our parents still talk about the fact that her teacher used to call her a prodigy. She could have played professionally."

"Wow," said Noah. "Why did you stop playing?"

"Um. You know what it's like when you're a kid. Always a new activity." The old lie tripped so easily from her tongue. She'd almost grown to believe it.

"Well, you've kept that talent hidden." The slight purr in Noah's voice indicated his appreciation for her other, unhidden talents.

"Why don't you show us around?" The pinpricks on Susannah's face turned into all-out flares. "I've been doing some preliminary research. I understand the building went up in 1881."

"Yeah." He continued to stare at her in that unnerving way, like a pet owner who'd just discovered his cat could talk, then shook his head. "From the start, it was connected to the University of Toronto, and for a few years, it operated as the U of T's divinity school. But as Toronto grew and became more cosmopolitan, there was a need for professional music schools. People here wanted what they had in Europe, and early musical leaders addressed the gap. So, in 1886, the focus here changed, and it became known as the Toronto Conservatory of Music. At that time, they taught everything. Piano, voice, theory, you name it.

Dr. Victor Asch was appointed its first director. Because of his contributions, the building was renamed for him after his death." He indicated the bronze statue in the foyer. "The man himself."

Susannah went over to inspect the statue. This portrayal of Asch was of him in his senior years. He'd been sculpted holding his cane, his head lifted toward the horizon in the posture of a visionary.

"By all accounts," continued Noah, "Asch had a good heart, and he was passionate about education. He was well-liked too. I'm sure it didn't hurt that he was charming, handsome and rich, a real society man."

"Must have been a hit at parties," Edwina mused.

"No doubt," agreed Noah, "but he was devoted to his wife, Elodie. Anyway, he wasn't just a pretty boy with easy money. Asch had the chops. He was an accomplished musician and choirmaster, and he'd led several local choral ensembles before taking the position here. Still, his appointment did ruffle a few feathers. Some considered him a young upstart, but he got the job done. Because of his influence, money flooded into the school and it gained an international reputation."

Susannah touched the polished knuckles on the statue. One of her more pleasant memories resurfaced. "I used to rub this for luck when I entered the building."

"It's a long-standing superstition here. If you rub Dr. Asch's knuckles before a performance or an exam, you'll have good luck." Noah grinned. "I used to do it when I studied here too."

"That's right," said Edwina. "Susannah said you're a big-time opera star."

Noah's face darkened. "That's kind, but I don't sing anymore." A staff member walked past them and down the hall. "Sorry, could you give me a second?" He called to the man and pulled him aside for a conversation.

Susannah wasn't sure why Noah would shut the subject down so effectively. He'd never wanted to dwell on his singing career any time she'd brought it up. Of course, she'd Googled him upon meeting him. Noah had been an acclaimed tenor and had sung on stages across Canada, as well as all over the world. She'd seen a couple of clips of his performances and had been blown away by his amazing voice and his stage presence.

She just didn't understand why he treated the topic as taboo.

Granted, she hadn't exactly shared much of her history with him either. He was allowed his secrets.

"Where were we? Oh, right." Noah rejoined them and gestured to the wall next to the entrance. "Now, in the old days, when you entered the school, you would have been greeted by Miss Melba Flanagan. She had her desk here. She was the secretary, registrar and librarian, and everyone connected to the Asch agreed she knew the workings of the school better than anyone else. For all intents and purposes, she ran the place."

Adelaide smirked. "Maybe they should have put her sculpture up in the hallway."

"You're right," said Noah. "She never got enough credit. Victor Asch relied on her in numerous ways though, and the two apparently worked well together. He called her 'My Melly.'"

"Did he?" Edwina raised her eyebrows.

"No funny business, just a lot of mutual respect," said Noah. "When Asch hired her, it was her first real job. She ended up staying for fifty years. That's how much this place meant to her. By the way, Susannah, I have a copy of her memoirs. I can get that to you."

"That would be great." Susannah moved closer to the main staircase. "And this is where Elodie Asch died."

"Yeah." Noah looked up the length of the stairs. "It's sad. Elodie was young when she died, only thirty-nine. My age, actually. She was a formidable woman, a great singer and an accomplished actress. She also taught voice here at the school for a short period of time."

"I read that Victor Asch was never the same after she died," said Susannah. "They seem to have been very much in love."

"That's the story." Noah smiled. "Asch still came to work and did his thing afterward, but it sounds as if his heart wasn't in it anymore. Melba remained at his side, and she became the guiding force here." He clapped his hand on one of the wooden banisters. "Anyway, they say Elodie Asch is one of our ghosts. The Gray Lady. She fell down the stairs and broke her neck. It was a tragic accident. She probably tripped on her long skirt. That hasn't stopped people from spreading all sorts of rumors about her death, of course. The most enduring tale is that someone pushed her, and that she now haunts the place, trying to bring her murderer to justice."

"That would certainly fit the profile of your typical gray lady apparition. Many of those spirits are supposedly women who died violently, or who pine for lost loves, hoping to be reunited." Susannah turned to Adelaide. "You getting any impressions?"

Her younger sister frowned. "Not yet. If Elodie is stuck here, it would make sense that she'd haunt the spot where she died, but I'm not getting anything."

"It's still early," Susannah replied. "I do think it makes sense to focus on Victor and Elodie Asch, as far as my research goes. People have been talking about their ghosts for years. Where there's smoke, there's fire."

Noah continued the tour by leading them down the hall. About twenty feet from the main entrance, Susannah noticed a photo of a young white man on the wall. He had a glorious head of chestnut curls, large brown eyes and a bright smile. There was a small plaque next to it, bearing a name and dates. She touched Noah's arm. "Who's this?"

"Ah. That's our Luca Brizzi memorial. Luca was one of our students. He passed away in 2002." Noah shuffled his feet. "He was my good friend. We were in the opera program at the same time. We were in a lot of the same classes, and we used to hang out after class every day with our other friend, Blake. The terrible trio." His hint of a smile clearly masked an enduring sadness.

Susannah bristled. Despite the fact that her work surrounded her with dead people, she didn't always do well with the subject of dying and she had trouble discussing it when they weren't dealing with long-gone historical figures. Only this was Noah's friend, and she wanted to support him. "I'm sorry. He was so young. What happened to him?"

"We were in class. German Diction with Professor Kraus." There was a faraway look in Noah's eyes. "He'd been fine up until that point. Maybe a little distant in the weeks before he died, but healthy, you know? Then, one day he just collapsed. They told us his heart gave out."

Susannah shot her sisters a look. They'd barely begun the tour, and had already encountered two deaths connected with the property. As difficult as it might be to discuss, they would need to find out more about Luca. She would need to ask Noah some difficult questions. "It must have been traumatic."

"Yeah. I still miss him," said Noah. "And, damn, he had a great voice! Luca could *sing*. Raw talent radiated out of him, but he'd been struggling. He never felt good enough, and yet I was in awe any time he opened his mouth. With a bit more coaching, he could have been another Pavarotti. I'm talking superstar status. His death really rocked the school community. We record a lot of the classes for educational purposes, so we still have clips of his performances in our library. I listen to them sometimes, so I never forget."

He still listened to his dead friend's voice. Susannah's heart hammered in her chest.

Suddenly, she wanted to hug Noah, to pull him close to her chest and stroke her fingers through his curls. But that wasn't something they did, and she didn't want to put him on the spot here at school, so she bit back her bizarre need to nurture.

She was uncomfortable expressing emotion, even around people she knew and loved. Whenever there was a family funeral, for instance, she was usually the person who offered quick condolences then spent the rest of the time in the funeral home coffee room, refilling cups and making sure everyone else had enough tissues. Keeping busy allowed her to block out all those devastating feelings.

But this hit her in a different way and she couldn't shut it out. Maybe it was because Luca looked like such a sweet young man. His expressive eyes were filled with hope, and he had such a cheerful smile. He seemed to be staring right at her, as if willing her to understand his story, to see how he'd been robbed of life.

Then again, maybe it was because she'd glimpsed the remembered pain in Noah's face. His grief was obviously still potent. She could almost taste its bitterness.

She fought the urge to break down, biting her bottom lip until the pain banished every last uncomfortable emotion.

Your emotions aren't appropriate here. You'll upset Noah.

Her sisters meandered down the hallway, but Susannah lingered at the memorial for a moment. In fighting her melancholy, a headache had erupted in her frontal lobe. She put a hand on the wall to steady herself, and massaged her temple, but the pain persisted.

Noah touched her back. "Hey, are you okay?"

"Yes." *Smile.* "Just fine."

"Your hand's shaking."

"Is it?" She held out her hand. *Huh.* Yet another example of her weakness. "Too much coffee this morning, I guess. I'm jittery."

"Right."

"Shall we continue?"

"Sure." A curious expression on his face, he patted her back, his hand lingering there for a few tingly seconds.

Susannah was more grateful for his touch than she would have expected to be. The memorial photo had been a sucker punch to her system.

She couldn't allow him to see her vulnerable again.

Noah continued to show them around the school. He led them to the basement, into a long hallway that housed several practice rooms. Susannah had never seen this part of the building before, and she wasn't sure it was a place she'd want to visit on her own. It wasn't that it looked old or ill-maintained. If anything, the walls sported a fresh coat of white paint, and it was well lit. It was more the fact that it made one feel isolated.

The hall was bordered by a number of individual small rooms. Even now, students practiced in many of them, and different voices could be heard, singing snatches of operatic pieces or exercises. There were pianos in each room so that students could use them to play along or just find their notes. Each door had a small window in it, and as they walked down the hallway, she saw lots of fresh young faces, singing their hearts out.

Adelaide stopped at the end of the corridor and pinched the top of her nose. "I don't feel good here. It's heavy. I can feel pressure bearing down all around me. There are so many feelings of inadequacy and desperation. The loneliness is almost overwhelming."

"That's not how I want our students to feel," said Noah. "Frankly, I've never really liked this basement, but it's well-used. We need a place where students can practice or prepare for exams, and not have to worry about how much noise they're making."

"I'd like to come back here at night." Adelaide glanced over her shoulder. "There's definitely some kind of presence in these rooms, and it's making me uncomfortable."

Susannah was uncomfortable too, but not in a way she was ready to vocalize. It was a cloying sort of dread. Inviting and repulsing at the same time. It throbbed all around her, as if mimicking the rhythm of her headache.

A cluster of tingles gathered at the base of her spine, but she exhaled quietly through her mouth and did her best to shake them off.

They slowly made their way upstairs. Noah showed them the new state-of-the-art theater that had been built in the Asch Institute's modern addition. Light and airy, it was nothing like the older part of the school.

"We have one hundred and thirty students in the opera program," he explained. "Throughout the year, we put on two full-scale productions in the theater. It's great training for the students, and it's well supported by our patrons. Opera has traditionally catered to a rich, white audience. We're working hard to be accessible and inclusive, and we refuse to turn this into a playground for a few privileged students. Instead, we have an aggressive recruiting program in place. We send scouts into the community to listen to church choirs, community theaters and small ensembles. That's how we found Ava Choi, our star mezzo-soprano. She was singing with a local Korean church when we found her."

"That's amazing," said Susannah.

"Yeah, and we have numerous scholarship programs in place to support the students. Most of them study here without paying a cent. People shouldn't have to go into debt for their education."

Warmth spread throughout Susannah's body as she listened to Noah speaking with such passion. He and his staff were helping their students realize their dreams, and in a way that didn't saddle them with future worries. It had taken her years to pay off her student loans, and she would never wish that on another young person.

Noah led them back toward the main staircase. "I'll show you the classrooms."

The moment her feet landed on the first step, making them creak as they had so many years ago, it hit her. An impression of gloom settled around Susannah, even before they arrived on the third floor. Accustomed to paying attention to detail, she listened to the signals her body was relaying. The unease began somewhere deep in her stomach, a slight turning over. It was like the feeling she used to get as a kid on long car rides with their parents. Whenever she sat in the back seat, she'd had to combat the urge to vomit.

She fought it now as well.

Noah showed them the first couple of classrooms, and she managed to keep it together. However, as they moved down the hallway, she could no longer ignore her discomfort. The vague roiling sharpened into spasms and dug into her ribs. "Whoa."

"Are you okay?" asked Edwina.

"Just a weird pain in my gut." As she glanced down the hallway, the cramps tripled in force, and she buckled over again. This time, she fell to her knees.

Noah was at her side in an instant, kneeling next to her, a hand on her arm to support her. "What's happening?"

"I don't know." Grappling with the strain, she lifted her head and looked down the hall, toward the last classroom.

Out of nowhere, an image shot into her brain. It was her, as a young girl, walking down this hallway. Her hair was tucked up into the ponytail she wore throughout her tween years. There was sheet music poking out of her pink backpack. Numerous bangles adorned her thin wrist. "That room at the end of the hall? That's where I had my piano lessons."

Noah glared toward the room. "I've seen a shadow figure up on this floor."

Susannah imagined a dark presence standing at the classroom door, looming over the image of her childhood self. The bagel that she had eaten that morning turned over in her stomach, and dill-flavored bile coated her esophagus. "Need some air."

Noah helped her to her feet and didn't let her go as they walked to the opposite end of the hallway. There was a small elevator there, and they took that down to the main floor. Susannah held her breath the entire time they were in the elevator, for fear of upchucking. Luckily, she managed to keep her bagel down. He spirited her through a side entrance, her sisters following, and they gathered together out on the walkway. It was only as she felt the fresh air on her face that she was able to breathe without being nauseous.

"Better?" asked Edwina.

Susannah nodded. "It just felt a bit close in there."

"I think," said Adelaide, gently, "that maybe you were more worried about coming back here than you thought you'd be."

"Nah, I'm fine." Susannah laughed it off, even though it made her stomach hurt. "It's an old building with some dark corners. We've dealt with worse."

Adelaide looked through the window of the side door. "I wouldn't be so hasty to dismiss this haunting. The word that keeps popping into my head is 'heavy.' I feel weighed down. There's something here, but I can't get it to come forward." She closed her eyes. "Maria, can you help me?"

"Who's Maria?" whispered Noah.

"Addy's spirit guide," replied Edwina. "She, uh, helps us out sometimes. Think of her as our not-so-silent partner."

After a minute or two, Adelaide opened her eyes. "Maria says there are several spirit people here. This building has seen its share of sadness and death." She let out a shaky hum. "But one of the spirit people has dominance over the others. It can influence the living too. She said you need to be careful, Susannah. Whatever this thing is, it seems very interested in you."

"Me?"

"You do have history here," Adelaide reminded her.

As if she could forget.

That was a long time ago. It has no power over you now.

The little girl inside Susannah disagreed, but she swept her away as well.

Adelaide said something else, but as she spoke, Susannah stopped hearing her voice. She could see Adelaide's lips moving, but the conversation simply faded away. Susannah's head began to spin, and she was overcome by the heaviness her sister had described. Struggling to clear it, she glanced up at the third-floor windows. Even though she saw nothing out of the ordinary, a voice sounded, deep in the recesses of her mind.

"How I've missed you, dear one. Shall we play?"

Chapter Four

Noah heard the person before he saw them. Footsteps echoed on the hardwood floor, somewhere down the hall.

Tap, tap, tap.

It was far too late for students to be wandering the halls of the Asch. Come to think of it, it was far too late for Noah to be working, and yet here he sat at his desk. His assistant, Brian, had gone home hours ago and the smaller office outside of Noah's was just as dark as the hallway beyond.

He checked the time on his phone. It was past midnight. How on earth had he lost track of his evening so badly?

Tap, tap, tap.

There was no way any of his students would still be here at this time of night. The noises must just be the building settling.

Get back to work. Only, suddenly Noah couldn't remember what it was he was supposed to be working on. A blank page lay before him on the desk.

Oh, right. He picked up his pen. He wrote a word on the page in big capital letters.

LUCA.

Then he wrote it again, and again. He wrote it so many times that the four letters bled into one another in several places.

There was a creak outside his office. *Tap, tap.* A pause. *Tap.*

It was closer now. Could a staff member have hung back?

A shadow moved in the hallway just inside his assistant's office.

Noah stood and followed. "Excuse me? The building's closed."

The shadow drifted down the hall. Although the hallway was unlit, he could make out the person's shape. It clung to the walls and dipped into the open doorways of the long corridor, a dark mass on the move.

"Hey. You need to leave. You don't belong here."

Upon hearing his words, the person turned back toward him. Or, at least, that was the impression he got as their shoulders shifted.

Something about those shoulders…something about that head of hair. *Curly, curly hair.*

A garbled noise emanated from the stranger. It was as if someone had come up behind him and clapped a hand over his mouth. Something crackled in the air and the lights turned on.

Luca stood there, staring at Noah. Almost everything about him was the same. His slim build. His brown curls. His warm eyes. The Sam Roberts Band T-shirt that he'd been wearing the day he collapsed in Professor Kraus' class.

Luca opened his mouth to scream but no sound came out. Even though Noah couldn't hear it, he knew the silent scream was a warning, and that it was for him.

Noah opened his own mouth to cry out in response, but no sound emerged. The shriek of terror remained in his throat, trapped forever.

His arms flailed at his sides, making contact with something firm. He clutched, and wads of fabric appeared in his fist.

Fabric. Sheets.

Specifically, his favorite steel-gray, eight-hundred thread count sheets.

He was in his bed, not in a dreary hallway at the Asch Institute. He hung his head in his hands, finding moisture all over his brow.

It was just a dream — a horrible one. That hadn't happened since the year Luca died. Back then, after seeing his friend, a healthy young man, just drop in the middle of German class, he'd had a lot of nightmares. Luca had been the first of his friends to die, and it had seemed like something out of a horror movie. Noah had been plagued by nightmares for about a year after that.

But this dream was different. Back in the day, he used to relive Luca's death in his nightmares. It had been a terrible memory, caught in a terrible loop, and Noah had merely been a spectator. In this one, Luca had looked right at him, imploring him to take notice.

Disoriented, Noah wondered at the crack of light under his window blinds. Morning already? He checked the time. It was almost seven.

"Shit." He rubbed his face and forced himself out of bed. On autopilot, he removed his boxer briefs and got into the shower. Without looking at the tap, he fiddled with it until the water was good and hot. He moved directly under the stream and closed his eyes.

Once again, the image of Luca prone on Professor Kraus' classroom floor vaulted into view.

Noah should have done something.

He often tortured himself with that thought, even though he'd known from Luca's glassy stare that nothing would have helped his friend. Besides, the teachers had tried to revive him and they'd been unsuccessful.

Still, Noah wondered.

After showering, he got dressed and shoved two pieces of toast down his throat. He had a packed schedule today. Staying home and moping was not an option.

The Darke sisters had worked a bit of scheduling magic and were free to do something called a night vigil this evening. Susannah had explained that they often worked at night because they believed the veil between this world and the spirit world was thinner then.

Although, if you asked him, he would swear that veil was already pretty fucking thin as it was.

Noah sighed. This was going to be one long-ass day.

* * * *

Noah checked the time. Finally six o'clock. The day had indeed dragged.

He stepped outside for some fresh air and a quick dinner at the noodle place across the street from the school. Carbs and sweet chili sauce would have to get him through the night.

As he ate, he checked his personal emails and sent a text to his mom and dad. They were both big fans of Susannah's YouTube show, and because he'd told them about the investigation, they'd been sending lots of questions his way.

If only they knew their son was sleeping with one of the women of Darke Paranormal Investigations. That, however, was a conversation for another day.

His thoughts had been drifting toward Susannah all day long. He couldn't wait to talk to her, to see how she was feeling after her funny turn at the school last night. Of course, he'd texted her early that morning but her response had done little to reassure him. He glanced at the message again.

Susannah: Hey, no worries! I'm fine.

She was always fine. He'd never known her to be anything other than fine. Even when her hands shook because she was fighting a wave of sadness, she was just fine. Even when she was on the verge of upchucking because some creepy shadow person seemed to have its sights set on her, she was hunky dory.

She might believe she was just dandy, but there was no denying she'd been affected by whatever was stalking the Asch Institute. It had been hard to see, harder than he would have guessed, and all his protective instincts had flared.

Truth be told, he'd lain awake that night, tossing and turning before finally falling asleep and into his own nightmare world. Ever since he'd enlisted the help of the Darke sisters, his sleep had been marred by frightening images. There had already been several times when he'd been tempted to stop what he was doing so he could walk over to her condo to check on her.

She's been investigating the paranormal for years. Relax. Maybe she really is fine.

He couldn't shake Adelaide's warning. *Whatever this thing is, it seems very interested in you.*

Susannah's face had gone white when she'd heard that, although she hadn't said anything. It didn't matter. He could still tell she was rattled. She'd retreated into herself, and her eyes had darkened in confusion.

Hell, he'd been rattled too. He might not know everything about Susannah, but he knew she took most things in stride. Seeing her off her game bothered him, and he certainly didn't want anything bad to happen to her. After feeling the tug of an ominous presence for the past while, it was unpleasant to have his own fears confirmed by what Adelaide had shared.

Whatever this dark entity was, it would have to go through him to get to his students.

And if it even considered terrorizing Susannah, he would...

Visions of violence slammed into his head.

Whoa, guy.

He'd never been the possessive sort, but the mere idea of someone hurting Susannah filled him with the need to wreak vengeance. Biblical-level vengeance.

He returned to the school and waited for the Darkes to arrive. At seven o'clock, he headed toward the main entrance to meet them. Because it was a Friday evening, the school was quieter than on most nights. The perfect time for them to explore and do what they needed to do. There might still be a few students scattered around the school, but for the most part, the building should be fairly empty.

His footsteps echoed as he walked on the old hardwood. As he passed Luca's memorial, everything suddenly felt somber and still. His dream flooded back in frightening Technicolor. He stared at his friend's smiling face, trying to imprint it back onto his memory to replace the unsettling spectacle from his dream. He wanted to remember Luca as he had been in life — happy and hopeful. Noah wasn't much of a praying sort, but he prayed Luca was somewhere beautiful, singing his heart out to an appreciative audience.

Taking a deep breath, he continued down the hall. He passed Dr. Asch's statue, giving its hand a swipe, and headed to the main doors.

Susannah and her sisters stood just outside.

Noah wiped his clammy hands on his pants. Damn, she looked pretty. Her long blond waves were caught up in a bun, high on top of her head, making her neck look like the most kissable place in the world.

You've kissed that neck before, you know. You've kissed a lot of things.

And yet, he couldn't seem to drag his eyes off the dainty column of flesh. He was already imagining himself licking a path between her earlobe and her collarbone. Despite the fact that he already knew the velvety softness of her skin and the flowery scent of her perfume, something about her felt new and exciting. He was consumed with the primal urge to mark her as his own and hide her away from prying eyes.

What the hell?

Enough's enough, dude. Open the door.

He pushed open the door with a bit more force than he'd intended, but the sisters didn't seem to notice. He stepped out under the archway. "Hello, again."

Susannah spun around first. "Noah. Hi."

Something about her crooked smile almost brought him to his knees right there.

Noah had never been the kind of guy to get hung up on looks. He was more interested in a person's charisma, in their spark. Nonetheless, Susannah's beauty always hit him in the gut. She was about five-nine and was taller than her sisters by a few inches. She had delicate features, like some goddess in a Botticelli masterpiece, but there was nothing two-dimensional about her. Curiosity and intelligence shone from her brown eyes and he found it intoxicating.

He opened his mouth to say something witty or interesting, but a strangled laugh popped out instead. He coughed a few times to set his head straight. "You all came back. Your bravery is appreciated."

Edwina slipped past him into the foyer. "We don't scare easily."

"But others have tried," said Adelaide, following.

He was left under the portico with Susannah. "How about you? Are you okay?"

"Of course. My favorite kinds of buildings are the ones that have lots of nooks and crannies, and ghosts of dead grannies."

He chuckled.

"We're tough, Noah. We can take whatever this place wants to dish out." They stood there facing each other, and neither of them moved a muscle. Susannah's gaze dipped as she checked him out. Although her face lit up with interest, her arms hung stiff at her sides. "I hope your day at work was, um, peaceful."

"So far, so good."

"Good. That's...really good." In the moment of silence that followed, she clenched her fists.

Noah knew her tells well enough to know she was holding herself back. She wanted to touch him.

The knowledge filled him with cocky glee because he wanted to touch her too.

Did she need him to make a move? Because he was more than willing to oblige.

With her sisters happily scrutinizing one of the artworks in the foyer, he drew closer to Susannah. She didn't pull away. If anything, she leaned in.

Just a touch.

His hands itching with the need to caress her skin, he wrapped his hand around the back of her neck and pulled her in for a kiss. All he did was brush his lips against hers.

She was the one who opened her mouth and deepened the kiss.

On a soft moan, she flicked her tongue at the corner of his mouth, then slowly traced his lips with her naughty little tongue. Inflamed, he took ownership of her mouth, sliding his tongue deep. Her body relaxed all at once, sagging against his, but then she stiffened.

For a second, he rested his forehead against hers. "I was worried about you."

"Really?"

"Yeah. I didn't like seeing you upset last night."

"Oh. There's no need to worry." Her face colored and the barest hint of a smile curled her lips. But as soon as it appeared, it was gone. She pulled away and ran a finger along the outline of her lip gloss to tidy it.

"I have something for you." He pulled a pair of panties out of his pocket, the ones he'd taken from her the last time they were together. "I washed them. I may be a thief, but I'm a polite thief who knows when to use the delicate cycle." He slipped them into her hand.

She gawked at the wad of silk, as if she'd never expected to get the panties back.

Had she liked knowing he was in possession of one of her most intimate pieces of clothing?

"Right." She shoved them into her bag, her cheeks coloring. "Thanks. We should go in. I'm hoping Addy will make contact with the Asches."

She walked inside, leaving him under the portico. Alone.

Even though his feet were planted on a solid stone step, he had the sense of drifting, floundering. Why did he suddenly feel like a little kid on a school trip who'd been separated from his class?

Susannah hadn't done anything wrong. They'd had a moment, an amazing kiss, and now it was over. They'd had plenty of similar moments that had ended just as abruptly. Why should this one feel any different?

There was nothing uncharacteristic about her behavior, and yet Noah couldn't help bristling from the tiny sting of rejection. It lodged under his skin, its needles pricking his flesh.

There was no reason to feel rejected. It wasn't as if she'd pushed him away.

But she hadn't thrown herself at him, either. And, for some reason, he'd sort of envisioned her doing that, had *wanted* her to do it. Only then did he truly understand how badly he had wanted to wrap her in his arms to make sure she was safe.

What was wrong with him? It wasn't like him to be so needy for affection. Her affection, specifically.

You love her.

Damn the gremlin to hell. It had a lot of warped ideas.

This wasn't about love. Maybe the dream of Luca had messed with his wiring. Grief, even twenty-year-old grief, could do strange things to a person.

No, it was simpler than that. He and Susannah tended to hook up every couple of weeks. He often got squirrely if he didn't see her for a while. That had to be his problem. They just needed to hook up again, to take the edge off.

It wouldn't be tonight, though. Susannah had warned him their night vigils usually took hours, running into the early morning.

Shit. He would need to be patient.

Unfortunately, his last shred of patience had flown away with Susannah's kiss.

Chapter Five

Susannah's nerves grated. The Darke sisters and Noah had been wandering the Asch Institute for a few hours now and hadn't witnessed a single anomaly. Not a single orb had flashed before their eyes. Not a single shadow had darkened the doors. Nothing had struck any of them as particularly uncanny.

Even worse, neither Adelaide nor Edwina had been able to make contact with Victor and Elodie Asch, or any other spirits for that matter. The school was like a bar after last call. It had emptied out.

She knew paranormal investigations could often take time and that results didn't come immediately like they did on all the TV shows. That being said, the Darke sisters had a secret weapon in Adelaide. She could sniff out spirit activity better than a hound dog after a bone.

"I don't get it. For a building that has a reputation for being so active, it just seems, well, dead," Susannah complained. "Is it possible the activity centers on the students? Most of them have gone home for the weekend. Maybe the ghosts aren't interested in performing for us."

Adelaide shook her head. "No, that's not it. There are several entities here. I can feel them watching from a distance, but they don't want to come forward right now. That, or something's preventing them."

"Maybe we should split up," said Edwina. "That might tempt them to talk to us. Addy and I will head upstairs. Suz, you and Noah take the basement. Then we'll meet somewhere in the middle. Keep your walkies on."

Susannah hesitated. She hadn't considered that she might be left alone with Noah during this vigil. He'd been in her thoughts so much lately, and it was starting to agitate her. And of course, there was that surprising kiss at the school entrance tonight. She hadn't planned on it, but he'd looked at her in that smoldering way he often did, and all her sense had flown out of the window. When he'd confessed that he'd been worried about her, making all her synapses fire, she'd almost lost it. In that moment, the only thing she'd been able to do was shove her tongue down his throat. It had taken all her fortitude not to grab him by the collar, throw him to the ground and mount him like a prized pony.

What the hell? Get it together. Remember your boundaries.

She'd hoped her sisters would act as a buffer all night long. Of course, they were only too happy to peel off and leave her to her own horny devices because they seemed to think she had "feelings" for Noah.

Hmmpf.

What did they know?

She'd learned how to master her feelings. Feelings didn't fit into her plan.

It wasn't that she had no emotional intelligence. She just preferred to keep lovers at a reasonable distance. Feelings caused messes, and Susannah couldn't deal with messes. Not in her professional life, not in her home, not in her appearance and certainly not in her relationships.

Love was the messiest thing of all, and she was a mess-free zone, baby. At least, she'd worked hard to become one.

There was a reason people called it "falling in love." It involved falling. Tumbling, plunging, plummeting, splat. No one ever survived the drop from a great height. She didn't want to dash her body on the rocks below.

Noah has always been respectful of your boundaries. There's no reason to believe he might tempt you to cross them.

Only they'd already stuck a toe over the line tonight. When he'd rested his forehead against hers earlier, something had snapped inside her chest. She'd heard it, clear as day. A resounding *thunk*.

Somehow, with a few words of concern, Noah had wrenched open one of the padlocks around her heart. That padlock now dangled there between her ribs, useless.

Geez. A little dramatic, don't you think?

"Susannah?" prodded Noah. "You all right with us splitting up?"

"Yeah, of course. Let's hit the basement." She charged toward the stairs well before any of the others started to move.

Noah caught up to her. "Someone's on a mission."

"I'm just disappointed there's been no activity tonight, that's all."

"I would have thought you'd already had enough to keep you going for a while."

"I'm conscious of the fact that we have limited windows in which to explore." She took the first few steps but stopped about halfway down. "We need to make the best use of our time."

"I appreciate that, but don't stress yourself out on my account." Noah reached for her hand. "The last thing I want is to cause you stress."

God, his hand was so warm, and it made all sorts of ideas float through her head, none of which were appropriate to the situation. Most of them involved taking said hand and positioning it elsewhere on her body. Actually, there were a few places she could think of and each image was more pornographic than the one that came before it.

He leaned in, his gaze focused on her mouth.

She extricated her hand from his. "Noah, let's not."

"Let's not what?"

"You know, extra touches and cuddles and stuff. They muddy the waters."

"And you don't *want* the waters to get muddied, right?"

"No. You don't either. We've talked about this."

He stared at her for a long, uncomfortable moment. "You're right. We have talked about this. I'm sorry. I guess I got carried away for a second."

"It's not just you. I did give you a great big wet kiss earlier. I should have known better, but investigations like these can bring up a lot of...feelings." God, she hated that word.

"Oh, yeah?"

"Yeah. A bit of paranormal activity, and the next thing you know, you're crawling all over the cute guy next to you. It happens. Hell, it happened to my own sister. Anyway, I shouldn't have acted on it. It won't happen again."

"Okay."

"It's important for us to be transparent with each other. I mean, it's not as if we're dating." She let out a strange laugh and continued to babble. "It's not as if I'm about to bring you home to meet my parents."

He blanched.

Maybe that last bit had sounded a tad cold.

Susannah Darke, you know full well your parents would absolutely adore this man. That was beside the point. "Do you understand what I'm saying?"

"Susannah, I get it." There was steel in his tone. "We're not dating. We fuck every so often. We're on the same page, I promise."

Now he sounded cold. "Great."

She took the rest of the stairs and he followed her. When they got to the door leading into the practice room hallway, he pushed it open and held it for her, staring straight ahead rather than at her.

Was it her imagination, or was his smile a little pained?

No, it was just the shadows in the basement. They added strange hollows to his face. Plus, he had dressed casually tonight, and it made him seem more boyish. Instead of one of his killer suits and a sexy pair of dress shoes, he'd worn jeans, a black T-shirt and running shoes.

Maybe that was part of the reason she felt off her game around him. She understood slick, professional Noah, the man who'd always made it clear what he wanted and how he wanted it. This Noah had an air of vulnerability about him, and she didn't know what to make of it.

All she knew was that it appealed to her on a visceral level.

Oh, sheesh.

It was entirely possible that she needed to take a little break from their fornication appointments. They'd been screwing for a year now and had successfully kept all emotions at bay. She and Noah understood each other. They were better off keeping it casual. Susannah didn't want anything more than that. Deep down, she knew Noah didn't either.

Keep it simple.

She could do that, and if Noah faltered for some bizarre reason, she'd just have to set him straight. She couldn't afford to let emotions creep into the deal. A few sweet declarations and she'd turn into a quivering ball of anxiety.

Nope. Not going there, and especially not with Noah.

Unlike their last visit to the basement, the practice room hallway was desolate. All the doors were closed and, aside from a handful of rooms, most of the lights were out. It was the perfect time to try to capture some EVPs.

Susannah pulled out her cell phone and hit the record button. "Hello. Is there anyone here with us? My name is Susannah, and I come here with respect. I'd like to communicate with any spirit people who might be here." She paused and let the recording run. "In particular, I'd like to make contact with Victor Asch and Elodie Asch. Why do you stay in this place? Do you have any messages for us?"

When they heard the woman's voice down the hall, they both took a step back, but they quickly realized the voice had no preternatural origins. It was coming from the practice room at the far end of the floor—a quiet, whimpering sound.

Frowning, Noah charged toward the practice room and looked in the little window. He knocked on the door then opened it. "Ava? Why are you still here?"

It must be Ava Choi, the student he'd mentioned.

Susannah followed and remained behind him. Ava stood before the mirror in the practice room, but she turned to face them. Her face was red, as if she'd been caught doing something underhanded. She was a lovely young woman with long black hair that was shaved around the ear on one side of her head. She was dressed all in black and had a backpack that was decorated with an intriguing variety of decals and buttons that showed her love of everything from BTS to opera to heavy metal. She must be about twenty if she was studying at the Asch Institute, but right now, she seemed younger.

"Hi, Dean Bellamy. I was just practicing."

"It's Friday night. You should be hanging out with your friends."

Ava's gaze darted between them. "Am I in trouble?"

"Not at all," said Noah. "This is my friend, Susannah. She's doing some research on the building. She's a historian."

Susannah stuck out her hand. "Hi, Ava. It's a pleasure to meet you. I hear you're one of the Asch's most promising students."

Ava's face fell as she shook Susannah's hand. "I'm really not."

"You're too hard on yourself," said Noah. "We talked about that, remember?"

Ava's eyes became unfocused. "I need to spend more time practicing. I've wasted too much time with my friends. I won't get ahead unless I focus and work harder."

"Who gave you that feedback?" Noah asked. "Not one of our teachers, I hope."

Ava blinked a few times. "Can I go back to my practicing now?"

"I think you've worked hard enough for today." Noah offered her a gentle smile. "It's time to go home."

"But—"

"Ava, I mean it."

"But if I don't work harder, I'll end up like Luca!" Her whole body shook with a cry.

Noah froze.

"Luca Brizzi?" asked Susannah. "The student who passed away?"

"Who said that to you? A staff member?" said Noah. "It's not appropriate."

"I'm sorry." Ava grabbed her backpack. She raced out of the room and through the door at the end of the hall.

Noah ran a hand through his hair. "Jesus Christ. When I find out who made that comment..."

As she turned to him, Susannah caught her reflection in the practice room mirror.

A hazy face appeared over her shoulder.

She gasped and jumped back.

"What's wrong?" asked Noah.

The image disappeared. "A face. There was a face in the mirror."

"I don't see anything."

A puff of air landed on her neck, right under her ear. Someone hummed a haunting sequence of notes.

That someone was in the room with them.

"Do you hear that?"

"Hear what?"

"Someone's humming."

"Sorry, no."

The noise stopped but the melody lingered in her mind, like a threat delivered on a sigh.

Something dark and dreadful gathered in her peripheral vision but, unable to see the sorts of things her sisters could, she wasn't able to identify it. Just like the previous evening, a sickening sensation assaulted her gut.

"I need to get out of here."

Noah was quick to spirit her away, but it didn't help.

The thing that watched was everywhere.

Chapter Six

When it became evident that the evening would result in no further activity, the Darke sisters decided to pack it in. Noah stood by in the school foyer, feeling helpless. Aside from Susannah sensing a presence in the practice rooms, there had been no other manifestations. Not a single misplaced footstep or ominous banging in an empty room.

Maybe it was for the best. He was still furious Ava had been given such a horrible message, and possibly from someone in a position of authority here at the Asch. Who else could it be? He would be following up with her teachers on Monday morning. It boggled his mind. He knew all of Ava's professors and coaches very well and couldn't even conceive of what might have caused one of them to warn her about ending up like Luca.

The image of a screaming Luca cut across his field of vision. He shook his head to get rid of it.

Also troubling was the fact that Susannah had been very quiet since their run-in with Ava, and she'd been reluctant to talk about what was brewing inside her.

It was just after three in the morning now and he was beat. They'd regrouped by the main entrance. There were dark circles of fatigue under Susannah's eyes, but she paced in agitation. Several long hairs had escaped her bun, and they now draped delicately over her neck. Noah wanted to brush those hairs off her neck and kiss her.

Watch it, buddy. No extra touches and cuddles, right?

She wasn't out of line in insisting on boundaries. Their boundaries were what had made their arrangement last so long.

It still stung, though.

"Addy, I can't believe you didn't pick anything up," said Susannah. "Like, not at all?"

"It can happen." Adelaide zipped up her jacket. "You know what I always say, communicating with the dead isn't an exact science."

Susannah marched over to the main staircase. "What about here, where Elodie Asch died? She's our best candidate for the Gray Lady. Maybe she doesn't realize she's dead. Maybe the rumors are true and someone killed her, and she really is trying to get some justice."

Adelaide shrugged. "I'm not getting anything."

"But you're always on the mark," pressed Susannah. "I mean, you stop strangers on the street to give them messages from the dead all the time."

Adelaide stared, clearly unimpressed with her sister's line of questioning.

Susannah whipped around to face Edwina. "What about you?"

When Edwina shook her head, Susannah huffed.

"What's with the attitude?" asked Edwina. "We can't *make* the spirits appear."

Susannah put a hand on her hip. "I don't know. You guys are the *special* ones who always have the answers. I'm not a medium, so forgive me for feeling a little disappointed that we can't give our client some information."

Geez. Now I'm "the client." Noah's ego shriveled a little more.

"We're supposed to be the paranormal investigators who capture amazing anomalies," Susannah ranted. "The ones who have a direct line to the spirit world. Instead, we've got nothing?"

"You're out of line." Edwina's lips compressed. "Look, we all need to take a break. It's been a long night. Noah, I'm sorry we couldn't get you any results. I have some work to finish up in Niagara-on-the-Lake this week, but we'll find a time when we're all free for another vigil."

"It's okay. I get it."

Susannah let out a bitter laugh and exited the building, shoving the door on her way out.

"Whoa." Noah had never seen her like this.

Edwina apologized again. "I don't know what's gotten into her."

"She told me she saw a face in the practice room mirror, and that she heard humming. She clammed up after that, not that I blame her."

"You didn't see or hear anything?" asked Adelaide.

"No. It must have scared her. I'm sure it hasn't been easy doing this investigation with me, either. She's been acting hot and cold. I get that our history might make things awkward."

"It's not that. Well, maybe a little," said Adelaide. "Look, I wasn't kidding when I said something here is interested in Susannah. I can't see the full picture yet, but it's clear she's been targeted tonight. We'll have to keep an eye on her. This place…it knows she's here."

"What does that even mean?" asked Edwina.

Adelaide squeezed her eyes shut then opened them again. "Every time I feel even a whisper of energy in the Asch, it seems directed at her. I can't explain it any better than that right now. Normally, when spirit people sense me nearby, they flock to me to tell me their stories. But in this place? It's like I'm staring into a pea soup fog."

Edwina sighed. "When she took piano lessons here as a kid, the building freaked her out, but I don't remember her ever saying why. Do you think she encountered something paranormal all those years ago?"

"Wait." Noah's head spun. "Are you suggesting this spirit *remembers* her?"

"I have a feeling that's exactly the case," said Adelaide. "I just need to find a way to tap in and confirm it. Something's been interrupting my connection from the moment I stepped foot on the property. That's partly my fault. I've been pushing myself too much lately, and my abilities suffer when I'm stressed. That being said, I do think we're dealing with a powerful entity."

"Do you think Susannah's in danger?" Noah wasn't sure how he got the question out without barfing.

Adelaide's face was grim. "Honestly? I don't know. What would help is for her to dig deep and tell us everything she remembers about her lessons here.

Maybe, outside this building, we can get her to open up about how she's feeling."

Hmm. Susannah's feelings. Noah had never been privy to them before, and she certainly didn't seem inclined to share them now.

He had to try to chip away at her defenses and get her to talk. He had to push.

Sounds like muddying the waters to me.

What if he pushed her away?

He might lose her altogether in the process, but if it meant she was safe, he'd make the sacrifice and be at peace with it. Her safety was more important than whatever strange feelings were riding him.

"Leave it to me," he said. "I'll check in on her tomorrow. I mean, later today."

Edwina and Adelaide shot him a look.

He could tell what they were thinking. They were worried he was going to fuck with their sister.

"I know Susannah can come off as unfeeling sometimes," cautioned Edwina, "but she's not. Be careful with her. She's softer than she seems."

"You have my word. I won't hurt her." He attempted a laugh, but it sounded pathetic to his own ears. "If anything, she might hurt me."

He traded numbers with her sisters before they headed out of the door, then walked them out.

Susannah sat on the portico steps, hugging her knees.

Something awful had reached inside her and had made her feel all alone.

The realization brought forth an anger in him that he didn't know he possessed. He wanted to walk back through the door, just so he could slam it.

It took everything in him not to sit next to her and pull her into a hug. Instead, he gripped the hand railing until his knuckles smarted. "Good night, Susannah."

She turned back to him, moisture making her eyes shine in the dark. Then the most extraordinary thing happened.

She stood, brushed off her pants and gave her head a little shake. She blinked once and any trace of her tears disappeared. Her face became a beautiful blank slate. With a nod, she turned and walked down the steps with her sisters.

Noah turned back to the Asch, practically seething. Before today, he'd never seen anything resembling a tear in her eyes. Seeing it now shook him to his core, even if it had only been a glimpse.

Something inside the walls of the Asch Institute had caused her sadness, and he would do anything it took to fix it.

However, what was even more disturbing, in a way, was the fact that she'd been unwilling to show him exactly how much the vigil had bothered her. He was in awe of how effectively she'd forced her emotions into submission.

And he needed to get her to open up? He didn't have a hope in hell.

Chapter Seven

From the moment my sister told me a new conservatory of music had opened in Toronto, I had been filled with an anxious sort of excitement. Dr. Victor Asch himself was accepting new students! Mother had procured for me an audition and I was very nervous to play the piano for the esteemed Dr. Asch. However, he made me feel right at home. He asked me about my background and my life in Kingston, and I explained how I assisted my father in his shop with various clerical duties. We talked for some time, and I was surprised he showed such interest in the mundane details of my life. A curious expression on his face, Dr. Asch finally asked me to play. When I was done, he continued to peer at me in the thoughtful way I've come to know.

"Well done, Miss Flanagan. You play well, but I'd like to discuss a different opportunity with you."

Imagine my surprise when Dr. Asch offered me a job at the conservatory! He had need of a secretary and registrar, and he believed I would be ideal for the role. I had never considered such work, but I confess I was intrigued by the possibility of working with him and the rest of the faculty.

Dr. Asch assured me I would fit right in. Me, a girl from the country! I wasn't sure how that would be possible, considering the faculty was comprised of such musical luminaries as Francesco Lombardi and Oscar Préjean. Signor Lombardi had once coached Adelina Patti! As for Monsieur Préjean, he'd taught all over Europe.

Nevertheless, my father constantly told me I had a sharp mind and an insatiable need to learn. Although I enjoyed playing the piano, it didn't fill me with passion. I'd always been a practical sort, and as Dr. Asch toured me around the conservatory, I became more convinced it was a far better situation for me than the rigors of performance.

I began a trial period in the position. I took the minutes at board meetings, I registered students in the appropriate classes, I officiated the first exams and I embarked on organizing the school library. These sorts of tasks gave me the sense of purpose that I had been searching for my entire life, and I so enjoyed getting to know the students. There was nothing I loved more than leaving my small apartment every morning and walking toward the school, wondering what that day would bring. It didn't take long for the Toronto Conservatory of Music to feel like home.

Life and Times: A Memoir by Melba Flanagan.
Registrar, Toronto Conservatory of Music, 1886-1936

She'd been run over by a truck.

At least, that was how Susannah felt on Saturday. Her muscles were sore, her throat was dry and her head pounded out a frustrating beat. She must have been run over by a truck when she wasn't paying attention.

She dragged herself out of bed at noon, even though she could have easily slept for a few more hours. Night vigils didn't usually exhaust her, but something about the vigil at the Asch had depleted her resources. Now, she wanted to retreat to a blanket fort and hide there for a week, with only a pile of salty snacks as her companion.

As she stumbled into the bathroom, she caught her reflection. Bleary eyes stared back. Some of her hair was still up in its bun, but most of it had fallen loose during the night, and the rogue strands hung like limp rags on her shoulders. Obviously, she hadn't bothered to clean up before dropping into bed. *Ugh*. Had she even brushed her teeth?

The night's activities rushed back in a jumble. She hadn't been very nice to her sisters, or to Noah, and there was no excuse for it. The wound sat ragged in her chest.

She'd been on edge all night long. The anxiety had started to build as soon as she'd approached the Asch building. Even as she'd walked up the front steps, she'd been walloped by something foreign and familiar all at once. Whatever it was, it had filled her with volatility. Even though she'd tried her hardest to maintain an even keel, it had burst from her at the end of the vigil.

Susannah had lost control, something she rarely did anymore.

She trudged out of the bathroom and grabbed her cell phone. She hit the Power button. It was at nine percent, another indication of her scattered head space. She never forgot to charge her phone, but that had been an issue as well. After plugging it in, she scrolled through her notifications. There were a couple of messages from her sisters, expressing concern. Guilt swarmed her. She'd have to call them back and apologize for freaking out on them.

Not once had Susannah ever blamed either of them for not connecting with spirits on previous investigations. She understood it wasn't a given.

What had gotten into her?

It was the Asch.

Returning to the school had done bad things to her nerves. Something there had played on her anxiety, making her act out. The kernel of insecurity that she'd been feeling about her sisters had popped and multiplied, spilling out all over the sidewalk. Now, she had to make it better.

There was also a text from Noah, and it had just come through a few minutes ago.

Noah: Hey, you. You're on my mind. It's a beautiful fall day. Feel like going for a walk?

The dam holding back the huge wave of guilt threatened to finally burst. The telltale lump appeared in her throat, but she swallowed it through sheer force of will.

Susannah glanced at her reflection again. Shit. She couldn't let him see her like this. She never let anyone see her like this.

Susannah: I'm not at my best.

Noah: I'd take you at your worst.

The lump returned. *Jesus, Noah.* Did he have to be so sweet?

Humor. What she needed was a good dose of humor to fend off these confusing sentiments.

Susannah: You say that now, but you haven't seen my PJ's. (winky face emoji)

Noah: Oh yeah? What kind of PJ's are we talking about? Silk kimono? French lingerie? Baby doll?

Susannah: The shirt has a picture of a sleeping hedgehog on it.

Noah: Fuck that's hot.

In spite of herself, she managed a laugh.

There. Order was restored. Her pulse was barely racing now. She could do this.

Susannah: Wanna come here instead?

Noah: (smiley face emoji) I'm not far. I'll be there in five, with coffee.

The weight on her chest lessened. He didn't hate her. Good.

She shot off a couple of quick messages to her sisters, apologizing for picking on them and promising to call them soon.

Edwina texted back right away.

Edwina: That's OK but I wanna know who said you're not special…so I can kill them.

Then she included a gif from a horror movie, of some masked villain wielding a knife.

Everyone needed someone in their circle who was willing to bruise heads for them. Edwina had always been that person for her younger sisters.

Adelaide was quick to respond as well, although her approach was different.

Adelaide: Forgiven, you are. Love you, I do.

She added a gif of Yoda dancing. Of course. A day didn't pass in which Adelaide didn't send gifs of Yoda.

Susannah ran to the bathroom and brushed her teeth. She gave her face a good scrub, removing as much of yesterday's makeup as she could, although a thin line of mascara remained under her bottom lashes. Combined with her bloodshot eyes, it was a truly gruesome effect. "Just pretend it's a smoky eye."

She didn't have time to fix her hair or change, and frankly, she didn't have the energy. Although Noah had already seen her in various states of undress, she wished she'd had some time to make herself presentable. She liked looking nice for her partner.

Not that Noah was her partner.

What if he didn't appreciate her in all her hedgehog glory? He was accustomed to seeing her in pretty underthings and outfits that showed off her curves, and she was most comfortable when playing the part of a well-dressed ice queen.

It would make for an interesting test, though. Would he take one look at her and bolt?

Within minutes, there was a knock on the door. She took a big breath and let him in.

Noah, who somehow looked as fresh as a daisy despite their nighttime adventures, smiled and kindly kept his gaze at eye level. He wore a denim jacket, jeans and a T-shirt from a classical music festival, and held a tray laden with two large coffees, sugar packets and creamers. She had a suspicion she'd be having fantasies about this exact moment. Noah in denim, offering her coffee and a shy grin, was an irresistible combination.

"Hey, you." There was a soft tentativeness in his voice. "How did you sleep?"

"Not great. How about you?"

"Not great."

"I'm sorry." She sighed, noticing the dark circles under his eyes for the first time.

"Can I come in?" He held out one of the coffees. "It's fresh and hot."

"Ohmigod, I love you."

His gaze met hers, questioning.

"Who doesn't love coffee, right?" She barked out a laugh and seized the cup. The coffee smelled rich and delicious, and she held the cup close to her chest. "Thanks. Make yourself at home."

Make yourself at home? The last time he was here, he ate you out in this very hallway. He has made himself at home plenty of times, sister. What a ridiculous thing to say.

Noah kicked off his sneakers and walked into the living area. "Where do you want to sit?"

"Love seat's fine." In her living area, she had two matching love seats, opposite each other. She plunked herself down onto one of them, hoping he'd take the other, but he sat next to her instead.

Proximity. Danger!

To make matters worse, he smelled good. Of course, he always smelled good. He wasn't a cologne guy, but his taste in soaps was impeccable. She suspected he bought the fancy bars that one only found at artisan markets and organic shops. His scent always made her want to draw near, to put her nose to that soft spot behind his ear. Today, there was a faint spiciness surrounding him, even a hint of pumpkin. Totally lickable.

What must she smell like? Weariness and denial, probably.

Noah set the coffee tray on the table. "I realized on my way over that I don't even know how you take your coffee, and for some strange reason, that bothered the hell out of me. I feel like I should know these things by now."

"I guess when we have met in restaurants, we've never really stuck around for coffee."

"True." He blushed. His tongue made a slow pass over his bottom lip, as if he were remembering their last encounter. "Anyway, I brought sugar and cream, just in case. How *do* you take it, by the way?"

"Black. One sugar."

"Perfect. I have you covered." He placed a sugar packet and a stir stick in front of her and proceeded to add sugar and cream to his. She took note of exactly how much he added to his cup. One sugar, one cream. As he stirred, he kept his gaze on his cup. "So. Those PJ's."

Susannah grimaced.

"What? They're adorable. And, um, I'm not trying to muddy the waters by saying that."

"I'm a mess. I don't like it but thank you."

"You're allowed to be something other than perfect, Susannah."

She did her best not to roll her eyes, even though his words found a home in her breast. She stirred her drink, wishing she could dissolve along with the sugar, and took one heady sip for courage. "Noah, I'm sorry for being weird yesterday. It was a strangely rough day."

He faced her and rested one arm along the back of the love seat. His shirt sleeve rode up, revealing his nicely toned biceps. "You don't have to apologize. If anything, I'm sorry this has been hard on you."

"The atmosphere at the Asch is...challenging, but that's no excuse for being rude to you and for sending out mixed messages."

"Hey, I know this is strange. Our relationship has pretty much only ever taken place in bed. I know we've had some nice conversations along the way, but this is the most we've ever hung out. It's bound to be tricky. If you need space, I can give you space."

"No, it's just the Asch. As soon as I got there, I felt like I was walking into a hot crater. Everything inside me just bubbled up." She tried to articulate the bizarre feelings ransacking her spirit. "It's like I went to a wedding, a funeral and an amusement park fun house, all in one day. I'm drained. You know it's not like me to wear my heart on my sleeve."

His eyes flashed and he nodded. No emotions. That was the name of their game. He rubbed his chin, drawing her attention to the faint stubble there. "Addy seems to think you were targeted."

"People can be targeted during hauntings. It just hasn't happened to me." Not in a long time, anyway.

"I don't understand what's going on at the school, but I know enough to realize it's powerful. I don't like seeing you sad. If you want to shut down the investigation..."

"No. The thought never crossed my mind. I want to help you and your students." Susannah remembered the fear in Ava Choi's eyes right before she ran out of the practice room. The young woman had been terrified, and Susannah's heart had gone out to her. She would just have to put aside her own fear for a while and stay focused. "I would never forgive myself if I walked away. I've faced lots of scary entities. I can handle the boogeyman of the Asch Institute."

Noah scooted closer on the love seat and touched her shoulder. His fingers felt good through the worn fabric of her PJ shirt. "Your sisters are worried that this *thing* has set its sights on you. I will not put you in danger." He squeezed her shoulder. "I can always call some other paranormal investigator."

His words, and the vehemence behind them, made her heart swell, but she tried not to dwell on it. "And hand this case over to someone else? Hell, no. I want to get to the bottom of this. Besides, we're the best."

"You love what you do, don't you?"

"I really do."

"What is it that attracts you to this sort of thing?"

She shrugged. "I guess my sisters and I all have our own reasons for wanting to hunt down ghosts and their stories. For Ed, it's the thrill of the chase, the chance to capture evidence on camera. Addy does it because she wants to give those lost souls some peace."

"And you?"

She thought about it. "There's a definite allure for someone like me. I'm a historian. I love doing my research and stitching all the threads together, weaving a tapestry of events and people. But it's also a lot simpler than that. Addy says a lot of spirits linger because they have unfinished business, that it torments them. That bothers me. I would want someone to tell my story if I couldn't do it myself. More than anything, I want to give a voice to the forgotten."

Noah stared at her, his lips slightly parted. "That's profound."

"I don't know. It's just the right thing to do. My sisters and I have the tools to help these spirits, so we do. They were people once and they deserve to find peace. Well, most of them, anyway."

"I admire you."

"Thanks. That means a lot to me."

His thumb traced soft circles on her shoulder, even while his gaze strayed. "I've been dreaming of Luca."

"I really am sorry about your friend. Do you want to talk about the dreams?"

"They just started with the investigation. It's like he's trying to tell me something, but he can't. In the dreams, he has no voice. He screams, but no sound comes out."

"Oh my God."

"The students have always speculated that Luca is one of the ghosts in the building." His eyes held a certain darkness, the sort born of fear. "You don't think—"

"No. I'm sure that's not the case." She tried to reassure him, even though she didn't quite believe her own words. Maybe it was best she didn't sugarcoat anything. "But if anything leads us to believe Luca isn't at peace, we'll do our best to help him. I swear to you, Noah."

He nodded, lost in thought. "I thought I'd grieved him, but I'm beginning to wonder if I ever confronted those feelings at all. I probably didn't know how. I mean, I was young too. I remember being sad in the quiet moments, feeling a hole in my life, but I just threw myself into my singing as a coping mechanism. And I remember being scared too, because we never got any closure on how he died. I never believed the bullshit they told us about his heart being weak. I still don't."

"You believe Luca's death was unnatural?"

"He was twenty. I can't help but wonder." He shook his head. "But what do I know?"

"I don't blame you for wondering. I'm here if you ever want to talk it through some more."

He arched an eyebrow. "Won't that muddy the waters?"

Touché. "I think talking's allowed, right?"

"Right." He paused. "Speaking of confronting feelings…"

Susannah stifled a groan.

"Addy thinks there might be a connection between the current haunting and your piano lessons years ago. You mentioned the Asch has always made you uncomfortable. Would you be willing to tell me why?"

She tried to find the words to describe the way the place used to make her feel, *still* made her feel, but none seemed adequate. "The Asch has just always felt *alive* to me, but at first, it was positive. When I started taking piano lessons, I was excited to be there. I was an anxious kid, and those lessons allowed me to step outside myself for half an hour at a time. They gave me something to look forward to. My mom would drop me off, I would race into the building, and stop to say hello to Dr. Asch's statue. I'd give his knuckles a rub and hurry upstairs. I loved music and I realized I was good at it. It was my happy place."

"But something changed?"

"It happened so gradually that I'm not even sure when exactly it started. I began to see things there out of the corner of my eye. Shadow figures, I guess. I was no stranger to ghosts. I've lived with Addy most of my life, and she's been seeing things since she was a baby.

But this was different. It wasn't just some restless soul, trying to share a final message. It was darker."

"That must have been scary for you, especially as a kid."

"It was." The hairs at the back of her neck pricked. "I heard voices too. *One* voice—a man's. It used to whisper in my ear all the time. That's why I freaked out in the practice room after we saw Ava. It was the same voice, Noah. I realize it's been years, but I'd know it anywhere. You don't forget something like that."

His brown eyes blackened. "What did it say?"

Susannah's heart began to palpitate. Just admitting that much filled her with dismay.

She couldn't go back to that place of foreboding. She'd worked very hard through the years to contain and compartmentalize her emotions and could not allow them to overwhelm her. And yet, even now, despite being blocks away from the school, the sensation of heaviness returned.

Change the subject.

No. She had to be honest, if only for the sake of the investigation. It wouldn't serve her to keep secrets, not about this. "It said, 'How I've missed you, dear one. Shall we play?'"

"The fuck?" His grip on her shoulder tightened.

"Look." Words tumbled out of her mouth. "For all I know, I was influenced by my surroundings. Maybe it was just some strange flashback. I think it's best we concentrate on the here and now, and on the facts. Our one aim is to help your students feel safe, and to make the Asch Institute a welcoming place."

He grunted.

"It's fine, Noah."

He gave her a side eye when she said the word *fine*.

Susannah fiddled with the worn hem of her hedgehog shirt, uncomfortable under his scrutiny.

He removed his hand from her shoulder in order to add a bit more creamer to his coffee. It didn't escape her notice that her skin felt cold from the lack of his touch. They drank their coffees in silence, sneaking the odd look at each other.

If there had ever been a moment to open up about her deepest, darkest fears, that was probably it. Susannah wasn't sure the opportunity would come up again.

Would she regret not being completely honest with Noah by not admitting how much the voice frightened her?

Hell, she wasn't even sure she'd been honest with herself about how much her time at the Asch had scarred her, and it had scarred her. Because of it, she'd had to abandon music, something that had given her immense joy and pride.

It's done. Let it go.

For several minutes, neither of them spoke. Susannah fidgeted in her seat, desperate to end the silence. "So, nice weather we're having. Very mild."

Noah aimed his penetrating gaze at her. "I know you feel a need to change the subject, and we can do that, but don't think for one moment that I won't be worrying my ass off about you. And don't think that I don't realize that we just had a conversation about actual emotions."

Her laugh fractured from uneasiness. "Who, us? Never. You and I are as cool as cucumbers."

Only Noah didn't laugh along with her. His gaze narrowed, full of a heat she hadn't seen before, not even in their sexiest moments. It made the hairs on her arms stand at attention. He returned his hand to her shoulder, slipping his fingers under her short sleeve, caressing her skin.

Then it hit her.

She'd allowed Noah to see her, really see her, if only for a moment. He'd also shown her a side of himself that she'd never seen before. Now, he looked at her with total awareness, and it just about knocked her off her perch.

Before this, their relationship had been based on sex, but they'd never had intimacy before.

The slow stroke of his thumb across her skin spoke of knowledge and of understanding.

Unfortunately, she didn't do communions of the heart.

Then why was she suddenly so curious about how it would feel to have him touch her, really touch her, with that same intensity in his eyes? Would it be a game changer?

Tumbling, plunging, plummeting. Splat!

No way, baby.

Her emotions were already all over the place, and it was growing harder to corral them. Adelaide was right. Susannah had underestimated how hard it would be to return to the Asch. The ominous presence was clearly fucking with her, and likely enjoying it too. She couldn't afford to add any other tension to the mix.

Susannah would have to be strong during this investigation, in more ways than one.

Chapter Eight

Elodie Kerr was a flamboyant peacock of a woman, one who captured hearts everywhere she went. She was loud and gregarious, had a flair for comedy and an infectious laugh. The daughter of a leather merchant, she had discovered her talent for drama and music at a young age. When she landed her first starring role at the Grand Opera House in Toronto, it was the start of a successful career. Her audiences couldn't seem to get enough of her.

Victor Asch was in one of those audiences when he first laid eyes on her. He told a friend years later that when he saw Elodie in person for the first time, everyone else simply faded into the background. After admiring her talents in The School for Scandal, a mesmerizing performance of Lady Teazle that inspired him to purchase tickets for several subsequent nights, he finally asked to meet her. Elodie was intrigued and allowed him to visit her in her dressing room after the show. A stately man from an old, moneyed family, Asch was tongue-tied and confessed afterward that he must have made a fool of himself. Elodie, however, was intrigued by his gentle manner and quiet charm. The two were quickly *besotted with each other. Inseparable from that day forward, they married within the year.*

Victor Asch: A Biography by Amy Farnell.

"Thanks, everyone. If Ava shares anything with you about who might have made those comments, let me know right away." Noah stood as the group of teachers exited his office, and followed them to the door, closing it behind them.

He'd messaged Ava's instructors after leaving Susannah's place the other day, and they'd all agreed to gather in his office first thing Monday morning before classes began. They'd all been genuinely shocked to learn someone had said something so vile to her, but they'd been adamant it wasn't them. Of course, there was always the chance one of them might be lying. Ultimately, his job was to ensure Ava's safety. He'd done his best to sniff out any bullshit in the meeting, but there had been no red flags.

He'd have to talk to Ava again and ask her specifically who she meant.

He wandered over to his office window and gazed out toward Bloor Street, stymied. It wasn't long before his mind wandered toward Susannah and her alarming words from the other day.

"How I've missed you, dear one. Shall we play?"

What the actual fuck? He'd barely gotten any sleep since prying the information out of her. Was this haunting more insidious than he'd originally thought?

Did this ghost really have his girlfriend in its sights?

She's not your girlfriend, pal.

True enough, but he couldn't stop fantasizing about it.

"Dammit." He gripped the windowsill and mulled over everything she had shared on Saturday.

He had glimpsed her guard falling. His had fallen too. Admitting he might not have grieved Luca properly? That was something that had never come up before. It had been twenty years. Although Luca had been a close friend, Noah had moved on.

Hadn't he?

He'd had another dream of Luca last night. As in the previous ones, Luca had appeared to him out of nowhere, struggling to cry out, but making no sound. Noah had woken up in a panic, drenched in sweat.

He was probably just dreaming about him because his name had come up during the course of the investigation. That's all.

Still, another of Susannah's comments hung in the air around him like a cloud. *"I want to give a voice to the forgotten."*

Luca hadn't been forgotten. Hundreds of people had attended his funeral. He had a nice memorial photo just outside Noah's office. Any student who spent time at the Asch Institute would hear about Luca and would know his name.

Maybe they hadn't done enough to memorialize him.

Could Noah have done more?

The image of Luca on the floor of Professor Kraus' class haunted him.

Stop it. There was nothing I could have done.

If Luca's spirit was upset at not being remembered, why hadn't he appeared to Noah sooner?

In his heart, he knew the nightmares were connected to the investigation. Stress-induced dreams and nothing more.

His thoughts drifted back to Susannah. When he'd admitted the depth of his admiration for her, he'd been speaking from a place of honesty. There had been something exhilarating in listening to her talk about how much she enjoyed her work and her pursuits with DPI. In fact, goosebumps had risen on his arms. He hadn't felt that sort of awe since the time he'd sung at the Teatro alla Scala in Milan, an experience that had been on his performance bucket list.

Noah had always known how much he loved fucking Susannah. He'd never been in the dark about how much he enjoyed just hanging out with her, but it was a revelation to understand how much he loved talking to her. Every time he saw her nowadays, he hung on her every word.

Because you love her, dipshit.

For Christ's sake. Could the gremlin inside his brain just give him a fucking break?

Truth be told, he'd been starting to align with the gremlin's way of thinking lately. He knew Susannah wanted to maintain a distance, but all his instincts screamed at him to draw her close.

His inner voice continued to taunt him. *You love her, bucko. The sad thing is that she'll never love you. You're a failure, after all.*

That cursed gremlin loved to remind him of his botched singing career and Noah always let it get under his skin, even though he knew he was successful in other ways.

He just hadn't ended up being successful at what mattered most to him, and he'd lost people because of it. Granted, most of those people hadn't been worth keeping, but it had still messed him up.

When the knock sounded on his office door, it startled him out of his daydreams. He opened it. His friend Blake Campbell stood outside, two coffees in his hands.

"Blake! When did you get back in town?"

"Last night." Blake leaned in for a hug, and Noah patted him on the back, so as not to spill the drinks.

"And the first thing you thought of today was bringing me caffeine?"

"I know." Blake handed him a cup as he walked into the office. "I'm far too good to you."

Noah took a grateful sip. "How did you know I needed one?"

"We have a psychic bond. I know how to anticipate your needs."

"How was Edinburgh?"

"Cold and wet, but beautiful as always. The audiences were great." A tenor with the Canadian Opera Company, Blake had recently traveled to Scotland for a touring production of *Giulio Cesare*, a production that had kept him away for a few months. He looked good. He'd grown out his ginger hair, probably because it was under a wig most of the time anyway, and had drawn it back into a short ponytail. His worn jeans and lumberjack shirt gave no hint at the expressive artist underneath.

Noah had missed him. "I'm glad to see you."

"I'm glad to see you too." Blake's smile tightened as he sat down. "But we need to talk."

It was only then that Noah realized how pale Blake was in the face. A freckled redhead, he was pretty much always pale in the face, but not like this. "What's wrong? Are you okay? Is Nando okay?"

"I'm fine. Hubby's fine. I just didn't get any sleep last night."

"Good reunion, I guess?"

"Yeah, but that's not the reason for my lack of sleep. I had this fucked-up nightmare." Blake's voice cracked. "About Luca."

An invisible force sucked all the air out of Noah's lungs. He leaned against his desk.

Back at school, Blake, Noah and Luca had been inseparable. Blake had also been in Professor Kraus' class the day Luca died. He was one of the few people from that time with whom Noah was still close.

"What kind of nightmare?"

"It was bad, like, really bad. He was screaming but there was no—"

"No sound?"

"Jesus. How would you know that? We really do have a psychic bond."

Noah set his coffee down on the desk, so he wouldn't crush the cup. "Actually, I've been having the same dream. Silent screams, like he needs help."

The two men stared at one another, but no matter how long Noah held his friend's gaze, he couldn't find any answers in it.

Noah had been ready to swear that his dreams of Luca were simply the result of an overwrought mind, but that didn't ring true anymore. Not if Blake was having the same dream.

Was Luca really trying to tell them something? Was he…somewhere horrible?

A terrible taste coated the back of his throat.

Needing to unburden himself, Noah spilled the news about the investigation at the Asch, and about the Darke sisters. Blake was immediately interested. After all, he'd also been a student at the Asch and he'd seen some shit too. No one walked away from the Asch Institute a skeptic.

When Noah finished his story, Blake just shook his head. "Why would Luca appear to us now, after all these years?"

"That's what I'm hoping Susannah and her sisters can figure out."

As Blake did a double take, a chunk of his hair came loose from his ponytail. "Oh my God. *The* Susannah. She's one of the famous Darke sisters?"

Noah narrowed his eyes.

"What? You never tell me anything! Oh, this just got good."

"Blake," he said in warning.

"You can't blame me for my curiosity. You throw her name around all the time, but you never told me she's a badass paranormal investigator. That's fucking hot." He grinned. "So, have things ramped up between the two of you?"

"Blake."

"I know, I know! You're very discreet, and I respect that, but you're also my best friend. I think I deserve a few details. The saucier, the better. I've had to listen to you casually dropping her name for a year, Noah, like she's the woman who delivers your mail and not the woman you sleep with. Throw me a bone."

"Susannah is amazing." He rolled his shoulders to ease the tension there. "She's smart and passionate and beautiful...and when I saw tears in her eyes the other day, I was ready to kill someone."

"Oh."

"Listen, it doesn't matter. She wants to keep things casual. *We* want to keep things casual. It just works better this way," he mumbled. "Why ruin a good thing, right?"

God love Blake. He didn't even raise one ginger eyebrow. "Sure thing, bud." He sipped his coffee. "Sounds like you kids know what you're doing, and I'm going to keep my opinions to myself."

"Blake."

"If you're going to keep calling my name, put some oomph into it."

Noah grunted.

"Your grunts might put the fear of God into your students, but they don't work on me. I've known you too long." Blake's blue eyes raked him from top to bottom and back up again, but there was kindness in his appraisal. "I know Colette hurt you."

"Colette? What does my ex have to do with any of this?"

"Like I said, I know she hurt you, and it made you leery of getting back out there again. But it's been a few years now."

"Christ." Noah began to pace. "I don't even think of her anymore. Colette Beauséjour is the last thing on my mind."

Only that wasn't exactly true. Every so often, she popped in, joining the little gremlin in his brain to remind him of his failings.

Désolé, Noah. You've lost your drive, your spark. You're not the same man, and franchement, I liked the old one better.

Another opera singer, Colette had left him during the lowest point of his life. To be fair, he hadn't been very fun to hang around with at the time, but he had promised her it would get better. It did too. *He* got better.

It just took a while.

She hadn't been willing to wait. Colette hadn't been interested in devoting more time to a man who was broken inside. Instead, she'd moved on. As far as he knew, she was performing at the Oper Frankfurt right now.

She'd been right to leave. He'd brought nothing to the table.

Hell, back then, he wouldn't have even known where to find the proverbial table.

"Well, I'm glad to hear it," said Blake. "Just promise me you won't push Susannah away because of what Colette said. At the end of the day, it was her loss, not yours."

"Right."

There was another knock on the door. Noah hurried to answer it, if only to get away from Blake's all-seeing eyes. He yanked on the door.

Susannah stood there, on her own, a large purse slung over her shoulder. Her blond hair was down, tumbling softly about her shoulders. She wore wide-legged pink pants, a thin white sweater and silver ballet flats, and she lit up the hallway better than a ray of sunshine.

For a second, he could only look at her. Heat streaked through his body, warming him from head to toe.

"Susannah." He held the door wide. "Nice surprise. I wasn't expecting you today."

She blushed, her cheeks turning the same color as her pants. "I know. I took a chance on popping in. I was just heading to the reference library, to do some research for the case. I can come back another time." She looked over his shoulder, toward Blake. "You're with someone. I'm sorry."

"No, it's fine." He touched her elbow and encouraged her to join them. "Susannah, this is my good friend, Blake."

Blake stood and pumped her hand, his freckles popping in delight. "I'm so pleased to meet you. I'll probably get in trouble for saying it, but I've heard your name many times."

"You have?"

Noah shot Blake a look that said *Do not go there.*

Blake turned his back on him. "Yes, I have. In fact, Noah was just telling me...how much he appreciates your work on this investigation."

"I'm happy to help. You two met in school, right?"

"Yeah," said Noah. "Blake and I go way back. We trained here together. He's a tenor with the Canadian Opera Company."

She let out a small gasp. "Awesome."

A hot streak of jealousy tore through Noah. He was proud of Blake's success, he really was, but he was aware that Susannah would never gasp like that over him.

"Thanks, but it's not as glamorous as it sounds. I spend most of my time waiting around drafty rehearsal halls, listening to a bunch of insecure people trying to out-squawk each other, and I know because I'm the most insecure squawker of all. What you do is much more exciting."

"It can be, but most of the time, we just hang around drafty old buildings too." She peered at the two of them. "Actually, while you're both here, could I get your opinions on something?" She pulled out her cell phone.

"Did you pick something up?" asked Noah.

"Yeah. I recorded an EVP. Actually, a class-A EVP, if I do say so myself. That means the voice can be clearly heard and hopefully understood by most people. Still, it's a bit staticky at the start, so I missed it on my first listen. Let me turn up the volume. I want to see if you guys can hear what I heard. Seeing as you both have more history here than I do, maybe it will make sense."

She played the audio clip. When the crackling voice came through, Noah's body went cold.

"Are you happy, Father?"

"That was clear to me," said Noah.

"Whoa." Blake shivered. "And the tone. Someone has daddy issues."

"Right? That's what I got from it too. Does that ring a bell for either of you?"

"No," said Noah, "but it's creepy as hell."

"And just like that, I've got material for a whole new set of nightmares." Blake picked up his coffee. "On that happy note, I should go. You teach class soon, don't you, Noah?"

"Yeah, in about fifteen minutes."

"I'm sorry," said Susannah. "I shouldn't keep you either. I just wanted to check in."

"Of course." Noah tried to keep his voice light. "Stay. Please."

Blake made his way to the door. "Susannah, it was lovely meeting you. I fully expect Noah to invite me the next time you two grab a coffee."

"I'd like that."

"Okay, *ciao*." He pointed at Noah. "Think about what I said. And call me. Soon."

"Yes, Blake."

When the office door was closed again, Susannah turned to him. "I like your friend."

"He's a great friend, my best friend, and I think it's safe to say he likes you too." Noah would probably never hear the end of it now. "So, I spoke to the staff members who work with Ava. I don't believe any of them made that comment about Luca. They seemed genuinely surprised when I told them about it."

"Okay."

"Also, a new development. You know how I've been dreaming of Luca? Blake had the same dream last night."

"I see."

"I think Luca's trying to tell us something."

"I think you're right, so we have to find a way to listen." She sighed and dragged her hand along one of the chairs in his office.

He couldn't help noticing her fingernails. Susannah always kept them manicured and polished. Today, they were painted a bright coral color...except for one. Her left pinky finger was bare. All that remained of the polish was tiny chips, and her cuticle was raw. She'd clearly been picking at it. He didn't care whether she polished her nails or not, but that bare pinky unsettled him because it was a symbol of her worry. It was almost as hard to see as her tears.

"You're busy," she said. "I should leave you alone."

"Would you...like to hang out and watch the class?"

"You wouldn't mind?"

"Not at all, and neither will the students. They're performers. They're used to having an audience. Actually, Ava's in the class, and she's on the schedule to sing today. You'll get a chance to hear her."

"I'd love that. I forget sometimes that these students will be gracing stages all over the world some day."

It was something he could never forget, no matter how hard he tried not to concentrate on it, or on what he was missing.

Noah grabbed his office keys and did a quick scan of his desk to make sure he hadn't forgotten anything else he might need. "We're in the theater today. The acoustics there are amazing. Wait till you hear it."

"I didn't realize you taught."

"Most of my day consists of administration and finding ways to improve the quality of education here, but I teach a couple of performance classes too. I like working with the students and it keeps me close to the music." Too close, he would sometimes argue.

"Of course, and I'm sure your students appreciate your input, considering your background is in opera." She paused and seemed to be choosing her words. "It must have been incredible to work in that world."

"Yeah." The familiar ache sliced into Noah's gut. *God.* Would it ever go away?

"You told my sisters you don't sing anymore. Not at all?"

His shoulders bunched up around the old knot of stress at the top of his spine. *Fuck.*

He hadn't had this conversation with many people, and on the rare occasion when he did, it brought up so many bad memories. He generally tried to avoid the topic at all costs.

But this was Susannah, and her brown eyes were full of warmth and caring, and for some reason, he didn't shy away from the subject the way he usually did. "I don't sing anymore because my voice isn't what it used to be. A few years ago, I had what was supposed to be a routine surgery to remove a cyst from my vocal cords. The doctor told me there was a risk I'd be left with scarring and persistent voice problems, but there was also a risk that the cyst would rupture and scar anyway. So, I took my chances with the surgery. It...didn't go well. My voice was damaged to such an extent that it didn't even sound like me anymore. My career in opera literally died overnight."

She stroked his arm. "I'm so sorry. I had no idea. I thought you retired."

"I was in my vocal prime before the procedure. If I hadn't needed the surgery, I could have sung for years to come."

"There was nothing they could do for you?"

"Nah. The doctor told me my voice might come back in time, so I canceled a couple of gigs, citing exhaustion, and took some time off. But the weeks turned into months, and even with all that rest, it never returned. I mean, I can vocalize, but what I was left with is in no way suitable for the demands of opera. If you were to hear me sing now, you would never believe I was a classically trained singer. So I let it be known I was retiring. It was a horrible time. If it hadn't been for Blake, I don't know what I would have done. I couldn't face telling people the truth. I just didn't want to keep rehashing the story. I still had ambitions and roles I wanted to perform, but I had to let those dreams die. I try not to think about them too often, to be honest."

"But could you sing in some other way? You know, choral stuff or even pop music?"

"I trained for the opera," he snapped. "You have no idea how hard I worked, the sacrifices I made."

"I'm sorry. You're right. I have no idea what that's like."

Shit. "No, I'm sorry. I don't mean to jump down your throat. Susannah, you're one of the few people who knows the truth. Blake's been great, but there were others who weren't so great about it. It's been a long time since I talked about it with anyone. I'd appreciate it if you kept it to yourself. It's still a sore spot."

"Of course. I promise." She nibbled her bare pinky finger.

Damn. Now he'd given her more to worry about.

Had he honestly expected he'd feel better for telling her the truth?

Bullshit.

If anything, Noah had hoped his burden might somehow be lessened in confessing to Susannah. Only the opposite had happened. Right now, it bore down on him, a Sisyphean weight, threatening to crush him yet again.

It was all because of the way she was looking at him, as if he was a puppy who'd just been torn from its mother.

You just had to spill it, didn't you? Now, she'll always look at you like that. And you thought there might be a chance at a relationship with this amazing woman? There's pity in her eyes.

He needed to get out of this office. He ran a hand through his hair and let out a huff. "I'd better get to class. I understand if you have other things you'd rather do."

"Not at all. I want to watch you teach. Is that still okay?" She smiled, but it didn't shine the way it usually did, and it caused another pang to cut just under his ribs.

"Yeah, sure." They exited his office and he locked up behind them. As they walked toward the theater, he didn't really know what to say so he kept his focus on the hallway. As for Susannah, she was quiet too. From his peripheral vision, he could see her sneaking glances at him.

More pity, great. Bravo, sport!

He opened the theater door. "Here we are. Have a seat wherever you'd like."

As he started to walk away, she tugged on his arm. "Noah, wait."

"Yeah?"

She glanced toward where his students were sitting, in the front rows of the theater. Some of them glanced back, and she released his arm. "Never mind. Have a good class."

He bounded down the central aisle toward the stage. He had to get away from her. All he could see right now were condolences. They radiated from her, bright and stinging.

He'd never wanted to be the object of anyone's pity, but especially not hers. He should have kept his mouth shut.

Maybe it was only kindness or empathy making her eyes shine. He supposed it was possible, but whatever it was, he couldn't handle it right now.

Abandoning all thoughts of his failed career, Noah forced a smile and greeted the accompanist at the piano. "Elmer, how are you?"

Elmer saluted. "Fine, thanks. You?"

"Just peachy." Noah called out to his class. "Hello, everyone. My friend Susannah will be observing today, so let's show her what we can do. Mr. Rivera, I believe you're up first. I'd like to hear the Donizetti that you've been preparing for our gala night. How's your breathing?"

Max Rivera, one of his young tenors, took the stage. "Much better, I think."

Noah took up a spot at stage left, next to the piano. "I'm sure you'll blow us away. Any time you're ready."

The young man handed some music to Elmer and moved to center stage. He then began "Una furtiva lagrima" from *L'Elisir D'Amore*, an aria Noah had sung many times during his life on stage.

Scenes from that production, and so many others, paraded through his memory. Only his memories were all distorted now, taunting him. On the rare occasions when he permitted himself to remember his experiences onstage, it was like witnessing someone else's triumphs. There had been a few failures along the way too, but for the most part, he'd had an incredible career. It just didn't feel like his anymore.

It never should have ended, not like that, and not so soon.

Max hit a high note, bringing him back to reality. The young man was doing well. He'd obviously been practicing and had absorbed the notes from their previous class.

As Max sang, Noah smiled, full of pride. Even still, his joints threatened to give out. He moved closer to the grand piano and gripped the glossy wood.

Just keep smiling.

Hopefully, it would disguise the waves of regret and envy that slammed into him again and again.

Chapter Nine

"My career in opera literally died overnight."

Susannah's mind was spinning with this information. Upon Googling Noah a year ago, she'd learned of his illustrious career, and the fact that he'd seemingly abandoned it without a second thought. Not once had she considered that it might be because he could no longer sing the way he needed to. After all, there had been no press release, no social media post to that effect.

People changed job paths all the time. She had simply believed that Noah had chosen to pursue another dream, that his passion was mentoring young singers.

Clearly, she'd assumed too much. Susannah had only scraped the surface of Noah's psyche, and suddenly, she wanted to know a lot more.

It had to be hard for him on some level, to be surrounded by music and performers all the time, and not be able to participate. He'd called it a sore spot, but based on his reaction earlier, it had to feel more like a gaping wound.

To make it in opera, Noah would have had to study it for years. How must it feel to dedicate a significant portion of one's life to a craft, only to have it all stolen away by chance? Singing would have been his reason for being, the thing that got him out of bed every morning.

Now it was gone.

If someone told her she could no longer do the things she loved, through no fault of her own, she'd be devastated. Her heart went out to him.

Even now, as Noah listened to the young tenor sing, there was a wistful look on his face, one she'd never seen before. His vulnerability, so open and on display, made her want to rush the stage in order to comfort him. It made her want to demolish her own walls, to bloody her hands as she pried the bricks from the mortar.

The young tenor finished his piece, and Noah was gracious as he gave him some pointers. He complimented the student's work, giving him specifics on what he'd done well and how he'd improved.

The student beamed. These young people wanted to please Noah. He obviously inspired them, even if he couldn't sing along with them.

He inspired Susannah, and in ways she'd never anticipated.

The man came to work every day, surrounded by the music he'd loved and lost, and he put aside his feelings. Somehow, he still found ways to coach and inspire others.

She wasn't sure she could have done the same thing if she'd been in his shoes. It would feel like a slap in the face.

Noah finished with Max, then called on Ava Choi.

The mezzo-soprano took the stage, deep furrows in her brow. She handed some sheet music to the accompanist and moved to center stage.

Noah smiled at her in encouragement. "How are you today, Ava?"

Ava stared into the theater, fixated on the lights, lost in her own world.

"Ava? What have you got for us?"

She jumped. "I'm sorry. I'll be singing 'Dido's Lament'."

The piece, composed by Purcell, was one of Susannah's favorite operatic pieces, and she couldn't wait to hear how Ava interpreted it. The accompanist struck the initial minor chord, notes so simple and beautiful they always caused her skin to prickle in excitement. Ava sang the first line in a voice that was clear and steady. She held back from using a heavy vibrato and the clarity of those first few notes caused Susannah to gasp. They rang through the theater, piercing its silence. Susannah sat forward in her seat, her hand on her open mouth, rapt.

Ava's voice was haunting. There was no other word for it. Listening to her was like entering another world, a warm, luxurious realm that made you forget where you came from. There was such depth to her sound, such layers of emotion. Every other student there looked on in wonder.

But as Ava continued, there was a commotion at the piano. All of a sudden, a sheet of paper flew straight up into the air. It took Susannah a second to realize it was a piece of sheet music. More rustling ensued. The accompanist's eyes widened as other sheets of music took wing, shooting off the rack one by one, then cascading to the ground.

Elmer looked back and forth between Noah and Ava. "I didn't touch them. They just flew off."

Everyone was silent for a few uneasy seconds.

Then, one of the students sitting near Susannah called out, "It's Luca."

There were nods of agreement and murmurs from the other students.

"Settle down, everyone. It's just a draft." Noah collected the sheets and put them back in order. He handed them to Elmer and turned back to Ava. "That was really good. Take a deep breath and start again."

She nodded, and closed her eyes for a moment, regrouping. She glanced at Elmer, giving him the signal to start.

Susannah's senses came to life. She watched, on guard.

Elmer played the opening chord. Ava then sang the first two notes.

Once again, the sheet music launched into the air as if propelled by an invisible force, then fell to the floor.

There was no settling the students this time. Even though Noah asked them to quiet down, they talked nervously among themselves. Susannah couldn't blame them. There was a skittishness in the theater that hadn't been present ten minutes ago. She could feel it oozing from the walls.

Okay, calm down. You've dealt with creepy-crawlies before. See if you can debunk the phenomenon.

From where she was sitting, she couldn't spot any sources of major drafts, no matter how Noah had tried to justify it. No one had been standing next to the accompanist. Elmer certainly hadn't thrown the sheets of music into the air. Why would he? Besides, she had a clear view of his hands, and they'd been on the keyboard the whole time.

Something else was here.

All of a sudden, the ceiling creaked above where Susannah was sitting. The only thing above her was a catwalk, one where technicians could access the lighting.

A second creak followed the first, a heavier one. Susannah craned her neck, wondering if a worker was doing maintenance up there.

A shadowed figure leaned over the catwalk railing.

Her breath caught.

It was too dark up there for her to be able to discern any details, but based on its hunched posture, it seemed to be looking down toward the seating area.

At her.

All at once, an invisible weight landed on her shoulders, as she peered into the dark void that should have been a face. All the emotions she'd struggled to banish on her previous visit overwhelmed her now. *Rage. Hopelessness. So much sadness.* It all manifested at once. A terrible ball of burning despair opened up in her chest, exposing her to anyone who cared to look. Susannah had the urge to cry, to scream and to run, all at the same time. Her skin itched, her hands shook and she wanted to tear at her hair.

"I see you, Susannah Darke. I see everything."

The voice was so clear, as if he spoke over her shoulder, and yet no one else seemed to hear him.

It was him, the presence that had filled her with dread when she was a child. As the entity continued to whisper, terrible thoughts entered her brain. This person knew her, and in a way no one else did. He knew every aspect of her, all the things she hid from others. Her jealousy, her fear and her insecurities. He knew her desperation and every unflattering opinion she'd ever wielded. It was a voice that made her want to abandon everything she'd ever held dear and surrender to nothingness.

"*Let's have some fun.*" All at once, the shadow person turned toward Ava.

No! Her head heavy, Susannah tried to stand to call out to Noah, but she couldn't make her lips work. Her head swam and her heartbeat tripped.

Somehow, in all this, Noah had persuaded Ava to sing again and the young soprano had started her aria a third time. The student began to suffer under the ghost's attention. The further she got into her aria, the more her tone deteriorated. She couldn't hit any of her notes cleanly, and her breathing became stilted. Her beautiful voice turned into something harsh and ugly.

That thing was hurting her.

Whispering words of protection that Adelaide had taught her, Susannah grabbed the seat in front of her and pulled herself to standing.

Dismayed, Ava stopped singing and stifled a cry.

"Ava?" Noah went to her, signaling for Elmer to stop playing. "It's okay. We all have off days."

"It's not that."

"What's wrong, then?"

"I can't," she cried. "Listen to me. I'm not good enough."

Susannah propelled herself out of her aisle and hurried to the stage. She gestured to Noah. "There's something here, affecting her. Up on the catwalk."

They both looked upward, but the shadow figure ran away. Its footsteps echoed above, pounding the boards.

The jarring sounds brought forth startled exclamations from the students.

"It's Dr. Asch."

"Or the Gray Lady!"

"No, it's Luca's ghost again."

"It's not Luca!" Noah's hand came down on the piano, and it echoed throughout the theater, loud and discordant. He took a moment to compose himself. "It's *not* Luca."

Susannah didn't believe it either. She didn't want to believe Luca Brizzi's spirit would wreak havoc on his fellow students.

Then again, what did she really know about Luca, other than he'd been Noah's friend and that he had died young? What if the smiling young man in the photo had somehow become malevolent?

"Everyone, stay here." Noah jumped off the stage and rushed up one of the aisles, toward the back of the theater. He disappeared around a corner, reappearing a few minutes later. As he walked back toward the stage, he caught Susannah's eye. He shook his head. "There's no one there."

Of course not. No one they could see, anyway.

His jaw ticking, Noah addressed the class. "I'm sorry, everyone. Let's finish early today. Keep working on your pieces. I'll see you next week." He then spoke to Elmer for a moment. The harried accompanist collected his things and left.

The students all filed out of the theater, many of them looking over their shoulders.

Rosanna Leo

As Ava began to walk away, Noah stepped toward her. "Ava, I think it's time we talked. Really talked."

The girl paled. "I can't."

Susannah joined them onstage. "Please, Ava. I saw that thing watching you and I know how it makes you feel."

Ava looked her up and down. "How could you possibly know?"

"I promise you, I do." Susannah turned to Noah. "Can the three of us go somewhere else? Preferably *outside* the Asch."

Chapter Ten

With so many brilliant people working at the Toronto Conservatory of Music, it didn't take long for certain personalities to clash. One such clash happened in the latter part of 1888.

Dr. Asch had gathered the faculty together for an announcement. As the others arrived, Dr. Asch pulled me aside. "I suspect my news might stick in a few craws today, Melly. Just you wait and see."

That was when he announced that Mrs. Asch would be joining the faculty as a vocal coach.

I, for one, was eager to have her on board. Dr. Asch had taken me to see a few of her performances at the Grand Opera House, and I was in awe of her considerable talent. However, there were some on the faculty who would be less enthusiastic.

Mrs. Asch often visited her husband at the school, and she had opinions on how certain things could be improved.

Of course, not everyone appreciates women with opinions, especially when they are correct.

When Dr. Asch broke the news, there was a bit of sputtering from Signor Lombardi. He was the eldest member of the teaching staff, and was always most skeptical of anything new.

It was, nevertheless, Monsieur Préjean who uttered the first objection. "But are you quite certain that Mrs. Asch has the…necessary qualifications? I mean no offense, of course."

Dr. Asch's blue eyes glittered with a dare. "No offense taken, my good man. Tell you what. If you have any concerns about Mrs. Asch's qualifications, perhaps you'd like to take it up with the lady herself. I'm sure she'd be thrilled to discuss them with you."

We never heard another complaint from Monsieur Préjean — on that matter, at least.

"What about you, Ambrose?" Dr. Asch aimed his gaze at Mr. Terence Ambrose, a talented young piano teacher. "Have you any concerns?"

But Mr. Ambrose spoke on Mrs. Asch's behalf. "None whatsoever. Mrs. Asch is a remarkable artist and I have no doubt she'll be an excellent instructor. I look forward to comparing notes with her. Personally, I think we ought to have more women on the faculty."

That comment drew a few flustered coughs from Messieurs Lombardi and Préjean.

Mr. Ambrose turned to me and smiled. Stricken with sudden amusement, I had to bite my lip to keep from giggling.

I confess I quite enjoyed working with young Mr. Ambrose. He was a much-needed breath of fresh air.

Life and Times: A Memoir by Melba Flanagan.
Registrar, Toronto Conservatory of Music, 1886-1936

Noah led the women out through the door and charged toward Philosopher's Walk, inhaling deeply to steady his nerves.

He'd lost control back there. A lot had happened back there.

Slow down. Breathe.

The fresh air was already doing him some good, and both Susannah and Ava seemed to calm down the further they got from the Asch. They walked south along the pathway. The leaves on the trees were starting to change, and the green space was now decorated with swathes of gold and red. He loved sitting on the benches in Philosopher's Walk because he could sometimes hear music drifting through the Asch Institute windows, but this time he chose a bench that was not in view of the school.

With the downtown traffic nearby, and students walking up and down the path, it all felt so normal. One could almost forget something very strange was happening in the building he loved.

They took their seats on the bench, with Ava in the middle. Concern was etched all over Susannah's face, and Ava just looked lost. Noah wanted to make it better for both of them. "Are you okay, Ava?"

She pulled a stainless-steel water bottle out of her backpack and took a healthy swig.

Noah would have liked a swig of something too, but not water. He struggled for what to say next but wasn't sure how to begin. This was bound to be one weird-ass conversation.

Whatever was on that catwalk could not have exited the building without him seeing it. Noah had checked the door to the fly room but had found it locked. The shadow figure had simply vanished.

Thankfully, Susannah took charge of the conversation. "Ava, I should introduce myself properly. I'm Susannah Darke, of Darke Paranormal Investigations. I know Noah said I was doing some research here, but there's more to it. My sisters and I are investigating the Asch Institute because we believe there are supernatural forces at work there."

"Wait. Are you the ghost hunters from YouTube? The ones who found that dead army guy in Niagara-on-the-Lake? My cousin showed me that episode. She likes scary shit."

"Yes, we're the ones who found Captain Kingston's remains."

"That was wild."

"We definitely had some wild moments on that case. We've only just begun our investigation at the Asch but it's clear something is haunting your school." Susannah drew closer to Ava. "And you, I think."

Ava shrugged. "Just another day at the Asch."

Noah jumped in. "Ava, what's happening is not normal, not even for the Asch. We want to help you, but in order to do that, we need you to be honest about what you've been seeing or hearing."

"It's Luca's ghost. He's restless, I guess."

Noah was growing weary of people attributing the activity to Luca's ghost. "Is that what you really believe? Because I knew Luca, and I don't believe he would do this."

"I'm sorry." The young woman fiddled with her backpack strap, but the distraction didn't work for long. Her eyes filled with tears. "I need to drop out of school."

"What?" Noah's heart tugged in sympathy, but anger sparked inside him as well. Something had tormented her so badly that she was ready to abandon her education. Even though he wanted to shout in frustration, he schooled his voice into a gentler tone. "Is that what you really want?"

"No, but...I don't know! Maybe it's better that way. For weeks now, I've just felt so unworthy. Like, to the point where my heart wants to break." Ava caught her breath. "I can't sleep. I can't rest. I love my classes. I love singing, more than anything else, but as soon as I get to the Asch, I'm surrounded by all these dark thoughts. That I'll never be good enough. That I'm wasting my time."

"Are those sorts of thoughts normal for you?" asked Susannah. "No judgment, if so. I'm just trying to understand."

Ava let out a strained laugh. "No. I'm actually perky most of the time, but since coming here, it's like I've forgotten how to be happy."

Noah unclenched his fists, unsure when he'd clenched them in the first place. It was possible they'd been tight for weeks. "The last thing I want is for you to feel unhappy here."

Susannah nodded. "Listen, Ava. I know you're nervous to talk about it, but you can trust us. Tell us what's been happening."

"I've been hearing voices." Ava let out a long breath. "It started about a week into the school year. I was in one of the practice rooms by myself, warming up for class. Suddenly, this dude's voice was all around me. It came out of nowhere and scared the shit out of me."

"What did it say?" asked Susannah.

"It said, *'Won't you sing for me, my dear one?'*"
Susannah blanched.

"I freaked out," continued Ava. "I grabbed my stuff and made a run for it. Anyway, later on, I felt so silly. I convinced myself I'd imagined it, so I went back to the practice rooms later that week. But I heard the voice again. This time around, I didn't run. I forced myself to stay put. I think a part of me wanted to see what would happen. And here's the thing. The man, whoever or whatever he is, was really nice to me. He complimented my singing and gave me a few really good pointers, then went away."

"So it didn't start out as a negative entity," said Susannah.

"No, it was like having a coaching session with Dean Bellamy. I felt better afterwards, even though it was super weird."

"But it changed?" asked Noah.

"Yeah." Ava gnawed on her lip. "One day, I went to the practice room before class to warm up. By this point, I'd heard the voice a few times. I expected to hear from him. In a strange way, I even looked forward to it. But that day, the voice was harsh and angry. It told me I had been a disappointment, that I would only ever be a disappointment. It shouted at me and made me feel small. I didn't understand what I'd done wrong, so I decided to leave. But when I tried to open the door, it was locked or stuck or something. I couldn't get out. That's when I saw the face in the mirror. It was a man. He was smiling, but there was something wrong with his eyes. They were dark—too dark, like a sinkhole. I just knew that if I stared too long, I'd fall into those eyes and never find a way to climb back out."

Noah's fingers curled into a fist once again, and he didn't bother to unfurl them. Ava's experience was so similar to Susannah's encounter in the basement. He wanted to go into each practice room and smash all the mirrors.

"I started screaming," said Ava. "I pounded on the door, and luckily another student heard me. He opened it, and was like, 'Dude, it's unlocked.' But it wasn't. I swear I couldn't make it budge."

"We believe you," Noah assured her.

Ava hung her head. "The voice stopped being friendly after that. Sometimes he tells me I need to push myself, to sacrifice everything for my music. Other times, he tells me I'm a fool to pursue my dreams, that I'll never have what it takes. I've tried to ignore it, but it doesn't work. When he speaks, I'm trapped in this horrible whirlwind of negativity. The pressure just bears down all around me. It's like I'm a fish caught on a line. His words...they tug on my cheek. They make me bleed."

Disgust rippled through Noah's gut. Whatever this thing was, it had a hold on her. No wonder Ava had been so distant lately. A grunt formed at the back of his throat, but he swallowed it down.

Ava's hand flopped in her lap. "I have to drop out. I can't deal with it anymore. I practice until I'm hoarse. I've been skipping classes to practice. I stopped seeing my friends. All I do is sing until I'm ready to collapse. I have no life anymore."

Susannah caught Noah's gaze. When she sighed, he knew she'd struggled with the same feelings years ago. Knowing these two brilliant women had suffered the onslaught of this vile entity was enough to make him want to tear the bloody Asch building down to the ground. Something told him it wouldn't fix the problem, though.

Susannah patted Ava's hand. "Ava, this entity has formed some kind of connection to you, but we're going to sever it."

"How?"

"I'm not sure, but we'll find a way." A shadow passed over Susannah's face. "I think that this thing thrives on people's insecurities. And I get it, because I've heard it too."

"You have?" asked Ava.

"Yes. As soon as I walked into the building, it was there in my head. This is an entity that feeds off your exhaustion and your isolation. It latches on and drains you of your spark. It steals your joy."

Ava's nostrils flared. "Why would it do that?"

"It's hard to say," replied Susannah, "but there are hauntings that can cause victims to feel oppression and heaviness. That certainly seems to be what's happening here. My job is to figure out who this person was in life, to find out what made him tick, so we can stop the activity for good."

"Sign me up. What can I do?" asked Ava.

"No." Noah was adamant. "We appreciate that you want to help, but you've been through enough. I don't want you exposed to this thing a second longer."

"But…"

"Dean Bellamy's right," said Susannah. "We need to remove you from this situation and keep you safe. Has the spirit ever manifested for you anywhere other than the school?"

"No, just at school."

"Good. In that case, I think it's best if you take some time away," said Noah. "We can arrange to have you study virtually for a while. I'll set it up."

"That's a great idea," Susannah agreed. "Is that all right with you, Ava?"

"I guess." Ava picked at a hole in her jeans. "I'm already behind in my classes anyway."

Her defeated attitude broke Noah's heart. "Look, Ava. You'll catch up. I need you to understand something. As singers, we're told that our voices are everything, that this box in our throats is our identity. That's why most of us freak out if we have so much as a cold."

"Been there, done that."

"Right?" Noah smiled. "But here's the thing. You're more than just a singer. It took me a while to figure that out, and I still struggle with it sometimes. Please take my word for it that you are so much more than what you do here at the Asch. You deserve a well-rounded life, one full of friends and family and dreams that have nothing to do with music. While you're away, connect with your friends. Grab a coffee with them. Go see a movie. You'll feel better once you start to reclaim those other parts of your life, I promise."

"I do miss my friends." Ava stood. Her posture was straighter than Noah had seen it in weeks.

"Then call them." Susannah handed her a business card. "And if you have any concerns, call me, day or night."

"Okay. I will. Thanks."

The weight that had been bearing down on Noah lightened a bit. He believed Ava would listen to them. She would be safe. He'd do everything in his power to make it so.

They watched as Ava left, making her way toward University Avenue.

Susannah angled her head, looking up at him with a shy smile. "You were very kind to her. Those were some wise words."

"Thanks. I remember what it's like to carry that weight. I'll probably always carry it."

Her smile faded away.

"Susannah, talk to me."

"It was just as Ava described. A man's voice coming out of nowhere, but also from inside me somehow. Every time I heard it, I felt overwhelming stress. It made me feel like I'd be a disappointment to others if I didn't work harder." She shook her head. "I was just a little girl. I internalized those messages. My playing suffered. My teacher told my mom I was distracted all the time. And all along, I felt this severe need to be perfect." Susannah ran the toe of her shoe over a rock. "I still have issues with that, and I'm beginning to think this place might have caused the problem."

"So, you stopped playing the piano."

She nodded. "After a while, I dreaded going to my lessons, and I eventually begged my mom to cancel them. I never touched the piano again. Sometimes, I swear my fingers itch from wanting to caress the keys. That entity took music away from me. I've always wondered what else it might have taken, if I'd stayed."

A terrible churning assaulted Noah's gut. "I remember Luca feeling the same way in the weeks before he died. He stopped hanging out with Blake and me. He never thought he was good enough. It ate away at him."

"I think that's exactly what this thing does. It destroys people from the inside out, to the point where they either walk away or drop." She sighed. "Noah, what if there have been others?"

"We can't have this. The Asch is supposed to be a place of nurturing."

"It can be again, but I need to find out who this spirit person was in life. Ava said the voice started out by sounding supportive and kind. That seems to fit the description of Victor Asch."

"But then it turned angry and mean." Noah didn't buy it. "That wasn't Asch's style at all. Why would he torture the students from his own school?"

"Someone else in the school's history must fit the profile. Something happened here that triggered this particular kind of haunting. In her memoirs, Melba Flanagan mentioned that there was a bit of tension among the teachers when Elodie was hired. She called out two men in particular, Lombardi and Préjean. Do you know much about them?"

"Yeah, they both taught here for years in the early days. But if you're asking whether or not there's anything seedy in their backgrounds or if they had skeletons in their closets, I wouldn't be able to tell you."

"I'm sure I can find out quickly enough." She checked her watch. "Unfortunately, I need to run. I have to do a couple of errands, but I'd like to check out the Asch library tomorrow. I think I've exhausted my other resources."

"I have a few commitments tomorrow morning, but maybe I could join you there at some point?"

"That would be great," said Susannah. "More than anything right now, we need a name. Addy has always said there are spirits who find power in anonymity. It gives them the upper hand. We need to be able to call it out by name and take its power away."

She was so brave, so determined. Noah just wanted to take her home and bundle her in his arms. It was getting harder for him to concentrate on anything that didn't involve Susannah. He cleared his throat. "It's a date, then."

"I'm meeting with my sisters tonight to work out a gameplan for the rest of the investigation. I'll catch them up on what happened today." She stood and straightened out the creases in her outfit. The creases in her forehead remained. "I should go."

"And I should get back." He stood. Unable to stop himself, he reached for her hand. "It's going to be okay."

"I hope so. I don't like what happened in the theater. The entity is clearly not content to hide in the practice rooms anymore."

Noah cupped her cheek. "Listen to me. I'll do anything it takes to keep that bastard away from you and my students. Anything."

Her lips parted.

The temptation to claim them was strong, but he wanted to respect her wishes. Even though it damn well almost took a year off his life, Noah stopped stroking her soft skin, and headed back toward the school.

When he looked back a few seconds later, she was still standing there. She brought her fingers to her cheek, where he had touched her, then she slowly walked away.

Chapter Eleven

Susannah ran around her condo, adjusting the couch cushions and straightening the pile of books on the corner of the coffee table. The books fell into two distinct camps: stories about famous hauntings and romance novels. The former she collected in the name of research and gruesome entertainment, while the latter was a softer sort of escape. Bookmarks of various textures and lengths stuck out from several of the books because depending on her mood, she might start one and finish it some other time.

Of course, there were certain types of books that she just couldn't read because they played havoc with her nervous system. She avoided stories with sad endings, disasters and apocalyptic themes and definitely couldn't endure the ones that involved the deaths of animals. Content warnings were her best friends. Luckily, the romance genre, with its assurance of a "happily ever after," kept her on an even keel. As for ghost stories, despite their morbid subject matter, they still fit into her happy place. Growing up with a ghost whisperer would do that.

She caressed the cover of the romance novel at the top of the pile. The model was dressed as a hunky contractor, and he looked a bit like Noah, thanks to his abundance of black curls.

Everything seemed to remind her of Noah these days.

"I'll do anything it takes to keep that bastard away from you and my students. Anything."

Lit up like a news station chyron, his words wouldn't stop cycling through her mind. Any time she was in Noah's presence these days, she could feel the foundations of her walls shifting. It was a grating sort of noise, mortar grinding into dust, creating holes in her battlements.

Girl, you have got to get a hold of yourself. All this restless yearning is so not appealing. Back to work.

Sighing, Susannah continued to tidy. Tidying helped her think. She couldn't process information when she was surrounded by clutter.

She had to find a way to positively identify the ghosts of the Asch Institute. The school had a wealth of history associated with it, but she had to narrow her scope. What had gone on underneath the surface of the prestigious music school? What kinds of personalities had roamed the halls, and what had they been willing to do to follow their dreams?

Her sisters were due any minute for dinner. She'd already ordered from her favorite Chinese takeout, and the food was warming in the oven. When her sisters buzzed, Susannah let them in.

"Hey." Edwina barreled past her at the door, kicking off her shoes. With astounding speed, she went to the kitchen, grabbed a fork, opened up the oven, speared a chunk of sweet and sour chicken and popped it into her mouth.

"Someone's hungry." Susannah raised an eyebrow.

"What? It was a long drive and there was traffic, so I didn't stop for a snack." Edwina began to pull the other dishes out, setting them on the counter.

Susannah turned to Adelaide, who was still unlacing her Chucks. "Hey."

Adelaide surprised her with a hug. "Hey, you." She gave her a tight squeeze. "You okay?"

"Of course." Something was up. Adelaide was probably being extra nice because the last time Susannah had seen them, she'd flipped out on them. She still felt guilty.

Edwina snuck another piece of chicken. "You mentioned you had updates on the case?"

"Give her a second. We literally just walked through the door." Adelaide patted her belly with the melodramatic air of a Victorian actor. "First, we dine."

Her sisters were such weirdos, but Susannah loved that about them. Of course, if anyone asked them, they'd gleefully inform them she was the oddball with her obsession for obscure historical details and her need for perfect order.

Edwina already had her plate loaded up with food and was eating as she approached the couch.

Susannah narrowed her eyes. "When did you last eat?"

"It's been hours. I'm seriously starving." She tucked into her fried rice and short ribs as Susannah and Adelaide loaded up. "I love my job at the Shaw, but damn, it's been hectic trying to squeeze everything in."

Edwina had been working with the famed Shaw Festival in Niagara-on-the-Lake, doing lighting and effects for one of the popular musical shows. The productions there tended to wind down in the fall, which meant she now had more time to devote to the case.

Adelaide made her living doing readings, and even though she did many, she could schedule them as needed. Susannah handed Adelaide a plate and watched in mild fascination as her younger sister diligently separated out all the items on her plate, so that the meat, vegetables and rice didn't touch each other. She'd been doing that since she was a kid, and it didn't look as if the old habit would ever die.

Adelaide brought her plate to her nose and breathed in the aromas with a dreamy expression. "Sweet and sour. My favorite."

They all got comfortable in the living room. Edwina regaled them with the adventures from her drive. Her home in Niagara-on-the-Lake wasn't exactly far, but depending on the traffic conditions, it could take up to two hours. Like Susannah, Adelaide lived in Toronto. Edwina planned to bunk with Adelaide for the next week or so, so they could concentrate on their investigation at the Asch.

It would be another opportunity for the two of them to get closer and to bond over things she couldn't possibly understand.

Come on now. Ed has stayed with you before. There was no need to keep score.

Still, their unfinished business sat like a barb in her skin.

They chatted about some family news, and the fact that one of their cousins was getting married. That meant there would be a bridal shower soon. Susannah bit back a groan, already dreading having to sit in a room with a bunch of near strangers, oohing and aahing over toasters and frying pans.

She fidgeted in her seat and braced herself for the moment when her sisters would inevitably launch a volley of questions her way, ones specifically about whether or not she and Noah should pursue a committed relationship.

Was this the reason Adelaide had been so lovey-dovey at the door? Were they planning to ambush her again?

Adelaide was the first to notice Susannah had gotten quiet. She peered at her in that unnerving, see-into-your-soul way of hers. "What's up?"

Susannah put her plate down and folded her arms over her chest. "I'm waiting."

They stared at her.

"We were talking about marriage. Ergo, I'm now waiting for the barrage of questions about Noah and me."

"We're not going to do that." Adelaide smiled sweetly. "Right, Edwina?"

Edwina sighed. "Yeah. By the way, no one says 'ergo' in casual conversation."

Susannah ignored the dig. "You mean it? No more pressure?"

"I'm sorry for pushing the issue with you before." Edwina put her fork down. "Look, I haven't exactly always been a passenger on the Good Relationship Train, so I should have cut you some slack. I just want you to be happy. You too, Addy. But I shouldn't assume that what works for me will work for either of you. I'm thrilled that I finally found my person. Simon is good for me." She hummed in contentment. "He's incredible, actually. He honestly surprises me all the time with how sweet and kind and sexy he is."

"Aw, we love Simon," said Adelaide.

"But listen, at the end of the day, if you're good boning Noah every few weeks, I'm good." Edwina shrugged and popped a mound of fried rice into her mouth.

"Wow. Thanks."

"I'll always be the big sister. I worry about you both." Edwina gestured to the stack of romance novels on the coffee table. "Although, for the record, that's a lot of happily ever afters for someone who doesn't believe they exist."

"I guess that's why I read them." Susannah picked at her left pinky cuticle. Damn, she'd made a mess of that finger. It looked awful. "Not everyone gets that kind of happy ending, and it's okay. I think it's possible to live a life of reasonable fulfillment without losing oneself in some all-consuming passion. These things don't always work out."

"Okay." Clearly still struggling, Edwina made a steeple of her hands and brought them to her mouth. "But why shouldn't it work out for you?"

Susannah's defenses shot up, but not out of anger. If anything, her sister's question, and her apology, made her pensive. "I already told you. Based on what I've seen—"

"I'm not talking about what happened to Paula or Rosalind, or any of your other friends," pressed Edwina. "Why shouldn't you, Susannah Victoria Darke, enjoy a toe-curling, pulse-pounding, sweat-drenched romance? Let's be honest, the signals are all there. You and your fuck buddy are clearly into each other. I mean, does Noah make your heart happy?"

Susannah opened her mouth but realized quickly that she didn't actually have an answer that sounded anything but flimsy. *Did* Noah make her heart happy? Her body certainly reacted whenever he was near. Her brain kept thrusting his image before her eyes.

"I'm sorry," said Edwina. "I promised I wouldn't do this. I should just shut up. It's your prerogative not to talk about it."

It wasn't that Susannah didn't want to talk to her sisters about it. They talked about everything. Or, at least, they had up until recently, and that lack of connection had become another near-constant source of worry.

Did Noah make her heart happy?

She didn't even have anyone recent to compare him to. It had been years since she'd allowed anyone to get close enough.

Her sisters ate quietly, awaiting her response.

Some words gathered at the back of her throat, but for some reason, they didn't make any sense and they wouldn't move past her tongue and teeth. They choked her. God, how they choked her. They lodged in her larynx like an undetected fishbone. Edwina's question was simple enough. She should be able to answer it.

Before all of this, she would have said there was only one thing that gave her fulfillment. Her work. There was nothing that excited her more than uncovering some previously unknown nugget of history. Lately though, she'd begun to feel the same sort of wild exhilaration in Noah's presence.

She used to think it was just the sex. He was really good at it.

But it wasn't just that anymore, no matter how hard she tried to convince herself of it.

She'd been learning more about him, and those details, the little things that made up the fabric of Noah, fascinated her. He was like an antique cabinet full of intriguing curios. She wanted to pry open each little compartment and discover the treasures within.

If she was honest with herself, she would admit she'd recently fantasized about being with Noah, about letting herself fall in love with him. Their moments together over the past couple of weeks had only added to the intensity of those dreams.

And yet, she'd carved out a comfortable life for herself. Everything was ordered and in its place. She was able to pursue her passions and make a living from it. She had a comfy home in a city that she loved. Thanks to her sturdy walls, no one made demands on her and she wasn't in a position to let anyone down.

She was able to do what she wanted, *who* she wanted, whenever the need arose. When her cravings for Noah became a distraction, she slept with him, and order was restored. Life resumed. She no longer thought about how his hands seemed made for caressing her body. She didn't contemplate the lines of his face for hours on end. She didn't feel the need to traipse her fingers over his stern eyebrows or wonder at the sensual timbre of his voice.

Or did she?

Truth be told, those cravings had started to bleed into other aspects of her life. Even now, she pictured the greedy way he went down on her, as if the taste of her restored order to his life. She remembered his vulnerability when he'd told her about not being able to sing, and how she'd wanted to make everything better for him. How she would have sold her own soul to get his voice back for him.

Did Noah make her heart happy?

When Adelaide spoke, it caught Susannah off guard. "We should drop it. It's clear you don't want to talk to us."

"It's not that." Susannah didn't want to put another wedge between them. Damn. She was an articulate person! What couldn't she articulate her thoughts when it came to Noah? Why did the subject leave her so untethered?

If you don't talk to them about this, they won't want to talk to you about other things. You'll be left out again. You'll drive them away, and you can't afford to lose them.

Susannah gripped the love seat upholstery.

Calm down. You're spiraling.

"I get it. Relationships are hard sometimes. Hey, you don't see me rushing out to find a life partner." Adelaide stabbed a chunk of sweet and sour chicken. "With my luck, when I finally run into my soulmate, he'll be a dead guy. They seem to be the only ones who have me on their radar."

"Addy." Edwina scoffed.

"I'm going to change the topic," said Adelaide, "but I'm not sure it'll be any easier to discuss. We really should have a chat about why you made that crack the other day about not being 'special.' You know, when you got upset at us at the Asch?"

You guys are the special ones who always have the answers. I'm not a medium, so forgive me for feeling a little disappointed that we can't give our client some information.

"Oh, that." Susannah shrank in her seat. "It was partly just the way the Asch was making me feel that day."

"But partly not?" clarified Edwina.

Here we go. Her stomach bottomed out. "Do you want the truth?"

Edwina frowned. "Of course."

"Okay." She cleared her throat and scraped at the nail polish on her thumb. *Shit.* She'd been hoping to restrict her nail polish carnage to only one finger. "I guess I've been feeling left out lately. It just seems that since Ed came into her abilities, you two have had a lot more in common with each other than with me. It's silly, I know. It's probably just me being overly sensitive."

"It's not silly at all," said Adelaide. "I'm sorry. We should have understood that it might make you feel left out."

Edwina nodded. "Yeah, I'm sorry, Suz. We didn't mean to exclude you. I just didn't want to waste your time while I hammered Addy with mediumship questions. I didn't want to bore you."

"It's not boring to me. We all investigate the paranormal, so I'm interested. If you're going on a journey, I want to be there with you. I want to support you, but I can't if you don't talk to me. And it's not that I expect to be invited every single time. It just feels like it's been adding up. We've always done so much as a unit, and I guess it stung." She huffed out a half-hearted laugh. "Although, I think a part of me has been hoping I might develop some mystical powers too."

"I don't know if that's in the cards for you, Suz," said Adelaide, "but it doesn't make you any less special."

"Yeah, yeah. I get it." She rolled her eyes. "We're all special in our own ways."

"Do you really wish you were a medium?" Adelaide blinked furiously, the way she always did whenever she was becoming upset. "Because I wouldn't have wished it on either of you. I'm at peace with it now, but you know it was hard for me for a long time."

"I know, Addy." Susannah had been there when her sister was bullied. "I haven't forgotten."

Adelaide fingered the gold necklace she always wore. It had a heart pendant with gemstones representing the birthdates of their grandmother's children. Their grandmother had had abilities too, and she'd passed the necklace down to Adelaide, who wore it to keep her grounded. "Here's what I think. You might very well have abilities. They do run in our family. In fact, I've always wondered if you might be an empath."

Little imaginary explosions went off in Susannah's mind. "An empath? That doesn't sound like me."

"No, it doesn't." Adelaide took a moment to choose her words. "Being a medium or a clairvoyant or an empath requires a certain level of openness and honesty, especially with oneself. You would have to be willing to embrace emotions, your own and those of others, and I know that's hard for you."

Pow. Right in the kisser. Susannah's hackles went up. "It's not like I have a choice." She needed her walls. They kept her safe.

"I know it's important for you to have boundaries," said Adelaide, "and I'm glad you feel comfortable being your authentic self with us. But maybe it's time to redraw those boundaries, and let one or two others in. I understand the need to keep certain sexual partners at a distance, but you don't even let your friends get too close."

"Are you saying I don't have friends?" Susannah was trying to regulate her voice as much as possible, but it rose with each word. "I have friends, lots of them."

"When was the last time you went out with any of them?" Adelaide continued calmly.

"I…" Like a trout struggling for air in a fisherman's cooler, her mouth opened and closed several times. "It's not always convenient."

"A DM? A text?"

Busted. She'd been meaning to reach out to a couple of them, but…hadn't.

She did keep people at a distance. In fact, she'd recently turned down a dinner party invitation because she knew a couple of high-strung acquaintances would be there, and she hadn't had the energy for their antics. She had a low tolerance for people who sucked the air out of a room, and she always avoided them, even if they were good people at heart.

It wasn't that she didn't care. She just hated feeling spent afterward.

So she was a bit of a loner, so what? She hung out with her sisters. For some reason, being with them didn't deplete her resources.

Edwina pushed her food around on her plate and gnawed on her bottom lip.

"You look like you're dying to chime in," said Susannah. "Go for it."

"I don't mean to keep harping on him, but you keep Noah at arm's length too. I understand why you would keep others at bay, but Noah seems really nice. He told us himself he would never hurt you, and I believe him. I know you don't like messy situations, but maybe this wouldn't be one."

"Noah and I both like it this way."

"Are you sure?" asked Edwina. "Because I've seen the way he looks at you."

Adelaide nodded. "Total smolder."

Susannah's mind reeled. Noah had agreed with her on keeping things light and casual. Why would he do that if he wanted more? He'd had plenty of opportunities to share his feelings if he had any.

Then again, maybe she hadn't made him feel safe to do so.

She'd always been the one to initiate those conversations about boundaries. Had he just been going along with what she wanted?

His recent text popped into her head. *I'd take you at your worst.*

Oh, God.

Did he have feelings? Had she steamrolled right over them in an attempt to preserve her own?

Her food sat like lumps in her gullet.

"Suz?" prompted Adelaide. "Are you okay?"

"Not really." Susannah sat back, no longer hungry. "I don't want to hurt Noah, but I won't open myself up to a world of pain. I can't."

Adelaide sat next to her and rubbed her back. "How do you know it would be painful?"

"It would be if I showed him the real me." She gestured limply at herself, at the mask of perfection she wore for others. "The real me isn't very pretty."

She'd shown her true self to others and had scared them away.

The comments had begun when she was young enough to absorb them. They'd come from her teachers, her schoolmates and even from her parents the odd time.

"Susannah's a smart girl, but she's a bit fragile."

"It's not worth crying over, Susannah."
"Oh, honey, you need to calm down."
"Why are you getting so emotional?"
*"Look at you. You cried so much that your face is a mess.
We don't want that, do we?"*
"We don't always need to share our feelings, Susannah."

Susannah didn't resent her parents for trying to calm
her down in certain situations. Even as a child, she'd
understood that she was a handful. She remembered
the first time her doctor had suggested she might be
"highly sensitive." It had felt like such an insult. So, she
felt things keenly. It didn't seem like it should be
problematic, and yet her behaviors seemed to annoy
others. Her mom and dad had done their best, too. In
no way were they bad parents. She'd grown up feeling
loved and appreciated. Nevertheless, somewhere along
the way, she'd gotten the message that she needed to
tuck her feelings away to make others feel better. That,
unlike the emotions of others, her feelings were messy
and unbecoming.

That sentiment was reinforced when she entered the
dating world and started to hear the same sorts of
comments from men. So, somewhere along the line,
she'd grown wary of sharing too much of herself with
anyone. It was so much easier just to assume the guise
of an ice queen, even though she was anything but on
the inside.

"Susannah," said Edwina, "do you honestly think
Simon loves me because I'm perfect? Hell, no! He loves
me because I'm opinionated, mouthy and I know the
difference between a ranged thermometer and a FLIR
thermal cam. I mean, obviously, the thermal cam is a
much more sophisticated piece of equipment because
of the way it records images for analysis, but that's

neither here nor there. Anyway, he loves my weirdness. I keep him on his toes. And I would guess Noah digs you for a similar set of reasons."

"It's easy for you guys to talk." The dam inside Susannah finally burst. "Your emotions were never considered a nuisance, or 'too much.' No one ever said your feelings were exhausting. I had no choice but to build up my walls. I learned early on that not only did my walls keep me safe, they kept others sane."

Her eyes filled with tears. For once, she didn't bother to blink them away. "Do you think it was fun being the kid who exploded into tears at the humane society commercials on TV? Sometimes adults would just shake their heads at me because they had no words. Managing my feelings made them tired, so I had to learn to manage them myself."

Edwina joined them on the loveseat, sitting on her other side. She and Adelaide immediately put their arms around her.

"Oh, Suz. I'm sorry you got that message," said Adelaide.

"Yeah," agreed Edwina. "For the record, you were never too much for us."

"You're my sisters." Susannah heaved a shaky breath. "The three of us grew up in this strange little bubble. When the scary shit happened, we were always together. You're the only ones who've ever helped me feel truly safe and accepted because we all have quirks. I love Mom and Dad, but sometimes they just didn't know what to do with me. For so long, I was told that being emotional means being weak. I was too high-strung, too impressionable. I was such an anxious kid and I became even more anxious trying to hide it. My fears used to keep me up at night. I could never stop my head from spinning or my stomach from hurting. So, yeah, I learned how to suppress my emotions. I had to."

"Oh, sweetie." Adelaide reached for her hand and squeezed it.

"It's why I keep others at a distance. Because when the shit hits the fan, I worry that it'll turn me into the blubbering mess I used to be. It's better to keep people away than to scare them away."

"Listen," said Adelaide. "If no one has ever told you before, your emotions are one hundred percent valid one hundred percent of the time. And if anyone tells you otherwise, fuck that jerk! I promise you that letting your guard down once in a while will not destroy you. Would it really be so terrible to let Noah into our strange little bubble?"

"Yes! It would be terrible, especially in Noah's case."

"Why?" they both asked.

"Because what if you're wrong? What if he doesn't actually feel the same way? I can't take that risk," whispered Susannah. "Have you *seen* him? He's incredible."

"You're pretty incredible yourself." Edwina reached for one of the romance novels and tossed it gently from one hand to another. "You know, I read my fair share of these books too, and if there's one thing they've taught me, it's this. At some point, you need to take a risk."

Susannah's skin crawled. She hated risks almost as much as she hated messes.

She had to be willing to lay it all out on the line with Noah. Intellectually, she knew it was the healthy way to live. She would never have encouraged her sisters to function the way she did, shuttered to profound emotion. She would want them to be happy, even if it meant they had to risk a bit of pain along the way. It just wasn't always easy for her.

"You must believe in love," said Edwina. "You encouraged me to go after Simon."

"Yeah, but that's different." Susannah sniffled. "That was you, not me."

Edwina hit her with a couch cushion, laughing.

"I know there's a lot of pain in the world," said Adelaide. "But there's a lot of joy too. Embrace it."

"That sounds frightening." Susannah smirked. "I think I'd rather talk to ghosts."

"It's not all it's cracked up to be," said Edwina. "I couldn't even do my groceries in peace the other day because a dead guy was following me around the store. It can be a lot."

She had a point there. Susannah wasn't sure she wanted that kind of energy in her life. She could barely deal with the dramas of living people. "Addy, do you really think I'm an empath?"

"Oh, you're totally an empath. Just a very stubborn one."

"So, you're saying I should tell Noah I have...feelings?"

"Yes!" Adelaide grabbed Susannah's shoulders and gave her a gentle shake.

"He absolutely wants you." Edwina waggled her eyebrows. "If you think the sex is hot now, imagine what it could be. I'm talking total annihilation of your nether regions. I bet he'd go to town on you for days."

"That might actually be worth the risk." Susannah wiped her eyes and laughed. "Whew. Weren't we supposed to talk about the case?"

"This was important too," said Adelaide. "Finish your dinner. Then we'll discuss our next steps. Deal?"

Susannah smiled. "Deal."

Chapter Twelve

When Susannah headed out to meet Noah early the next afternoon, it was with more than a measure of trepidation. Even now, despite it being a cool fall day, a line of nervous sweat broke out on her upper lip and hairline.

She was supposed to tell Noah she had feelings. For him, specifically.

Bloody terrifying.

As she entered the Asch Institute, she took a moment to collect her thoughts. It was the middle of the school day. Students and faculty members hurried back and forth on their way to class. There was a different energy in the air today, a buzzing sort of vibe, like everyone had ants in their pants. It was probably just her.

It would be difficult to be honest with Noah about her feelings. Yes, she'd had a breakthrough with her sisters, but she knew she was safe with them. Noah was a whole other matter.

Baby steps.

She'd seen a therapist a while back for some coping mechanisms, and he'd suggested she be honest with people about how baring her soul was hard. Noah already knew that about her, so she was part of the way there.

Which reminded her it was probably time to book another appointment with the therapist.

As Susannah walked around the school foyer, she was drawn to the area where Melba Flanagan used to sit. There was a little alcove built into the wall there, and Susannah could easily see how a desk would have fit into that space. She had now read much of Melba's memoirs and it was clear the exceptional young woman had been dedicated to her job. Perhaps because of that dedication, she'd also been discreet. Susannah had been hoping Melba would have revealed a bit more about her colleagues, but aside from her detailing the odd disagreement, much of the book was about the day-to-day running of the school.

What Susannah needed was something juicier. She hoped her research in the school library today would shed some light.

Susannah turned to Dr. Asch's statue and was about to give his knuckles a rub out of habit, but then stopped herself. "I really don't want to believe you're the dark presence here, Dr. Asch. If it's not you, help a girl out, okay?"

She then checked herself. Yes, Victor Asch was remembered as the benevolent first director, but it was entirely possible there was a side to Asch that she had yet to uncover. As a historian, she had to be willing to accept the fact that this process might reveal some unsavory details.

Steeling herself, she headed toward Noah's office.

His assistant, Brian, must have gone out because the outer office where he sat was vacant. The door to the inner office had been left open. She popped her head around the corner.

Noah sat at his desk, talking on the phone. Upon seeing her, his eyes lit up and he waved her in. Her heart did a funny little somersault in response. He motioned that he'd just be a moment longer, so she took a seat in front of his desk.

To distract herself so she wouldn't openly gawk at him, she took the opportunity to check out the details of his office. There were some amazing period moldings on the wall, but despite the vintage architecture, he'd furnished it with modern touches. The chairs were made of sleek leather and there were a couple of gallery-worthy paintings. Susannah had never been a fan of modern art, but the surroundings suited Noah. His condo was decorated in much the same way, with industrial colors and simple embellishments.

She was stricken with the desire to see his condo again, so that she could take note of all the little details she had previously disregarded. How much of him had she missed in her haste to leave at the end of all those evenings?

"Yeah, Julius, that sounds great. Tell Marek I said hello. Will I be seeing you both at the gala?" Noah said to the person on the other end of the line.

A gala. Hmm. Susannah smoothed out a crease in her pants and tried not to look like she was listening to the conversation.

He laughed and the joyful noise made her chest constrict. It was a great laugh, three short bursts of joy.

She wanted to hear it again and again, and to be able to laugh along with him.

"Excellent. See you then." Noah ended his call and focused his gaze on her. A slow, sensuous grin curled his lips. "Hey, you."

God, she loved when he greeted her that way. His sexy tone went straight to her crotch. She tried to think of something engaging or intelligent to say, but all that came out was a hushed "Hi."

He stood and slowly walked around the big desk toward her. For some reason, it seemed to take forever, allowing her a chance to drink him in. He was wearing one of his gorgeous suits, a well-fitting gray ensemble with a slim pinstripe. At his neck, he wore a purple tie, one that put all sorts of interesting flecks into his dark eyes. It also put a lot of interesting ideas into her head, specifically about being tied down with it. She snuck a glance at his shoes. Burnished brown cap-toe brogues. Probably Italian. A devastating combination. Power-house Noah was back in the building.

Help!

He was coming closer and her breaths were getting shallower. For a crazed moment, she wondered if he would keep his distance, as per her request. Then again, maybe he would throw caution to the wind and kiss her with all his pent-up lust. She already knew she'd kiss him back, tongue and everything. Then again, maybe he would have mercy on her and throw her down on his desk to fuck the hesitation right out of her.

She was kind of hoping for option number three. For her, a physical reset always resulted in a mental reset, and God only knew she needed some of that shit right now.

Only she'd previously asked him to cool it, so the desk fornication wouldn't happen. She already knew it.

And yet, he still managed to surprise her. Noah stood before her, studied her for a tense moment, and reached for her hand. He slid his cool fingers against hers and played with her ugly, unpolished pinky finger. When he saw what she'd done to her thumb, he frowned. "How are you?"

"I'm okay." *Liar!* "How are you?"

"Okay."

Susannah wanted to pepper him with questions about his day, and whether he'd slept well last night. She wanted to know if he'd watched anything good on TV, or if he was reading anything interesting, or if he'd gone to bed and had another disturbing nightmare. They'd both previously confessed their dislike of small talk, but suddenly she wanted to know about the minutiae of his day. What did he have for lunch? Had he enjoyed his morning coffee? Did he take it strong, or did he prefer a medium roast? She wanted to know how long it had taken him to choose his tie and what had inspired him to pick the paintings for his office.

Since having that difficult conversation with her sisters, and since promising she'd tell Noah how she felt, she wanted to know it all.

But she couldn't put any of that into words while he was caressing her pinky finger. In fact, the only word that popped out was another weak, "Hi."

Noah's shy grin opened into a smile. "You said that already."

"Did I? Oh. Um, did I hear something about a gala?"

"Yeah, a fundraising shindig for the school. It's coming up in just over a week."

"Really?" *Do not fish for an invitation. Do not fish for an —*

"So." Noah dragged out the word. "I was planning on going alone, but it occurs to me that it could be interesting for you...you know, from a research perspective."

"Research. At a fundraising gala."

"Several of our biggest patrons are former students. I wouldn't be surprised if some of them had stories they could tell you." He scrunched up his face. "Actually, that's a cop out. No one does research at a gala. The truth is I'd love it if you came as my date, but I don't want to push your boundaries."

Her boundaries, not *their* boundaries.

Her sisters were right, and she'd been wrong. So, so wrong.

No, not wrong. It was okay to have limits. But maybe she was ready to test them with Noah.

Be honest. "I'd love to go with you. I think we'd have a great time together."

There was a ripple along his stern eyebrows. "Really? Okay, then. That's great. I'll text you the details."

"Sounds like a plan." She smiled, marveling at the fact that she hadn't imploded upon admitting her true feelings. Well, one little feeling. There was still a lot more to admit. *Again, baby steps.*

She checked in with herself, as Adelaide had advised. How did she feel right now? A little nervous, a little shaky and barfy, but also kind of excited. She wanted to put on a nice dress and attend a ritzy gala with Noah. It could lead to a second date. It could lead to all sorts of interesting things.

Don't go there right now. One thing at a time. Plus, you're still on the job.

He released her hand, and she drummed her fingers on her thighs, needing to do something with them. "So, about that library."

"You sound excited to see it."

She snorted out a laugh. "It's a library. If I told you exactly how much I want to see it, you would finally understand that I am a total, irredeemable nerd."

He gnawed on his full bottom lip, his teeth meeting with plump flesh. "Susannah, I would never dream of redeeming you."

Okay, she needed to get out of that office, pronto, or she would throw him down on his own desk. She stood on trembling legs. Thank goodness she hadn't worn heels. "Lemme me at those books."

"I'll walk you down." He held her gaze for a long, fraught moment. He'd been doing that a lot lately, and it scared the shit out of her because his gazes always managed to make her feel naked and disarmed. Still, she didn't look away, and she silently cheered herself for holding her own. *Yay, you.*

He finally took mercy on her and led her out of the office, and she took a deep breath. Had he seen her defenses slipping? Probably. Was it terrible? A little. Her body registered its confusion in various ways. There was a giddy sensation high in her chest, a fluttering somewhere under her ribs.

It was also…nice. Lovely, actually, but still scary.

Plus, he was so hot she could weep. As they walked together, her gaze slipped toward his pinstriped glutes. She imagined clutching on to those two firm mounds as he pumped her hard. Her mind wandered even further, and she pictured herself standing nude before a clothed, pinstriped Noah. She envisioned herself letting him see everything, all the imperfections that she'd never managed to correct. Her bunions, the kidney bean-shaped mole on her shoulder, the crooked tooth that somehow never straightened, despite years of braces. Would he still like what he saw?

They passed Luca's memorial, and she doused her rampaging desire. *Remember why you're here.*

Noah glanced at the photo and frowned.

"Any other dreams?"

"Every night."

"I'm sorry."

"Who needs sleep, right?"

Noah led her to an area behind the theater and down a set of stairs. They were on the same floor as the practice rooms but appeared to be in a different wing. They arrived in front of the library entrance. Susannah was drawn to the name emblazoned on the wall, the Elodie Asch Memorial Library.

Noah ran a hand over the sign. "As you can see, Asch named it for his wife."

"Well, who wouldn't want a library named after them? It seems like a real gesture of love."

Although the library was small, it had its charms. There were posters of famous opera singers on the wall, including one of Noah as Rodolfo from *La Bohème*. In it, he wore a bottle-green vest and had a purple scarf slung around his neck. His face was filled with passion as he sang. Susannah could have gawked at the poster forever, but Noah hurried past, averting his gaze.

It seemed his own walls were still firmly in place.

There was a long line of carrels on one side, several currently occupied by busy students. A couple of soundproof study rooms sat off to the side, so that people could meet in groups. Susannah spied some interesting old volumes on the shelves, and she couldn't wait to dig in.

Noah spoke to the library technician on duty and explained Susannah was his guest, and that she should be allowed access to anything she needed. He then took her into the stacks and pointed out a few shelves. "These are some of the oldest materials. You should find something helpful here. If you need anything else, just ask at the desk." He blushed. "Of course, you don't need me to tell you how to use a library."

"I've seen a few in my time."

A strand of her hair fell across her forehead. He reached out to tuck it behind her ear and he met her gaze. "You're good, then?"

His hand was warm and his touch was gentle, and she wanted badly to just give in to temptation and lean into it. "Yeah."

"Great. I, uh, guess I'd better get back to work. FYI, it's the library's early night. It closes at five."

"Some people like to close down bars. I like to close down libraries."

"Of course, you do. Would you mind if I joined you in a while, to find out what you learned?"

"I'd like that."

They stood in the library stacks, both of them seemingly unable to break eye contact, and unable to move. They stood very close to one another, probably closer than was advisable. His breath, warm and alluring, landed on her cheek. His lips parted, and his tongue slipped out to wet them.

She should be stepping away from him. He'd already said he had work to do, and yet, she just couldn't seem to move out of his sphere. She liked it in his sphere. It smelled good and it made her skin tingle.

For the first time, she noticed Noah had a tiny mole just under the full curve of his bottom lip. *Huh.* How had she never seen it before? It was just a regular mole, more like a freckle actually, nothing that she should have found remotely fascinating. And yet, she couldn't drag her eyes off it. All of a sudden, there was nothing in the world that intrigued her more than that mole.

She would have kissed that mole before, a hundred times even. Her lips would have smashed against it. Her tongue would have already moistened it. On its own, it didn't merit her attention at all. It shouldn't capture her imagination. However, her gaze homed in on that mole, and on the full lip right above it.

God, she wanted to kiss him.

Susannah suddenly wanted to explore the little divot under his bottom lip with her tongue, wanted to place open-mouthed kisses all over his face and body. She wanted to take him home and slowly remove all his clothing, learning what made him tense and clench. Normally, they just tossed their clothes aside without a care, and sometimes they only removed key items. But right now, she wanted to see everything and she was possessed by a strange need to lie bare and vulnerable before Noah.

If she told him all her secrets, would he keep them close to his heart?

She stepped toward him, but then stopped herself. *What are you doing? You're in a library. You have work to do. Fornication is not the answer!*

Noah moved toward her, his eyes glazed and focused on her mouth as well. "Susannah…"

"I should get to it, I guess." Her voice rang out in the quiet library.

He snapped to attention. "Right. I'll check in with you later." He turned to leave.

She was supposed to tell him she had feelings for him. She was supposed to…say something. Her arm moved of its own volition and she yanked on his sleeve. "Wait."

"Yeah?"

Once again, her walls sprang up around her as she envisioned all the numerous ways this could go wrong. *Not now. If you're going to do this, do it right, not on the fly.* "Thanks for pointing me in the right direction."

"No sweat." He slipped out of the stacks and headed toward the library entrance.

She should have felt relief, a reprieve, but she didn't.

If anything, she was consumed by the need to chase him and throw herself up against his hard body. She checked her watch.

It would be hours until she could see him again, and she already knew she would be counting every last minute.

Chapter Thirteen

Fuck, fuck, fuck.

Outside the library, back in the basement hallway, Noah sought out a quiet corner and faced the wall. He willed his erection to disappear and forced himself to think of all sorts of unsavory things to accomplish it. *Dead fish. Smelly feet. Coffee that's grown cold.*

They'd had a couple of moments back there, very confusing moments, and they'd left him rock hard. As he focused on his breathing, his dick settled down again.

What the actual fuck?

First, Susannah had asked him about the fundraising gala with that coy look in her eyes. Then she'd agreed to attend with him. Even more surprising was the sexual tension in the library just now. She'd been on the verge of kissing him. Had he imagined it?

No. Noah was almost forty years old. He wasn't some horny kid, misreading the signals. Besides, he understood Susannah's signals better than most things.

He'd had plenty of time to learn them and appreciate their nuances.

Nevertheless, her words still rang loud and clear in his mind, much clearer than any nuance.

No muddying the waters.

Had she changed her mind? Would she even tell him if she had?

There was only one course of action, as far as they were concerned...whatever "they" even were, at this point.

Let her come to you.

It would be hard, when every particle in his body screamed for her, but he was determined to respect her wishes. There was no other choice. If she wanted him, she would have to say the words.

Noah headed back upstairs, toward his office. There was plenty to occupy him there. They were in the midst of hiring a couple of new teachers, one for Italian diction and another for acting and stagecraft. He'd promised to call a couple of patrons back, as well. And he'd made it a priority to secure a new government grant for students who needed financial assistance. A near-bottomless pool of bureaucracy awaited him. He shouldn't have any excuse to dwell on thoughts of Susannah.

Even though all he wanted to do was dwell on thoughts of Susannah.

When he got to the main floor, he glanced down the hallway leading to the practice room stairway.

A flash of long black hair down the hall caught his attention.

Ava?

It couldn't be. She was supposed to be studying from home.

When the person with the long hair turned the corner, he glimpsed the distinctive shaved patch near her ear. Definitely Ava. He didn't know any other students who wore their hair the same way. Oblivious to his attention, she headed toward the practice rooms.

No!

The hallway was busy with students, and Noah didn't want to call out and alarm anyone. Quickening his pace, while trying to look calm, he headed toward the practice room stairs. A couple of students called out to him, but he dodged those conversations as politely as possible, promising to catch up with them later. He made it to the door, shoved it open and ran down the stairs.

Even though the upstairs hallway had been busy, the practice room hallway was strangely quiet. Most of the doors were propped open, a sign that the rooms were empty and available. It was also dark. That caused Noah's hackles to go up. The lights in the basement were supposed to be on at all times during the school day. Someone had turned them off. He paused and flipped the switch, illuminating the space.

He listened in for a moment, trying to determine if anyone was actually down there, but it was still. Eerily still.

"Ava?" He was sure he'd seen her. He waited a moment, but there was no response.

There was another exit at the end of the hallway, but it was a heavy door and he would have heard it if someone had let it slam shut.

"Is there someone here?" Noah took a few steps.

The lights in the hallway flickered and went out. He stopped in his tracks, surrounded by darkness once again.

The only light switch in the hall was the one he'd just touched. He looked over his shoulder. No one was there.

Okay, so I need to get someone to check out the lighting. It's an old building. He was constantly ordering repairs. This was just another one.

Only every instinct told him this wasn't an electrical issue.

He was officially freaked out. It was hard not to be. Despite the early hour, the basement was surprisingly dark when the lights were out because there were no windows in that area. He turned around and reached for the light switch.

From the far end of the hallway came a low moan. Noah froze. That noise…he knew that noise. He whipped around, his fists clenched.

The lightbulb down the hall flickered a few times. Just outside the last practice room, a figure stood in the fitful light. This person did not have long black hair. He had curly brown hair and a frame Noah knew all too well because he'd watched this person perform many times. He'd sat next to him in class and had hung out with him on the weekends. Dark eyes beckoned. They were eyes Noah would never forget. Their memory was reinforced every time he walked past the memorial upstairs.

Noah's throat seized, but he managed to croak a single word. "Luca?"

The lights above Luca flashed on, brighter than they'd ever shone. They illuminated his old friend's face, a face that was paler than it had ever been in life. Luca raised his arm, pointed at the final practice room, and uttered a single word. "Hurry."

For a moment, Noah stood still. After all the nightmares of Luca silently screaming, hearing his voice came as a shock.

Somehow, that shock roused Noah from his funk. He tore toward the practice room. As he did, the lights were somehow restored to their normal brightness.

Luca faded as Noah drew near. Noah raged internally, wishing he could bring his friend back and communicate with him properly. He wanted to tell him how sorry he was, and how he wished there'd been something he could have done that day in Professor Kraus' class, other than gape in astonishment and terror.

The room at the end was closed, but he wrenched it open. Ava was curled up in a ball on the floor, her hair draped over her face.

"Ava!" Noah knelt next to the young woman and tapped the floor next to her head. "Ava, can you hear me?"

She pushed her hair out of her face. Thank God she was unhurt. She turned confused eyes toward him. "Dean Bellamy?"

He helped her sit up. "Are you okay?"

Ava's gaze landed on the piano, on the mirror, then cycled back to him. "How did I get here?"

"You don't remember? I saw you come down here when I was upstairs."

She slowly shook her head. "I was supposed to stay home. I know that. I had logged into Professor Bankole's class earlier and was just doing some homework." Her lip quivered. "I don't know how I got here."

Noah took note of the subway pass in her hand. She didn't seem to have a backpack or handbag, though. "You must have taken the subway."

The pass fell out of her hand. "I guess so? I don't remember."

"And no one was here with you in the practice room?" He retrieved the pass and gave it back to her.

She hesitated, her face flushed. "I heard his voice. He was angry."

Noah stood and glanced around the room. Of course, the creepy prick was gone now. "Do you remember anything he said?"

She thought for a moment. "Actually, yeah. I thought I heard him call me Terence."

"Terence? Are you sure about that?"

"Yes. The voice said, *'I'm disappointed in you, Terence.'*" She shook her head. "This is so fucked up."

"Okay, here's what we're going to do. I'm going to call a cab and we'll get you home. I'll see you to your door. Would that be okay?"

"Yeah." She took his outstretched hand and stood.

"Are either of your parents home?"

"They both work from home."

"Okay. I think we need to tell them what's been going on. Is that all right with you?"

She nodded, her eyes moist. "I'm scared."

"Listen to me, Ava. We're going to fix this. That is the last time it messes with you, I promise." He shouldn't be making promises, but he had to give her some hope. Susannah had seemed convinced the evil ghost couldn't reach Ava at home. Clearly, the sonofabitch had some kind of hold on her, if he could make her get on the subway and return to school in a daze, without her parents noticing. Without her even realizing it.

Dammit. What if she'd walked onto the subway tracks? A number of horrible scenarios presented themselves.

Noah led her out of the practice rooms and back toward the stairway. As he reached the light switch, he glanced over his shoulder at the empty hallway.

Luca was well and truly gone, and it left an even bigger hole in his heart. Seeing him disappear had been almost as bad as watching him fade away the first time.

But Luca had found a way to help Ava. In fact, if it hadn't been for Luca, Noah might never have looked for her in that last room.

God only knew what the evil entity might have done then.

Chapter Fourteen

Elodie Asch dead after fall downstairs
Toronto – Mme. Elodie Asch, formerly of the Grand Opera House, died yesterday after a fall at the Toronto Conservatory of Music. Mme. Asch, wife of the Conservatory's director, Dr. Victor Asch, had recently assumed a teaching role at the conservatory, and was beloved by staff and students alike. Mme. Asch is best remembered for having played the roles of Juliet and Lady Teazle. Memorials have been placed outside both the Toronto Conservatory of Music and the Grand Opera House.
Globe, Dec. 10, 1890

Susannah kept going back to the old newspaper clipping. Elodie Asch had only taught at the school for a few months before her fatal accident. Her death had apparently come as a big shock to everyone.

Elodie had been a singer and actress at Toronto's Grand Opera House, a theater that no longer existed, but that had once stood on Adelaide Street West.

During its heyday in the late nineteenth century, it had been a center for elite entertainment and had attracted a number of international acts. Theater legends such as Sarah Bernhardt and Maurice Barrymore had trodden the boards there.

Over the years, Susannah had read about numerous tragic deaths that had caused hauntings. It made sense that if anyone was still lingering at the school after death, it would be Elodie, certainly as the infamous Gray Lady.

Then why hadn't they seen her? Was it because she'd only worked at the Asch for a few months before her death? Maybe her connection to the school wasn't strong enough.

And why did Susannah and Ava keep hearing the voice of a man?

Susannah located another biography of Victor Asch. She skimmed the index, looking for any mention of Elodie. For the most part, the biographer made little mention of her, which annoyed her to no end, but he had included a paragraph that caused Susannah's pulse to race.

Victor Asch never recovered from the loss of his beloved wife, Elodie. He retreated from society, as well as from several of his duties at the Conservatory. For the next couple of years, much of his work was handled by registrar Melba Flanagan.

Devastated, Asch spent more and more time in the company of spiritualists. One in particular, a Madame Liliana, claimed to be in contact with Mrs. Asch's spirit. Asch was a regular attendee at Madame Liliana's seances, even going so far as to host several at his opulent Rosedale home. It was the spiritualist who first insinuated that Mrs.

Asch hadn't been the victim of an accidental fall at all. Madame Liliana claimed Mrs. Asch had been murdered.

No one believed the nonsensical claim, of course. There was no evidence to support it. Francesco Lombardi, a longtime colleague at the school, said, "It's a shame to see Dr. Asch being led around by that distasteful spiritualist woman, but the very fact that he entertains this rubbish is a sign he's no longer fit to run the Conservatory. I don't like to say these things, but they must be said."

"Well, well."

Francesco Lombardi's name had popped up again. He'd been one of the ones whose feathers were ruffled when Asch hired Elodie. She would have to do more digging on him.

And who was this mysterious Madame Liliana? Had she been legit, or was it possible she'd been a scammer who was taking advantage of a vulnerable widower? Victorian spiritualists were renowned for misleading and cheating their clients. Dr. Asch certainly could have fallen prey to a scam. It didn't sound as if he'd ever come to terms with his wife's death.

Of course, Susannah's own sister was a medium. She didn't want to assume Madame Liliana was a crook. Perhaps she'd merely been trying to help but had been under the wrong impression about the alleged murder.

But what if she'd been onto something? What if Elodie Asch really had been killed? Someone could have pushed her down the stairs, and it still might have looked accidental.

Susannah flipped to a photo of Victor and Elodie on the lawn of their home. Dr. Asch had fair hair parted down the middle, thick sideburns and an impressive mustache. He wore fine clothing and had a twinkle in his eye. Elodie was every bit as handsome as her husband. With raven hair piled high on her head and a sensuous mouth, she must have captivated her audiences. They were an impressive couple, and it was clear they were smitten with each other. Even in this photo, Victor's hand curled possessively about Elodie's waist, and she leaned into his touch. Love, as well as a healthy dose of sex appeal, just sparkled around them.

Susannah flipped to a later photo of Asch, one taken a mere five years after Elodie's death. In this one, the twinkle had gone out of his eye. His hair had turned white and his shoulders sloped. He looked nothing like the proud statue in the entrance of the institute.

Her death had shattered him.

Or was she seeing something else? Victor and Elodie had clearly had a passionate relationship. Could the passion have soured somewhere along the way? What if they'd argued? Maybe, ardor had turned into rage, and he'd pushed her down the stairs when no one was looking. Or, perhaps he'd jostled her, and she'd simply fallen. If so, was it possible that his guilt had aged him? Worse still, could it have transformed him into the terrible shadow man?

Could Victor Asch actually be the dark entity?

As much as she was trying to remain open-minded, it just felt wrong. Her body hummed in agitation, as if resisting the very idea. Every instinct was telling her that she was grasping at straws.

And what of that EVP?

"Are you happy, Father?"

Even though the EVP had been staticky, the tone had been clear. Whoever had asked that question had asked it in bitterness and desperation.

Could it somehow be connected to Elodie's death?

On a hunch, she reached for one of the collective biographies that she'd been perusing. The book was about early Canadian contributions to the classical music scene, and several of the Asch Institute characters had featured in it.

She turned to the page on Francesco Lombardi and quickly skimmed the information.

"Born in Naples in 1835, performed as a pianist in Adelina Patti's concert tour, blah, blah, blah," she mumbled. "Got married, had a couple of kids, moved to Canada in 1870. Come on, gimme some spicy stuff."

What she needed was a red flag, something that would indicate this dude might have been driven to murder his boss's wife.

There was nothing. Susannah closed the book.

She just didn't buy it. Lombardi may not have agreed with Asch on certain things, but there was no indication he hated him.

And what did all of this have to do with Luca?

Frustrated, she reached for her cell phone, just in time to feel it vibrate with an incoming text. As soon as she saw the text, her heart dropped into her shoes.

Noah: Won't be able to meet you at 5. I found Ava at the school, in a bad state. She's okay but I've brought her home. Just talking to her parents now.

Susannah: OMG. I'm sorry. Do what you need to do.

She didn't expect to get a response back, but her phone pinged a few minutes later.

Noah: Can I see you tonight?

She didn't hesitate.

Susannah: Yes.

She already understood it wasn't a request for updates on her research. Noah wouldn't be looking for a coffee and a chat. If he'd found Ava in distress, he would be upset. There was every possibility he was going to need something more tonight, perhaps even the comfort of her body, and Susannah already knew she would give it to him.

Distracted, she checked the clock. The library would be closing in half an hour. Frankly, she didn't have the energy to do any more research. Her head was already swimming. She began to gather her things and put her library books in the returns area. She swung her bag over her shoulder and headed toward the entrance.

The library technician was tidying up the service desk for the evening. On a whim, she decided to trouble him one more time. "Hi. I realize you're closing soon, but Dean Bellamy said you had recordings of a student named Luca Brizzi."

He rifled in a drawer. "Yeah, they're just in-class recordings. Poor kid never had a chance to sing professionally. Actually, I have one handy because a student returned it earlier. You'd be surprised how often I get asked for recordings of Luca." He leaned in conspiratorially. "Between you and me, I think he has a bit of a fan club among some of the students. Anyway, he had a beautiful voice. It's a shame he never got to realize his full potential." He handed her a DVD case. "A young Noah Bellamy makes an appearance on this one too."

"Really?"

"It's a tenor duet from *Elisabetta Regina d'Inghilterra* by Rossini. 'Deh! scusa i trasporti.' You can borrow it, if you'd like."

She thanked the library tech and headed outside, moving at a good clip. Her head in the clouds, she almost plowed into a man on Bloor Street West. Somewhere on the short walk from the Asch to her condo, she realized she was cradling the DVD near her heart. Feeling foolish, she stuck it in her bag for the remainder of the journey. In a way, she didn't blame herself for treating it as precious cargo. Noah and Luca's voices were captured on that fragile disk, and neither of those voices existed anymore.

As soon as she got home, she pulled it out of her bag. She wasn't even sure why she wanted to see it. Inspiration, maybe?

Susannah didn't even watch DVDs nowadays because she streamed most things, but she still had a DVD player in her TV cabinet. She plugged it in, adjusted the settings and popped in the disk.

The class had taken place in the Asch Institute theater, and it featured performances by various students. The grand piano stood in the same corner of the stage as it had when she'd observed Noah's class, only it was a different accompanist. A few students took their turns singing, and their teacher coached them. Finally, Luca and Noah were called up to the stage.

Susannah leaned forward, her hand trembling. She'd seen recordings of Noah singing before, but this was a young Noah, and she felt protective of him right now. He took the stage, adorable in his Tragically Hip T-shirt, with torn jeans and unkempt hair. This was a Noah who hadn't yet seen his friend die, a Noah who hadn't had his own dreams cruelly ripped from him, and there was only hope and light in his eyes. He seemed unhurt, undamaged by the world, and she wished she could keep him that way.

And, of course, there was Luca, whose voice she'd never heard before. It was the same young man from the memorial photo. Unruly curls, warm brown eyes and a beautiful smile. He wore torn jeans too, ones that looked just like Noah's, only they were torn in different places. On his wrist was some sort of leather bracelet, and he had a band T-shirt on as well. The Sam Roberts Band. Susannah smiled because she loved their music. Here, captured in this recording, Luca was buoyant and whole, and it made her heart hurt to see him.

She wasn't familiar with Rossini's opera about Queen Elizabeth I, but she had a feeling it wouldn't take away from her enjoyment of the duet. The accompanist played some introductory notes, and Luca began. His voice rang out through the theater, rich and resonant. Noah was right. For such a young person, Luca had had a natural ability, the kind of voice that only comes around every so often.

As he sang, he and Noah traded looks. They were both trying their hardest to be serious, but merriment shone from their eyes. It was clear they enjoyed performing together. She quickly Googled the scene and learned it was about an attempt by the Duke of Norfolk to deceive the Earl of Leicester. Courtly intrigue notwithstanding, the young men bubbled with playful energy. It almost looked as if one of them had cracked a joke before going on stage, and now they were both struggling to maintain the seriousness of the scene.

When it was Noah's turn to sing, Susannah held her breath. His voice had a different timbre than Luca's, a mellow tenor that wrapped itself around each note with a caress. For the first time, she really listened to him, and finally had a sense of all that he'd lost. His sound was magnificent. Paired with Luca, they were a thrilling combination.

Very few people would have seen what she was now seeing, and the gravity hit her with full force.

The world had lost out on seeing those two artists perform together.

Before the duet ended, she stopped the recording. She couldn't listen to it anymore. It was making her sad and sentimental and angry and...she wasn't quite sure what else, but it boiled inside her like a forgotten pot of water on the stovetop.

Susannah marched into her kitchen and poured herself a glass of orange juice, downing it in one go. Why did she feel like punching a wall? Her hands itched with the need to do something, anything, to help Noah. But there was only so much she could do. She certainly couldn't restore his voice.

Maybe she could help him understand he was amazing, whether he still sang or not.

More than anything, she wanted to hold him, to assure him she understood, at least as much as she ever could.

Her talent, her joy, had been taken too, and she was only now starting to realize the impact of that loss. All of a sudden, she wanted to go home, to her parents' home, where her old upright piano still stood in the corner of the den. It probably needed a good tuning after all those years of neglect.

How would it feel to touch the keys again? It would be painful, no doubt. For the first time in ages, she wondered if she could possibly recapture that joy.

Her phone buzzed where she'd set it on the table.

Noah: Can I come in?

She pressed the button that unlocked the entrance in the foyer. Her throat thick, Susannah waited inside her door and counted the seconds it would take for him to take the elevator up to her floor. *Fifteen, sixteen, seventeen, eighteen.* He barely got three knocks out before she opened it.

He stood in the hallway, staring at the carpet, but he slowly raised his head. His skin was pale. Stress had brought out dark circles under his eyes, and lines in his forehead. He still wore the killer pinstripe suit, but he'd loosened the tie and the top button of his shirt.

"Is Ava okay?"

Noah nodded. Other than that, he didn't move, and seemed to have forgotten how.

"Noah?"

"I saw Luca. At the school."

The harmonies from the recording still haunted her, like a tinkly echo after a music box had been slammed shut. She pulled him through the doorway and into her arms. As she embraced him, she kicked the door closed. He buried his face in her neck, clutching her tight around the middle. She ran her hands through his thick hair and kissed his jaw. "I'm sorry. I'm so, so sorry."

Noah looked at her, his eyes full of confusion. "There's no need for you to apologize."

Then why was that untrustworthy organ in her chest thumping for all its might? Why did she want to erase the memory of anyone who'd ever hurt him? Why was she suddenly feeling so much for this man, so much in fact that she wasn't convinced her poor heart knew how to process it all?

Say something to make it better.

She wasn't sure anything would make it better. Here in her condo hallway, when he was holding onto her like a lifeline, no words were adequate.

So, she kissed him. Hard, and full on the mouth.

For a few crazed seconds, the kiss remained relatively chaste. But then she opened, offering him more, and he took it. He plunged his tongue into her mouth, like he was marking her, warning others away. She was happy to wear that mark. She wanted it all over her body.

Noah groaned, his grip tightening. He ran his hands up and down her back, then toward her ass. He massaged it and grunted, presumably because of the barrier of clothing.

She wanted it gone too, and fucking yesterday.

Their lips still connected, straying here and there to each other's necks, she dragged him into the condo. She would have stopped at the couch, but she wanted a bed for this, so she led him those extra steps into her bedroom.

Once there, Noah took a beat, cupping her cheek. "Are you sure?"

"I'm sure." To reassure him, she unbuttoned her shirt.

Noah watched her fingers, focused on each tiny button as it slipped through the fabric. She cursed her outfit. This morning, she'd been happy with her selection—gray trousers, a button-up blouse and ballet flats—but now it just seemed like too many clothes. Too bad she hadn't worn a loose dress that she could simply throw over her head and onto the floor.

He started to ease his suit jacket off, but she stopped him with a touch.

"No?" he asked.

How could she explain her burning desire to reveal her heart to him, without sounding like she'd lost her mind? "Sit."

"Okay." He eyed her warily, but not unenthusiastically, and sat at the edge of her bed.

Her breath shallow, she continued to undress. She removed her blouse and let it fall to the floor, conscious of Noah's gaze. He followed every movement with interest. He'd seen her naked before, but his eyes narrowed with a new appreciation. She unzipped her pants and stepped out of them. Dressed only in her underwear, she stood still and let him look his fill. At least she'd put on nice underwear. Knowing he was coming over, she'd changed into a pale pink bra with a lace trim, and matching bikini undies.

Noah licked his lips. "Do I get to take my clothes off now?"

"Not yet." Susannah climbed atop him, straddled his lap and kissed him again.

"Fuck," he murmured against her mouth.

He tangled his tongue with hers and a corresponding heat pooled low in her belly. As she ground on top of him, trying to get as close as she could, moisture seeped into her delicate panties.

Suddenly, the cotton and lace irritated her skin. She might have been wearing burlap for all the comfort the garment gave her.

Noah seemed to be enjoying their texture, though. He grabbed her ass over the underwear, digging his nails into her flesh, then slid his hands under the fabric.

Yes! Skin to skin.

See me. Understand me.

His tailored suit did nothing to disguise his erection. He strained against her, and she writhed against the hard ridge, desperate for release. The more they moved, the more the wave inside her gathered strength. It was still distant, looming on the horizon, but it wouldn't be long before it crashed to shore.

Noah could tell too. He positioned her further on his lap, away from his cock.

Susannah could have cried, she wanted it so much.

"Not like this, sunshine."

"Sunshine?"

"Yeah." Pink streaked across his cheeks. "You light up my darkness."

Susannah tried to think of something to say, something terribly profound, but he saved her from having to string any words together when he pulled the cups of her bra down. Exposed, her nipples stiffened.

Noah ran his hands over her breasts, thumbing the nipples, clearly determined to see how hard he could make them. "Fucking beautiful." He lowered his head, taking her left nipple into his mouth while tweaking the other.

Susannah moaned. It was ecstasy and it was brand new. He'd done this before. She'd felt this before. But something was different.

They were different.

He sucked and nibbled, causing her to dance on his lap, almost to the point of falling off. She would come like this if they weren't careful, and she still hadn't allowed him to take any clothes off. Noah's hand inched toward her backside again, rounding over the fleshy mounds. And he didn't stop there. He moved his fingers closer to her core, almost detonating the charge inside her.

Okay. She needed to be naked. Now.

Susannah scrambled off his lap. She probably looked a sight with her wet panties, her boobs out, and her hair sticking up in places. She didn't care though, because Noah was looking at her like she was the goddess Athena, newly sprung from her father's head in full armor.

Standing before him, she removed her bra.

He let out a huff of breath. "Panties off."

She obeyed, slowly sliding them over her hips and down her legs. Then, to taunt him about their last panty interaction, she dangled them from a finger. "Want to borrow these ones too?"

The noise he made was animalistic, the sweetest sound she'd ever heard. "Give them to me."

She dropped them into his outstretched hand, and he brought them to his nose. Noah closed his eyes and inhaled. When he exhaled, it was on a shattered breath. He opened his eyes, tucked the panties into his jacket pocket, and stood. "Get on the bed."

She liked the reaction her teasing elicited and decided to draw it out a bit more. She crawled onto her belly, lifted her hips and wiggled her ass. "Like this?"

They'd indulged in some rougher play before, and they knew each other's preferences and limits. So, Susannah knew what was coming.

When he slapped her ass, she cried out in delight. "Yes."

He ground over her, whispered in her ear, "You like that, don't you?"

"You know I do."

To reward her honesty, he slapped the other cheek. He urged her legs apart and stood between them, kneading her ass. "As tantalizing as this is, it's not quite what I was getting at, and you know it. I need a taste of you, Susannah. On your back."

She didn't dare disobey him. Noah had never denied her pleasure before, and she knew he wasn't about to start now.

She rolled over and made eye contact with him. There was something lighter about his face, and that probably had a lot to do with the fact that she was nude and writhing in front of him, but she didn't like the haunted air surrounding him.

Make it better. Give him something else to think about. Susannah spread her legs.

His gaze never straying from the juncture of her thighs, he removed his suit jacket and draped it over the chair in the corner of the room. He then returned to her and knelt at the edge of the bed. Wrapping his hands around her thighs, he pulled her toward him. The first lick caused her to sigh, the second to groan. The third, accompanied as it was by a suck on her clit, forced a cry from the back of her throat.

God, already so intense. He'd planted a bomb inside her, and it would only take a certain touch to set it off.

Was Edwina right? Was it possible that this whole experience could be heightened if she made herself truly vulnerable?

Susannah decided to test her sister's theory. She tangled her fingers in Noah's hair and opened her mouth to say something, but he fluttered his tongue against her clit and she forgot how words were formed.

He heard her gasp and looked up. His eyes were hooded with satisfaction and he wore her juices like a balm. When he smiled with that wet, wicked mouth, she forgot her own name.

His, on the other hand, was slowly being etched into her heart. She could feel each cut of the invisible knife as it pierced at her flesh, leaving her raw and jagged.

"Noah," she whispered, because a whisper was all she could manage.

"Yes, Susannah?" He toyed with her, teasing his finger into her seam.

Why shouldn't romance happen for you?

It would be so easy to just make him get her off quickly, to have an impersonal fuck and send him home. He'd do it, no questions asked.

This was so much harder.

His expert finger traced her lines, knowing exactly how to prolong her torture. "Say what's on your mind. You can tell me anything. You're safe with me." His face had lost all trace of amusement. There was a shadow in his dark eyes, but she glimpsed hope there.

"I," she began, fumbling, "I...feel it."

That was it? That was all you could spit out? Oh, Suz, brace yourself. This is where he leaves. Pathetic.

But Noah didn't leave. He dropped a kiss on the inside of her thigh and smiled. "I feel it too, Susannah Sunshine."

Hearing her name linked with that sweet little nickname brought tears to her eyes. She blinked madly until they disappeared. She would *not* cry! Certainly not while his face was between her legs.

He'd understood how hard it was for her to utter those three words. He probably understood everything. Noah saw her, truly saw her, and he liked her.

True to Edwina's prediction, something devilish flashed across his face. He cocked his head, regarding her. He was still stroking her with his finger, as if he had all the time in the world. "How much do you think this pretty pussy can take?"

"I don't know. How much can you dish out?" Of course, now that they were talking about sex, she'd miraculously rediscovered her ability for speech.

Sex was easy. The other stuff? Not so much.

His nostrils flared in determination and he removed his hand and went back to work with his naughty mouth. Her hips bucked in response. Her nerve endings had enjoyed a brief respite during her moment of emotional discharge, but they rocketed back to life now. Because this was Noah, and he'd always made it his mission to study her orgasms, he knew exactly how and where to touch her. A few soft licks here, a tongue swirl there and a series of devastating sucks. That was all it took. Susannah dug her fingernails into his shoulders and shouted as the blast shattered her.

Noah didn't let up, not even as her arms fell from his body and her legs turned to mush. When he finally took pity on her, he pulled away, his breathing ragged. He stood before her, all pinstripes and stern eyebrows and wet lips. A thing of beauty, if she'd ever seen one.

Noah wiped his mouth with the back of his hand. His gaze fierce, he yanked on his tie. "The waters are muddied. You know that, right?"

Oh dear. "Yeah."

Susannah began to tumble, to plunge, to plummet. She knew where this was headed.

Splat.

Only, right now, she welcomed the carnage.

Chapter Fifteen

Noah couldn't get his clothes off fast enough. Something had changed in Susannah and it filled him with urgency. He was overcome by the need to put his stamp all over her before she changed her mind and decided she didn't want him at all.

And yet, he was sure they'd turned a corner.

I...feel it.

Those three words, as small and insignificant as they might sound to a stranger, meant the world to him. Susannah was guarded, and he knew how hard it was for her to say even that. He knew it was Susannah code for "I care for you." It might even run deeper than that. Although she'd fought back tears, he'd spotted them and his heart had hammered in response. It was the most meaningful exchange they'd ever shared, and he wasn't about to waste his chance.

He would show her how good they could be together, even if he had to keep her naked and squirming for the next few hours to do so. He tossed his tie to the floor and got to work on his shirt, cursing each button. Susannah watched, her tongue flicking at her open lips.

She liked what she saw. She never would have fallen into bed with him that first night if she hadn't been attracted to him. But there was something new in her gaze tonight, a sort of hunger and surprise, and it brought out the beast in him.

Her gorgeous pussy was still on display. It was the most tempting thing he'd ever seen. She didn't go completely bare. Although she'd removed some of the hair, a smattering of brown curls still decorated the area above her lips. He fucking loved it. Revealing the sensitive skin underneath was like unwrapping a decadent present.

He wanted her to be all his.

They'd never been exclusive before, and they'd both been honest about taking other sexual partners, but he kept coming back to Susannah. He fully realized now that those other one-night stands had been attempts to forget her, but it had never worked. He craved her, and lately, that feeling had ratcheted skyward.

Bare from the chest up, he started to remove the rest of his clothes. His hands shook as he peeled off his socks, pants and boxer briefs. He retrieved a condom from his wallet and set it on her bedside table.

She slid her hands toward her breasts, encircling her nipples. "Noah."

Her voice was the purr of a hungry cat. He could listen to that sound all day long. Gripping his rock-hard cock, he stroked it nonchalantly.

Susannah's pupils dilated, the black pinpricks swallowing the umber iris.

"Tell me what you want."

She'd never been shy about discussing her desires before, but she was at a loss for words today. Her throat moved as she swallowed.

Still stroking, he moved closer. With his other hand, he touched her knee. "Susannah, tell me what you want."

"I…can't." A hint of moisture kissed her eyes.

Oh, no, no. He couldn't have her crying. He knew it was difficult for her to discuss her emotions, but if she was still struggling, then he hadn't made it comfortable enough for her. Noah knelt before her at the side of the bed and pulled her to sitting position. He clasped her hands. "Hey, hey, hey. Listen to me. I know something's happening here, and I think you know it too."

Her head dipped in a nod.

"And I want you to know I would never rush you or take your feelings for granted. I want you to feel safe with me, Susannah, so safe you never second-guess yourself or worry about how something will sound. And if there's something I haven't done to make you feel protected, I'm asking you to tell me so I can fix it. The last thing I want is to hurt you. So, let me be clear. I care for you, and I want us to give this a try. I have no interest in anyone else. I don't want to fuck anyone else, or to bare even a part of my soul to someone who isn't you. You're the one I want."

She held back her tears but ended up making a funny hiccupping sound. He smiled and cupped her cheek.

"So, in the interests of helping you feel safe," he continued, his chest tight, "I would really like you to tell me what you want right now, because I will do it. If you want me to eat your pussy for the next day and a half, sweetheart, I will clear my schedule. If you want to climb me like a tree and ride me until you have no strength left in your legs, I will be your mount. If you want me to fuck you until my stamina is nothing more than a memory, consider it done. And if you just can't deal with any of this right now and you want to stop, that's okay too. If you want me to collect my sorry ass and walk out of the door, I'll do it for you. All you need to do is say the word."

She took a second to reply, and he hung on her words. Luckily, she didn't tell him to take a hike. Instead, Susannah nodded toward the condom. "Put it on."

Thank Christ. Noah reached for the packet, tearing it open and putting it on with lightning speed.

She then lay back and pulled him on top of her. As he nestled between her legs, she touched his cheek. "I want to feel close to you."

"Yeah?" He nudged her opening. "Like this?"

She nodded.

Heart to heart. Excellent choice.

Noah entered her slowly, enjoying the mad rush of sensation that accompanied his movements. He offered her an inch of himself at a time, and her whimpers grew the deeper he drove. She grabbed his ass, holding him tightly against her, and buried her face in his neck. She'd come so hard last time, but he was determined to make her come again. Missionary wasn't normally their jam. When they met for their quick hookups, they typically chose positions that facilitated speed and efficiency. But he was happy to take his time now, and if this was how she wanted it, this was how he would give it to her. Even if it killed him.

She sighed. "You feel so good."

"So do you." Noah claimed her mouth, continuing his leisurely seduction. They rocked against each other, their timing so perfect. She always showed so much appreciation for his moves. He'd never known anyone who seemed so in sync with his instincts in bed. Her touches drove him wild. Her breath was always so sweet and her kisses fed him better than a gourmet meal.

He was already close. He didn't dare increase his speed, for fear of coming too soon. He refused to come until she did again.

Withdrawing a little, he moved a hand between them. Her clit was so swollen. As he stroked it, she cried out. "Yes. Oh, Noah, yes."

"You like that? Want me to suck that pretty clit again?"

Her eyes widened. "Could you?"

He chuckled. "Nothing would make me happier." Noah slid from her body, almost groaning from the loss of contact. It wouldn't matter. There was no way he was losing this erection. Besides, he could come from sucking her off, it was that good.

Shaking all over, he descended to his knees again. He'd spend the rest of his life on his fucking knees if she let him. His touches more desperate now, he yanked her toward his mouth. There was no preamble this time, no sweet kisses on the thigh. Noah sucked that delicious clit until it fairly bulged between his lips.

Within seconds, her arms were flailing. "Yes! God, yes."

Noah grunted and did that thing with his teeth that always drove her over the edge. She fell apart beneath him, clutching the sheets and gasping.

His cock strained. He was more than ready. As her moans softened, he got up and speared inside her with a brutal thrust. "Fuck! Yes." Over and over, he drove deep inside her.

Susannah's cries were manic. She kept calling his name, God's name, and probably those of a few angels and demons too.

All the pain Noah had been harboring since seeing Luca and finding Ava, all the shame he'd masked since telling Susannah about the loss of his voice, poured out of him in a mighty rush. He lost himself in his thrusts, indulging in a punishing rhythm that left him changed by the end. When it was over, his throat was raw and thick, and his own emotions played havoc with him.

Everything was a mess.

How would he ever help Luca, and how could he keep Susannah and his students safe from the insidious presence at the school?

Out of nowhere, a voice echoed in his head. This time, it was Colette's. *Do you honestly think Susannah will give her heart to you? In the end, she won't want you.*

Even now, his pain distorted Colette's memory and her words, making them harsher than they ever had been in reality. Even now, they wounded him. When would it ever stop?

Oblivious to his inner turmoil, Susannah caressed his back. "You're perfect."

"Oh, sunshine. I promise you I'm not."

He pushed Colette's ghost away and tried to hold on to what he had with Susannah, whatever it was. He wasn't sure how long it would last, or how much she had to give. But Noah was greedy, and he would take whatever she offered.

Chapter Sixteen

Susannah's growling stomach roused her from a luxurious near sleep. She turned her head to look at the bedside clock, and even that small movement brought forth new aches in her body. *Eight o'clock.* They had missed dinner and must have fallen asleep after their sex fest. She should probably order some takeout. They had a lot to discuss.

However, she snuggled back into Noah's side and closed her eyes. It was nice there, warm and cozy. His armpit made the perfect pillow for her head and his chest hairs tickled her nose.

Why hadn't they ever snuggled before? Snuggling was seriously awesome.

A few minutes later, his stomach growled too. He chuckled and turned toward her.

No. I want my armpit pillow back.

He dropped three soft kisses onto the corner of her mouth. That was seriously awesome too. "You look so soft and satisfied."

She opened her eyes. His hair was mussed and stubble dotted his jawline. God, he was beautiful — achingly beautiful. "I am satisfied."

"Me too, but I wouldn't feel right if I didn't feed you. I'll order something for us." Before she could offer to do the same, he slid out of bed. Still nude, he walked over to where he'd left his suit jacket and pulled out his phone.

She rolled over to observe him better. Noah had once confessed he rarely had time for the gym, but his body still bore the memory of previous workouts. He was just solid everywhere, with nice pecs and a high, round ass. No wonder he filled out those suits so well. In her opinion, he was bloody perfection. He was hairy too. She liked that, and she knew for a fact that he loved the odd tug on those wiry hairs.

Then there were the marvels beneath his waist. Her gaze drifted toward his crotch. His cock was semi-erect, and still remarkable.

He glanced over his shoulder. Did he like having her watch him?

Judging from his wink, he did.

Good. She was beginning to realize she hadn't spent nearly enough time doing so.

He scratched his hip, drawing her attention to another mouth-watering piece of flesh. "What are you in the mood for? Pizza? Wings? Pizza and wings?"

If only he knew her appetite lay elsewhere right now. *Settle down.* "Pizza and wings. I'm starving. Any pizza's fine. Just no anchovies or mushrooms, please."

"How hot do you like your wings?"

"As hot as you can tolerate them."

He clutched his chest. "Susannah, are you trying to steal my heart away? A fellow hot wing lover. Awesome."

She laughed along with him, amused by the idea of stealing his heart with a few chicken wings. Nonetheless, his words tickled her.

Does Noah make your heart happy?

He'd certainly made parts of her extremely happy over the last couple of hours. But it wasn't just the life-affirming sex. He'd been so kind, so generous. She'd shared her feelings, in the only way she'd known how, and he'd helped her feel treasured and secure.

Maybe with a bit more time, and a lot more effort on her part, she could share more. Maybe this could actually work.

He finished placing his order and walked back over to the bed. Even though she was snug under the sheet, his gaze raked her as if she was on full display. "Do you have any idea how sexy you look right now?"

"I, um, was just having similar thoughts about you."

"Oh, yeah?" He groaned. "I really want to get back in bed with you, but we should talk."

"We should."

He reached for his discarded suit pants.

"Want to wear something more comfortable? I have a tracksuit in the closet that might fit you."

He hesitated to answer and she realized what he must be thinking.

"It didn't belong to some ex," she clarified. "I actually bought it a few weeks ago for Simon, Edwina's husband. His birthday is coming up. But then I decided to get him something else, and I forgot to return it. It's brand new. You look about the same build as him."

"You don't have to explain. I know you've been with other people."

Just as Noah had. A terrible thought occurred to her. Had he collected any of *their* panties? The rush of jealousy brought heat to her face. "Right. Anyway, I just thought I'd mention it in case you don't want to put your suit back on."

"You're sure you won't need it?"

"I'm sure." She slid out of bed and walked over to the closet.

Noah crept up behind her. He slid one arm around her waist and cupped her bare ass with his other hand. "Mmm. You're hard to resist."

Her knees started to liquefy, but she held her ground. Before his fingers started to wander, she pulled out the tracksuit. "Here you go. If you like it, you can keep it."

"Thanks." He pulled her close and nuzzled her neck. "I guess we should get dressed, huh? This pizza place always works quickly and I doubt the delivery person wants to see my naked ass at the door."

She gave his butt a playful slap. "This ass? You'd make their day."

He looked at her, one eyebrow raised in curiosity. "You like my ass?"

She toyed with his chest hair, overwhelmed by emotion yet again. It churned inside her, filling her lungs while choking off her words. Was this what it would always feel like? A tsunami of feeling? She wouldn't survive it.

He tipped up her chin, making her look at him.

"You know I like...all of you, Noah. I like all of you very much."

Something warm and wonderful flashed in his eyes. To have that light aimed at her was both awe-inspiring and intimidating. "I like you too, Susannah Darke. Every last inch of you."

He kissed her softly, but it still scored her with heat. Before that heat enveloped her, she extricated herself from his embrace. She needed to think, but she wouldn't be able to if Noah Bellamy was naked in her presence much longer.

They got dressed. Noah looked cute in the tracksuit, even though it was so different from anything she'd seen him wear. The dove-gray fabric suited him. In a weird twist, he was no less distracting in a tracksuit than he was completely nude or in a slick suit, but she did her best to keep her gaze at eye level.

She threw on some flowered leggings and a loose T-shirt that skimmed her hips. After grabbing a couple of beers, they sat in the living room and awaited their delivery.

As they waited for dinner, he told her about finding Ava in the practice room, and about Luca's appearance. The stress returned to his face as he recounted the details. Susannah held his hand, listening quietly, so he could unburden himself.

"Ava had agreed to tell her parents about how she'd ended up at the school, but she changed her mind at the last minute. She begged me not to say anything about hauntings or about her getting on the subway without realizing it."

"I get it. People struggle with the idea that the paranormal could exist. They probably struggle even harder with the thought that others will judge them for believing."

"Have you always believed?"

"Growing up with Addy? Hell, yeah. I mean, when your little sister tells you she's playing building blocks with her invisible friend Maria and those blocks start moving by themselves? You become a believer quickly. But not everyone can process that stuff. Geez, up until last year, even Edwina was still pushing back on Addy, and she grew up seeing the same things I did. I understand why Ava wouldn't want to worry her parents."

"She made up some story about feeling lightheaded at school. Of course, they were concerned, but she laughed it off, saying she hadn't eaten a proper breakfast that morning. I had to go along with it. Ava's an adult. I can't force her to tell her parents anything."

"I'm sure they appreciated you looking out for her, whatever the reason."

The delivery person buzzed Susannah's unit. When he arrived, Noah collected the food from the door and brought it in. They piled up their plates with gooey slices and sticky wings and sat at her kitchen table.

She let him get a few bites in before she brought up her research. She told him all she'd discovered at the library, including the part about Dr. Asch's grief and his visits to Madame Liliana. "I've been working under the assumption that this medium might have been a scammer, that she was taking advantage of Asch, but there are other possibilities. Let's say her intentions were good. Even if she was trying to help, Madame Liliana could have inadvertently opened up the school to all sorts of activity. Addy always says you have to be very careful who you invite through the door."

"Are you saying the school could be some kind of portal?"

"It's one theory. I'm struggling to find others. If Elodie is haunting the place, she isn't making herself known. Even Addy couldn't sense her. The Asch Institute appears to have been a place where, for the most part, people were kind and had the students' interests at heart. But maybe something awful slipped through, something that can affect the living in a negative way. Look what it did to Ava. What if the same thing hurt Luca too?"

"Christ." He didn't say anything for a long time, and when he did, his voice was uneven. "He's suffering, isn't he? Luca's been suffering all these years."

"Let's not get ahead of ourselves. Like I said, I'm spitballing here. You said yourself that he'd only just started appearing in your dreams, as well as Blake's. Why wait twenty years to do so? Maybe Luca came back to warn us about Ava."

"We have to help them, Susannah."

"And we will, I promise."

"Ava said something that struck me as weird. When I found her in that room, she said the voice called her Terence."

"Terence?"

"I know, right? But she was insistent. The voice apparently said, '*I'm disappointed in you, Terence.*'"

"Interesting. It's another name to research." She dabbed her mouth with a napkin. "But it's clear my research is only going to take us so far. I may need to find my answers somewhere else. I think it's time I confronted this thing head on."

"What are you suggesting?"

"It remembers me, Noah. It came for me before. Maybe I can tempt it to come for me again."

"I don't like how that sounds."

"Provoking spirits is what we do. Trust me. I'm prepared for this. My sisters and I have done plenty of solo investigations. Sometimes, you have to poke the bear. Or, the bear's ghost, in this case."

"Wait. You want to go in there on your own?"

"The rest of you would still be in the building somewhere, but yes, I want to visit the practice rooms by myself. We'll set up cameras and video, and you could watch. You'd all be nearby if something went wrong."

Noah pushed away from the table.

"I'll be perfectly fine, I promise."

"You do that a lot, you know." His jaw ticked. "Tell people you're fine when you're not."

"Noah..."

"You're nervous, I can tell. Your hand's shaking, and you've scratched the nail polish off three fingers now."

Had she? Damn. She clenched them and brought them to her lap. "We have to do something. What if this haunting has nothing to do with the Asch Institute at all? It's not lost on me that this could be connected to the land itself. For all we know, there could be some ancient evil attached to the place. What if this has been going on since even before Elodie Asch hit that bottom step? Maybe this entity has been quietly picking people off over the years, and no one has noticed because they've attributed those deaths to something else, like a fall down the stairs or a weak heart."

"But to use you as bait?" He held out his hand and she grabbed it. "I don't want you to get hurt."

"Look, I'll admit I was scared to come back to the Asch, but I went in with eyes open. And now, after seeing what this thing has done to Ava, to Luca and to you? Now, I'm fucking pissed. It's time for a reckoning."

He glared at her, but there was respect in that glare.

"Can you trust me?"

"I do trust you."

"Good. I promise you, Noah. We will clear your school of any evil. That shadowy fucker might think he has a few tricks, but my sisters and I have a few up our sleeves too."

He pulled her from her chair and brought her to his lap. She straddled it, immediately aware of the bulge at his crotch. Susannah moaned and rubbed up against it.

Noah ran his hand up into her hair and gently tugged, exposing her neck. He kissed it, nipping at her skin. "You're a fucking badass, and I don't want any more pizza. I want you."

"Good. I want you too."

They scrambled off the kitchen chair before their movements broke it. Noah threw her down on the nearest available surface, the couch, and yanked on her leggings. He spread her legs and began to kiss her there. It only took a few artful licks for her to tumble through space.

Susannah grunted in pleasure, digging her fingernails into his shoulders.

Noah thought she was a badass? She could live with that.

Where this man was concerned, she would be a grade A, top-of-the line, badass, and she would gladly put herself in harm's way to keep him safe.

Chapter Seventeen

"I'm so glad I get to join you on your ghost hunt tonight." Blake fist-bumped Noah as they headed to the Asch Institute loading dock behind the building. "It was lovely of you to invite me. Oh, wait. You didn't invite me, which was rude, by the way."

"I'm sorry, but there was a reason for it." Noah stopped walking. He hadn't excluded Blake for the purposes of making him feel bad. If anything, he'd hoped to spare his friend any additional grief, but he should have been clearer about his intentions. "Blake, I have no idea what might be going down tonight. I've already lost one friend. I don't want anything to happen to you."

"Oh." Blake swallowed hard, his Adam's apple bobbing. "Don't worry about me. I'm tough as nails. Besides, Luca's been visiting me in my dreams all week. I need to have a part in helping him find peace."

"I know. I just wish it didn't have to be this way."

"Come here." Blake held his arms open.

Noah embraced him hard, patting him on the back. "I miss him."

"Me too. We have to help him." Blake managed a pathetic laugh as they pulled apart. "He's still wearing that ratty Sam Roberts Band T-shirt. I was really hoping he might have upgraded his wardrobe in the hereafter."

Noah chuckled. "Hey, we were there when he bought that T-shirt. That concert was awesome."

"It was." Blake smiled. "And I still have my T-shirt tucked away in a drawer."

Somewhere during the exchange, they'd both shed a few tears. They both wiped their eyes. "It's going to be okay." Those words had become Noah's mantra lately. He found himself pacing around his office or his home, whispering the same phrase all the time. He wasn't even sure if he believed it anymore, but there was something reassuring about saying it out loud.

It's going to be okay. It has to be.

In truth, he was glad Blake was here tonight. He would be a welcome addition to the team, and there was something to be said for strength in numbers. Besides, he would keep Noah on an even keel when Susannah headed off on her solo investigation.

A fucking solo investigation. What the ever-loving fuck?

He'd been saying "fuck" a lot lately too.

Hey, listen. If you want a serious relationship with this woman, you'd better get used to this. It sounds like she does this shit all the time.

He'd tear his hair out.

Noah could already picture their weekends. Instead of driving out of town on a nice day to a farmer's market, or catching a movie or a ballgame, they'd likely be wandering around graveyards at midnight or breaking into abandoned houses to check out the vibe.

Was he ready for this?

If he meant he got to spend time with Susannah, he sure as hell was. As nerve-wracking as the idea might be, he wouldn't have it any other way. When Noah remembered the sweet vulnerability in Susannah's eyes or the way she shattered in his arms, he knew he was ready for the total package.

You love her.

This time, he didn't snipe at his gremlin. Noah just hoped she was prepared to accept him as he was.

He rolled his shoulders, trying to stretch out his muscles. Something told him this ghost hunt was going to be tense, but he had to have faith that Susannah and her sisters knew what they were doing.

They headed outside and onto the loading dock. Blake craned his neck. "A car's pulling in. Your *casual friend* and her sisters are here."

Noah hadn't filled him in on the developments between him and Susannah. Firstly, he didn't actually need to know all of his business. Secondly, it was so new. Noah wasn't taking anything for granted. Yes, Susannah had taken a huge step in admitting she cared for him, and even though he was grateful and hopeful, he remained guarded. This could all still fall apart.

If she hurts you, you won't recover. Your heart will be effectively broken, buddy.

"Whoa," said Blake. "Check it out."

Noah glanced at the black Jeep that had parked below the dock. The Darke sisters got out of the vehicle. The setting sun illuminated them, casting a rosy glow. As he got a good look at them, he had to clap his mouth shut.

Susannah and her sisters all wore the kick-ass gear that they normally wore on their YouTube episodes. Cute black polo shirts with the DPI logo, black cargo pants and Doc Martens. He'd seen them wear the outfits online but had never seen it in person.

Forget broken hearts. He might not recover from this insanely hot vision.

"Come on." He pulled Blake by the arm. "Let's go help them."

Adelaide greeted them first. She had ornamented her rough-and-tumble look with a sparkly comb on one side of her bobbed hair. "Greetings, earthlings."

Edwina stood next to her. She had her auburn hair up in a ponytail and wore her usual dark red lipstick. She nodded toward Blake. "Hey. Who's your friend, Noah?"

Noah made the introductions, his gaze straying toward Susannah.

She had been rummaging in the backseat of the Jeep, but she emerged now and his heart issued a pathetic series of beats upon seeing her up close. She swept her long blond waves out of her face and walked around the Jeep toward him, and for some reason, his addled brain insisted on showing it to him in pornographic slow motion.

Holy fuck.

Her shirt was tucked into her cargo pants, cinching her waist and accentuating her curvy hips and mouthwatering breasts. Her scuffed Doc Martens made it look as if she'd just returned from a rumble, one in which she'd kicked the ever-loving shit out of the other guy. Her lips were pale and pink and she wore a dark eyeshadow that made her look like an old Hollywood temptress. A breeze carried her soft scent toward him, and he had to ground himself on the sidewalk so he wouldn't fall over.

Blake walked over to embrace Susannah before Noah could react. "Hello again. This smoky eye?" He brought his fingers to his lips in a chef's kiss, then turned to Edwina and Adelaide. "The three of you are too gorgeous for words."

"Stop." Adelaide's sly grin said, *"Don't you dare stop."*

"We decided to bring our gear this time," said Edwina. "I've got some new tech that I'm eager to try out. Seeing as we'll be filming, we figured we should dress the part. Noah, are you still okay with us filming? The students are gone for the day, right?"

Noah gazed at Susannah, lost in a pervy dream about sticking his hands in her cargo pants pockets. *Hmm, so many pockets ...*

"Noah?" Blake elbowed him. "Edwina asked you a question."

"Right." He snapped to attention. "Filming. Sure." God, he'd lost the ability to string a proper sentence together.

Susannah gave him a bashful sort of smile, her smoky eyelids shimmering, and his gut whimpered at the sight of her.

She might very well be the death of him. It had only been a couple of hours since he'd seen her, and his body still craved her.

She bumped up against him. "Hi."

"Hey, you. I was planning on playing it cool, but I really want to kiss you. Would that be okay?"

"I wish you would."

Noah cupped her cheek and brought his lips to hers in a soft caress, one that wasn't nearly long enough for his liking, but that promised longer ones. Her perfume teased him, making it hard for him to pull away. "What is that perfume?"

"Lily of the valley. Is it too strong?"

"No, it's perfect. I want to eat you up. Make sure you buy, like, boxes of it."

She laughed quietly. "Never fear. I have a full bottle."

The chatter around them had stopped. Noah looked over his shoulder.

The three of them weren't even bothering to pretend not to watch. Edwina and Adelaide grinned, and Blake's mouth opened and shut.

Time to deflect. "Are we doing this ghost hunt thing?"

"Yes. Everyone grab a case and let's go." Edwina grabbed the handle on one of the equipment cases and headed toward the entrance. The others did the same. "I'll need some time to set up my stuff. I haven't brought all our tech with us, just some of the basics. Cameras, motion detectors, EMF readers, that sort of thing. And, of course, my new ghost box communicator. If all goes well, we should get messages from the dead."

"For real?" asked Noah.

Edwina beamed. "Yes! It's the coolest thing. It displays words and numbers and allows spirit people to use those terms to answer questions. It also scans the environment for spikes in EMF and temperature changes. As soon as a spike occurs, I get an audio alert, and the display lets me know which sensor was triggered."

Noah leaned toward Susannah and whispered, "I didn't understand any of that."

She grinned. "It's okay. She does."

"Well." Blake's eyebrows shot up in mild horror, probably at Edwina's enthusiasm for ghostly communication. "You folks know how to have a party, don't you?"

"You still have time to back out," said Noah.

"No." Blake shook his head. "I want to be here. For Luca."

They made a couple of trips back to the Jeep to collect a couple of other pieces of equipment, and the Darkes proceeded to set it up in places around the school. They moved quickly and efficiently, and it was obvious they had done this many times.

Once they were finished, Adelaide gathered them all together in front of the main staircase. She closed her eyes and said a short prayer. She also called on her spirit guide, Maria, to help them throughout the night. When she opened her eyes again, she pinned her gaze on the staircase, and whispered, "Finally."

Even though Noah didn't have her abilities, he immediately understood they weren't alone. Chills shot down his back, sending cold right down to his toes.

"There's a spirit person here," said Adelaide. "It's Dr. Asch."

They all turned toward the stairs. Noah peered but couldn't see anything out of place.

"Thank you, Dr. Asch, for coming to us. My name is Addy. I want to assure you we're here to help." Adelaide frowned, zeroing in on a spot about six feet up from the bottom step. "He's not paying attention to us. He's muttering something and pacing back and forth in front of the stairs. He keeps saying, 'It's a dreadful business, Melly.'"

"Melly," said Susannah. "That's Melba Flanagan."

"Residual activity?" asked Edwina.

"What does that mean?" Blake whispered the question.

"It means a sort of imprint of past activity," explained Edwina. "It plays over and over again but isn't an intelligent haunting. It doesn't interact with the living."

"No. He's definitely here." Adelaide shook her head. "But he's too distracted by his own memories to talk to us."

"Is he looking for Elodie?" Susannah asked.

"About Elodie?" Adelaide was adamant. "She's not here. I didn't sense her before, and I don't sense her now. I believe that when she died, she moved on right away. Maria's telling me she's at peace. Victor's upset about what's happening at the school."

"Is he the one causing the oppressive feelings?" asked Noah.

"Absolutely not. The vibe I get from him is concern," said Adelaide. "If you were to run into him, you'd likely hear footsteps or the tapping of his cane on the floor. I don't think he wants to scare anyone. He loved this school, and still does."

For some reason, Noah was relieved. He'd always felt a kinship with Dr. Asch and didn't like to think he might be the ominous presence.

Blake avoided looking directly at the staircase. "Can you help him go into the light or something?"

"At some point, I'd like to help him move on," said Adelaide. "Although, I get the sense he knows how to cross over. He just doesn't think it's appropriate right now."

"Because of the 'dreadful business'?" asked Noah.

Adelaide nodded. "He feels it's his responsibility to stay until it's resolved. He won't leave his students."

"Can you get him to talk, Addy?" asked Susannah. "Maybe he has some answers. Does the name Terence mean anything to him?"

The youngest Darke sister stepped toward the stairs, her voice calm and clear. "Dr. Asch, there's a dark entity here at your school and I know it worries you. Help me banish it. Please tell me what you know."

The hardwood steps creaked in several places, as if someone was walking upstairs.

"He's gone," said Adelaide a few moments later. "He's upset, but he's also unsure of how to help. He feels he has to stay on the move, almost on patrol." She glanced toward Susannah, her own face full of worry. "I'm sorry. I couldn't break through to him."

Susannah rubbed her arm. "It's okay. We all know you're doing your best. You've helped us narrow things down."

Noah was glad to see that the sisters had patched things up after their last visit to the school. He could tell they meant the world to Susannah.

Edwina handed them each a flashlight. "All right, everyone. I'm going to hit the lights." She walked over to the central electrical panel and threw the main switch, plunging the school into darkness.

They all pressed the buttons on their flashlights, but only Noah's and Susannah's illuminated.

"Shit. I just put fresh batteries in each one right before we drove over." Edwina fiddled with her ghost box device. "The battery's dead on my spirit box too. For fuck's sake." She grunted.

Adelaide held a small recording device. "My recorder won't turn on."

"Of course not." Edwina pasted on a smile. "It's okay. I had a feeling we'd have some issues. That's why I brought spare batteries. Give me a sec. I'll run back to the Jeep."

"I'll go with you," said Adelaide. "It'll be dark out there. You shouldn't be alone."

As the two women started walking away, Blake looked back and forth between Noah and Susannah. "So." He drew out the word.

Noah grinned. "Yes, Blake?"

"I, uh, am going to go help them put batteries in the flashlights. I think that could be a three-person job." He scurried after them.

Noah's nerves came out in a chuckle. "We've been deserted."

"Looks like it."

Alone with Susannah, Noah took the opportunity to pull her close. "We're off to a good start this time. Ready for what comes next?"

She wrapped her arms around his torso. "Ready as I'll ever be. I'm glad Addy's already been able to make a connection. I have a feeling it's going to be a busy night. It feels different in here. The air's electric."

"Oh, yeah? I'll take your word for it." He dropped a soft kiss on her lips.

She closed her eyes for a moment, moaning quietly into the kiss. When she opened them again, her gaze drifted over his shoulder and down the hallway. She sucked in a breath.

"Are you okay?"

"We're not alone." As she spoke, her eyes grew wider and wider. She aimed her flashlight down the corridor.

His back hunched with nerves, Noah slowly turned.

A woman stood at the end of the hallway, by the stairs leading to the library. Although she was far enough that he couldn't make out the details of her appearance, he caught a few key items. She wore a form-fitting gray jacket over a white lacy blouse, the kind with a high Victorian collar. Her bustled gray skirt was made from the same fabric as her jacket, and it dusted the ground. She had curly blonde hair, which was gathered up high on her head.

The Gray Lady.

Her figure was diaphanous. As she moved, Noah was able to make out the line of the wall molding behind her.

Susannah's voice was hushed. "Please tell me you're seeing this."

"I see her."

The Gray Lady raised her hand and gestured for them to follow her.

"What do we do?" asked Noah. "The others are still outside."

Susannah's jaw was set. "No time to wait. Keep your light on her." She grabbed her cell phone from her cargo pants pocket. "I'll quickly text my sisters."

The spirit woman turned the corner toward the library stairs, disappearing from view. However, as they followed, they found her waiting halfway down the staircase. Once again, she crooked her finger and continued walking. Aside from the delicate swish of her bustled gown, she moved silently. The scent of roses trailed behind her.

She stopped in front of the library and allowed them to catch up. As she waited, she ran a dainty hand over the letters of the Elodie Asch Memorial Library sign.

"It's not Elodie," whispered Susannah. "Elodie had dark hair."

Noah couldn't shake the sensation that he'd seen the blonde woman before. He angled the flashlight in her direction. She was tall, about five-eight, and she held herself high. Her eyebrows were blonde and sparse, almost invisible. Her blue eyes were set close together, a trait that was exaggerated by her pince-nez glasses. Although there was a translucence about her, he couldn't miss the detailing on her gown. It was well made, with fine finishes. The gray color gave it a somber air, but there was a hint of extravagance at her throat. There, she wore a silver and pearl brooch. It nestled delicately in a flourish of lace. She turned and glided into the dark library.

Noah didn't understand how Susannah was keeping it together. He was about to lose his shit big-time.

A real ghost.

Then again, he'd already seen Luca's spirit. He was getting to be a pro at this sort of thing.

The spirit woman's presence, while mystifying, didn't fill him with the same dread and grief that Luca's had. If anything, he couldn't help but gaze in wonder.

"I'm going to try to get an EVP." She hit the record button on her phone. "Thank you for coming to us. Are you here about the evil spirit haunting this school?"

The ghost nodded and continued her quiet journey. She led them into the rare book room and stood before a glass case filled with old school memorabilia. She pointed to the bottom corner of the case.

"What are you trying to show us?" asked Susannah. "Can you talk to us?"

The spirit woman's lips pursed in frustration. She continued to point at the display case, her arm shaking with vehemence.

"Okay, we understand. Noah, can you shine your light where she's pointing?"

He did so. "It's an old opera program from one of the school's productions. Wait. There's something behind it. It looks like the edge of a photo. It must have fallen behind the other items at some point. I'll get the keys for the case."

He went behind the service desk and grabbed the pertinent key ring. He unlocked the case and pulled out not one, but two yellowed photos. He set one down on a nearby table and they looked at the other. "This was taken in 1890. It's a group photo of the faculty. I don't think I've ever seen this before."

There were nine men in it and two women. Their names were all listed under their figures. Dr. Asch sat in the middle of the front row, leaning back, his legs crossed at a casual angle.

To Asch's left sat his wife, Elodie. The other woman, a blonde, sat on Asch's right. She was the mirror image of the spirit woman standing in front of them now.

Susannah gasped. "You're Melba Flanagan."

Melba nodded.

"What's keeping you here?" asked Susannah.

The spirit woman whispered, "Him."

Noah glanced at Susannah and back at Melba. "Dr. Asch?"

But Melba shook her head.

"What's happening here at the school," began Susannah, "doesn't have anything to do with Elodie's death, does it? She really is at peace, isn't she?"

Creases of wistfulness formed around Melba's eyes. She raised a gossamer hand and touched the photo, brushing the faces of Victor and Elodie. Then, she touched the brooch at her throat.

"The Asches gave you that brooch?" asked Susannah.

Melba smiled. "They were my friends."

"They admired you and appreciated all you did for the school, Melba." Noah took a step toward her. "We all do. I want you to know that. Your dedication hasn't been forgotten."

Melba's chest rose and fell with a breath of apparent gratitude.

Noah wasn't sure if his expression of thanks would be enough to give Melba peace, but he hoped it would help. He didn't want her to suffer. She'd given everything to the school—her entire career.

She put him in mind of some of his own teachers here at the Asch. Early on, he'd had a couple of vocal coaches who had nurtured and guided him through the stresses of those early auditions, when no one knew his name. Hell, if you'd asked him then, he would have gladly taken a bullet for them. As an educator and vocal coach, he now modeled himself on his early mentors, and hoped he inspired his students to go out and do incredible things.

He wanted to be what Melba had been for so many.

"Melba," Susannah said, "if Dr. Asch isn't the one who keeps you here, who is?"

Tears gathered in Melba's eyes. She dabbed at them with a handkerchief that was as translucent as the rest of her. Her shoulders shook with a quiet sob.

Susannah held out a hand. "I know it takes a lot of energy, but please try to talk to us again. Who is keeping you here?"

The spirit woman gestured toward the second photo—the one Noah had set on the table.

Noah grabbed it and held it between the three of them. It was a photo from the same time period, and it displayed two white men, an old man sitting in a chair and a younger man standing behind him. The older gentleman's face was etched in harsh lines, giving him an air of disapproval. The younger guy clutched the back of the chair, but he looked as if he wanted to be anywhere but there. He had a pleasant enough face, with kind eyes and a freckled complexion, but his shoulders were slouched in apparent defeat. He read out the caption. "William Ambrose and Terence Ambrose."

Susannah jumped when she heard the names. "Terence! It's coming back to me now. Terence Ambrose was a piano teacher here at the school. His father was some sort of big-time music publisher, wasn't he?"

"Oh, yeah. Ambrose & Co. was one of Canada's first music publishers. The company's not around anymore, but I've picked up some of their music at antique stores and estate sales."

Melba's sentimental gaze landed on the younger Ambrose's image.

"Terence worked here. Is he the one who's responsible for all the negative activity?" asked Susannah. "Please talk to us."

But Melba just shook her head in frustration.

"Melba, listen to me," Susannah implored. "Someone's hurting the students, scaring them. I know that must upset you, considering how much of your life you spent caring for them. Help us understand. Who would do this? If it's Terence, we need to stop him."

The spirit woman's face took on an aspect of horror. She held her hands over her face and her shoulders heaved with a silent cry. Melba then reached out to them in a final appeal. As she faded away, another waft of rosy fragrance permeated the air. She whispered a few more words. "Please help him. I can't reach him."

For a moment, Noah and Susannah just stood there, in awe.

Noah's body trembled with a shiver as any icy draft wafted around them.

Susannah stared at the photo of Terence Ambrose. "I need to find out everything I can about him. So far, I've come across very little."

"I don't believe Terence worked here for long. If I recall, he died a few years after this picture was taken."

"Right, I read about that. He died of fever, but he was at home, not at the school. I didn't think anything of it because it didn't seem connected to what's going on here. I skimmed his bio, but nothing stood out as a red flag." Her eyes widened. "Wait. The EVP. *'Are you happy, Father?'* That must have been Terence."

"And there was voice that Ava heard. *'I'm disappointed in you, Terence.'*" Noah quickly replaced the old photos back in the display case, but he made sure to prop them up against the back of the case so they could be seen. He then shut and locked the case, and replaced the keys. "So, none of this has been about Elodie's death at all. All those rumors people have spread throughout the years, all those ghost stories were fairy tales. Meanwhile, she's at peace."

"There's something to be said for that, at least. I guess when Melba was first spotted in her spirit form, people just assumed the Gray Lady was Elodie. I made the same assumption." Susannah sighed. "I feel foolish."

"Why?"

"Because I've been barking up the wrong tree since day one. Whenever I go into an investigation, I always keep an open mind and I never take things at face value. But this time, I bought into all the hype surrounding Elodie's death. I was sure she was the Gray Lady, just because others had said so. I feel like I've wasted your time."

"Susannah, no. We all believed the hype, but now Melba's given us some new information. We're onto something."

"And we have the real Gray Lady to thank for it." Susannah slipped her hand into his. "When Melba was alive, she took care of the people here. She's still doing so. It's not fair that she's stuck here."

It filled Noah with anger and a need to understand. All that was left of that dynamic woman was a grieving, frustrated wraith, who'd possibly been wandering these halls for decades.

Right there, he made up his mind to commemorate Melba Flanagan's contributions to the Asch. It should have been done a long time ago.

"Onwards and upwards, I guess. We still have a vigil ahead of us. I think it's time we address the Ambrose men." Susannah led him out of the library with the determination of a Valkyrie. They held hands as they raced upstairs to join the rest of the group.

Another series of chills skittered across Noah's back. All of a sudden, he sensed eyes on him. It wasn't

Melba's gentle presence, either. It was something grasping, something desperate and terrible.

From out of nowhere, his head began to throb. The pain started at the base of his skull and spread to his forehead. Dark clouds appeared before his eyes. As he struggled against the sudden onslaught of pain, his stomach turned over. Bile coated his throat. He tried to tell Susannah, but his throat closed on his words. As they went upstairs and rounded the corner on the stairs landing, he swallowed hard, trying to get rid of the foul sensation.

The most terrible thoughts assaulted him, weighing him down. *You're not good enough to run this school. What makes you think you'll be able to help anyone here? You can't even sing. You're dried up. Finished.*

With difficulty, Noah glanced back at the library entrance.

Out of the corner of his eye, he spotted a man in a dark suit. His mournful stare captured Noah, his eyes burning with black fire.

No!

Even though he stood at a distance, when the man reached out his hand, something odious seeped into Noah's being and latched on.

Chapter Eighteen

Susannah caught her breath as she hit the top step. The first thing she heard was several sets of footsteps running down the hall.

"Ohmigod," Edwina cried. "What happened?"

"The Gray Lady, she's Melba Flanagan." Still shaking and a little disoriented, Susannah let go of Noah's hand and proceeded to tell them what Melba's ghost had relayed. As she spoke, Susannah glanced toward Noah. Even in the dark hallway, his face was a sickly white. He stood aside from the group by a few feet and leaned against the wall. "Noah, are you okay?"

He nodded and gave her a thumbs-up.

He was probably winded after their run up the stairs and the strange encounter with Melba. God only knew she was.

Adelaide reached for Susannah's hand. "Are you guys all right?"

"Yeah," said Susannah. "Melba directed us to an old photo of Terence and William Ambrose. Terence, the son, taught piano here at the school for a few years in Melba's day. William was a music publisher, but he doesn't seem to have been connected with the school. I think Terence might be our guy."

Adelaide cast her eye around the hallway. "Something's here. I can sense a spirit man hovering. It's a horrible energy."

"The bugger wants to come out and play, huh?" Edwina chuckled darkly. "Okay. Come on out, Terry. We'll play."

"We need to be careful," cautioned Adelaide. "Maria keeps telling me something's not right."

It was often easy to forget Maria was around, at least until Adelaide reminded them. When she did, it could be off-putting. Maria had died of whooping cough in 1907, a mere toddler, and she'd somehow latched on to Adelaide years later. Even though Maria revealed herself to Adelaide as an adult, she had a distinctly childlike way of manifesting in front of others. Whenever Maria needed to warn them of danger, a disembodied childish cough could be heard. It was a horrible, racking cough, probably just like what she would have suffered from in 1907. Even after all these years, the sound still caused Susannah's body to turn to ice.

Susannah and Edwina had seen Maria's full-body apparition only once, during the Niagara haunting at Simon's bed and breakfast. Sure enough, she'd appeared as an adult. After that, they'd stopped thinking of her as the creepy Edwardian kid who followed their sister around.

"Maria says he's confused and angry," said Adelaide. "This entity doesn't realize he's dead, and he thinks we're the ones interfering. He doesn't want us here. He wants us out...now."

"Is it Terence Ambrose?" asked Susannah.

Adelaide rubbed her forehead. "I can't tell. All I see is a dark mass."

Susannah rose to her full height and shouted into the air. "We're not going anywhere, dude. You need to understand this is not where you belong anymore. It's time for *you* to leave, and to stop hurting the students!"

"Susannah, don't," cautioned Adelaide. "He's so mad right now."

"Well, he can stay mad. I'm mad too. I need to get into a practice room for a solo vigil. I have questions."

"That's a bad idea." Adelaide fingered her heart pendant. "This is a powerful entity. We should stay together."

"I'll be fine, Addy. We've all done solo vigils before."

"Yeah, but this guy specializes in isolating people," said Adelaide. "If we separate now, it'll give him the upper hand."

"Susannah's right, Addy," Edwina interjected. "We have done this before. We'll keep an eye on her."

"Want me to stand on guard outside the room?" asked Blake "I have no idea what I'm doing and I'll probably pee myself, but...."

From out of nowhere, a child's hacking cough sounded in the hallway. The pained noises echoed all around them.

It was Maria.

Blake's eyes widened. "Uh, did someone bring a kid to this shindig?"

"No, it's my spirit guide, Maria." Adelaide stood firm. "That cough is her way of warning us of danger. You heard her, Suz. We need to stick together."

"But, Addy—"

"I said no."

The coughs grew in volume, to the point where Susannah was tempted to cover her ears.

Oh, come on. Why was her sister trying to hold her back, now that they'd finally made some headway on this case? Frustrated, Susannah looked to Noah for support.

Only then did she notice that he was gone. She looked up and down the corridor, but he was nowhere in sight. "Wait. Where's Noah?"

They all looked around.

"Shit." Adelaide's hand shook. "When Maria started getting upset, I thought it was because you wanted to do the solo vigil. She was actually trying to tell us to watch out for Noah. We have to find him! Blake, come with me. Suz, take Ed with you. Stay connected on the walkies." She grabbed Blake's arm and they began to check the nearby classrooms and offices, calling for Noah as they went.

Susannah's pulse quickened. *No, no, no, no. Not my Noah, please.*

How had she lost track of him? And how had he slipped away undetected?

For someone who'd quashed her emotions for most of her life, she sure was feeling them now, and each one centered on Noah. If he was hurt or traumatized in any way, she'd never forgive herself. Why had she been so insistent on doing that stupid solo vigil? She'd let pride get in her way, and now Noah might pay for it.

Her head throbbed as she tried to process her distress. Darkness encroached on her field of vision, narrowing it. She blinked several times in an attempt to clear the shadows.

"Hey." Edwina grabbed her by the shoulders. "Breathe."

"Ed." Susannah tried to suck in a breath, but it never reached her lungs. "If he hurts Noah…"

"Look at me. He couldn't have gone far. He's in here somewhere. We'll find him. Let's go to the practice rooms."

Clutching her hand, Susannah followed her sister, grateful for her willingness to take charge. Now, as fear swarmed Susannah's heart, she would follow Edwina's lead.

It had always been that way. Edwina had always been their fearless leader, charging into battle. A vision from Susannah's childhood popped into her head. It was of the sisters, walking to school. Edwina strode ahead of them, her dark hair tucked into a braid. Her eyelids were lit up with a smear of brilliant blue shadow, makeup that their parents hadn't allowed her to wear, but that she'd smuggled into her backpack for a fast application around the corner from their house. Edwina tugged on Adelaide's hand, urging their younger sister to pick up her pace. However, Adelaide's face was buried in a comic book. She wore her favorite Yoda barrettes in her hair and had a matching green T-shirt. When she did look up, she spoke nonsense into the air.

She was talking to Maria, of course. That was something Adelaide had done out loud a lot when she was younger, and it had led to her being bullied in school.

In the memory, Susannah followed them, watching from behind. She had been a slim little girl with a blonde ponytail and knobby knees. Even back then, she'd been obsessed with tales of haunted castles and villainous royals. One time at a vintage sale, she'd found a costume replica of Anne Boleyn's famous B pendant. Being Team Anne, she had begged her parents to buy it for her. She'd worn that B everywhere, which had led to a fair bit of confusion at school, considering there wasn't a single B in her name.

The bullies had loved that too. *Those Darke sisters are such freaks.*

As Edwina led her through the halls of the Asch Institute, pangs of nostalgia swept through Susannah. Along with that nostalgia came raw anger, and a desire to protect her loved ones from the bullies.

That included Noah now.

She must care strongly for him, or else she wouldn't be so afraid to lose him.

They entered the practice room hallway and Susannah turned on the lights. All the doors had been propped open for the evening, and she ran down the corridor, quickly scanning each room. There was no sign of Noah.

"He's not here. Let's go back." This time Susannah took the lead, racing up the stairs two at a time.

Once she was back on the main floor, she stuck her head around the corner to see if Adelaide and Blake were there.

But she saw someone else instead.

A young man stood outside Noah's office, staring at her. In that half-second, she felt each hair on her body lift in awareness.

"Luca."

Edwina joined her, seeing the apparition. "Holy shit."

"Hurry!" Susannah raced toward Noah's office, and Luca faded away as she got closer. She tore into the reception area but found the inner office locked. She pounded on the door but it wouldn't budge. "No!"

"Leave it to me. It's probably just stuck." Edwina opened up the small cross-body bag that she always used during investigations and pulled out her keychain. Attached to the key ring was a mini pry bar. She wedged it into the seam of the door and applied pressure. After a couple of tries, the door popped open.

Noah lay on the floor in front of his desk. Susannah raced over and threw herself to her knees. His eyes were open and wide, but unmoving and unseeing. Was he in shock? She wasn't sure, but at least he was breathing. They could work with that. She touched his cold check. "Noah? It's me, Susannah. I need you to come back to me. Please."

He didn't even blink.

"Noah, listen to my voice. Whatever's going on in your head, just tune it out and listen to me. You're stronger than this. *We're* stronger than this. Please come back. I'll never forgive myself if I led you into danger." As she begged him to awaken, her eyes filled with tears. Several fell onto his face, near his own eyes.

Whether it was out of sheer reflex or something else, Noah finally blinked. His eyes focused, landing on different points in the room, but settled on her. "Susannah." His voice was gravelly and sounded sore. "You're crying."

An indelicate sob burst from her as she hugged him.

He sat up and pulled her into a tight embrace. "It's okay. You found me."

Edwina cleared her throat. "I'll go tell the others you're all right."

For a while, all Susannah could do was hold him and give silent thanks for Edwina's love of gadgetry. He smelled so good and she buried her nose in his neck, trying her hardest to burrow deep so no one could ever pry her away.

Was this love?

If so, it didn't come with the awful *splat* that she'd come to expect. She braced herself for some terrible impact, but if anything, it cushioned her and helped her feel secure. Every piece of joy that she'd ever stifled came rushing forward in a blaze of light.

Noah was okay, and she might actually be in love with him.

She was starting to wonder if she'd always felt this way, ever since that first night at the group dating event with the bad wine and limp spring rolls.

Baby steps, remember? You don't need to label this right now.

"What happened? One minute, you were with us in the hallway, then you were gone."

"I don't remember how I got to the office, but I do remember seeing a man as we left the library. His eyes just bored into me."

She understood the creepy sensation all too well. "Yeah, well, he wasn't the only one watching you. I saw Luca. He led me to you."

The heaviness of the world came out in Noah's sigh. "Of course, he did. He was always a good friend."

"Let's get you out of here. That's enough investigating for one night." She helped him up and they headed back to the school entrance to meet up with the others.

Edwina was already dismantling some of their equipment. Remaining in groups, they quickly collected the rest of their tech and packed it up in the Jeep.

Adelaide got into the passenger side of the Jeep. Edwina turned to the others. "Anyone else need a ride?"

"I'm good," said Blake. "I live close by, and I could use some air." He turned to Noah and crushed his friend in a hug. He let him go with a sniffle then hugged him all over again.

Susannah realized how much the two men were still suffering over the loss of Luca. It must be horrible to never get closure, to never have the chance to say goodbye. Her thoughts drifted back to the recording of Noah and Luca singing together all those years ago. Those three boys had never seen this coming, not any of it.

She would get them the closure they needed, no matter what she had to do to achieve it.

Susannah grasped Noah's hand. "I'd like to see you home, to make sure you're okay."

His answering smile caused a hundred butterflies to crawl out of their cocoons. They fluttered high up in her chest. She kept her mouth closed, for fear of letting them out and losing the sweet moment of giddiness.

"All right. We'll check in with each other tomorrow," said Edwina. As the others wished each other a good night, she pulled Susannah aside. "You okay?"

"Yeah. Thanks, Ed. I love you."

"Aw." She hugged her. "I love you too. Now, go make that man a hot toddy or something. He's seen a few things tonight."

As far as Susannah was concerned, they'd all seen more than enough. She glanced back at the windows of the Asch and quietly cursed the dark spirit.

Its reign of terror was over. She would see to it personally.

Chapter Nineteen

When they got back to his place, Noah was surprised to see it wasn't as late as he'd thought. It hardly mattered. He still felt as if he was recovering from a bad flu. Everything ached, his head pounded and his throat was dry.

But Susannah was with him, and he was fairly sure she'd saved his life tonight.

Luca and Edwina had helped, of course. He couldn't forget that.

However, it was Susannah who now held on to his arm as if she was afraid to let him go. They'd walked back from the Asch like that too — touching each other, their fingers or arms always entwined.

When he'd regained consciousness in his office, she'd looked so scared. He never wanted to see that look on her beautiful face ever again, so he needed to get his shit together now.

He locked his condo door behind them and took a deep breath. "Here we are. Can I get you anything?"

She dropped a soft kiss onto his mouth. "Sit down and rest. Let me get you something."

Fair enough. He was parched. "Water would be great. Actually, there's some really good whiskey in the corner cabinet. Could I have a bit of both?"

She shooed him into the living room so she could get the drinks. He sat on the couch, sinking into the soft upholstery. When she returned with the two glasses, he threw back the water first, then the whiskey. Susannah poured herself a measure of whiskey too, and she shot it back. Neither of them cared about savoring the drink tonight, it seemed.

She was still standing, so Noah patted the seat next to him. She put her glass down and flew to him, snuggling in tight and draping her arms around his chest.

He chuckled and stroked his fingers through her hair. "I'm not going anywhere, you know."

"I didn't like seeing you like that."

"It was just like when I found Ava. She couldn't remember how she got to the school that day."

Susannah pulled away so she could look at him. "Has anything come back to you?"

"All I really noticed were those eyes. They were terrible."

Her lip curled. "The entity must be able to jump people, to possess them in a way. I just don't understand why. If it is Terence, what's his motivation? He was a teacher in life. I don't remember reading anything about him that struck me as creepy. Melba said in her memoirs how much she enjoyed working with him. Heck, even in the photo he looked kind of sweet. Downtrodden, maybe, but still sweet. William, on the other hand, looked like a total asshole, but he wasn't even connected to the school. I don't understand why this is happening."

Just talking about Terence and William Ambrose made his head feel heavier. "Could we talk about it tomorrow?"

"Of course. You must be exhausted. I remember how I felt after he came to me." Susannah gnawed on her bottom lip. "I can go home, if you'd like."

"No." Noah slid his hand around the back of her neck and brought her forehead close to his. "I wouldn't like that at all. I want you to stay."

"I'd like that too."

They put their glasses in the kitchen sink and Noah led her to his bedroom. He gave Susannah one of his T-shirts, in case she wanted to sleep in something, and they took turns using the bathroom. While she finished up, Noah stripped out of his clothes, leaving his boxer briefs on.

As much as he wanted to forget he'd ever seen that ghostly face, it was the man's voice that continued to haunt him. It was like the spirit man understood his insecurities, maybe even better than Noah did himself.

The words cut into his tender flesh, just as Colette's had all those years ago.

Maybe it was time to acknowledge that wound out loud. He never really had.

Susannah emerged from the bathroom, wearing his shirt and her panties. God, she took his breath away.

She deserved his honesty.

Susannah went over to his window to shut the blinds. He joined her there and reached for her hand. "Can I tell you something?"

"Of course."

He brought her to the bed and they sat. He glanced at his bookshelf over Susannah's shoulder, and his gaze landed on the framed photo of Luca, Blake and him. It had been taken the year Luca died. Part of the reason Noah had worked so hard to make his singing dreams come true was because Luca never would. For that reason, his failures stung even harder. "What happened tonight…it brought up some bad memories, and I feel like I need to talk about them out loud."

"Okay."

"It has to do with an ex. Do you mind?"

She hummed in agreement, but her nerves manifested as she scraped at one of her fingernails.

Noah didn't want to upset her with talk of exes, but maybe Susannah deserved to hear what Colette really thought of him. It might even change the way she looked at him, but he had to take that chance. "A few years ago, I was involved with a woman named Colette. She's an opera singer too. We met during a production and hit it off, but everything soured after I had my surgery. Like I told you before, it was a dark time for me. When I wasn't feeling sorry for myself, I was raging against an unfair world, one that had taken everything from me. And because I didn't share the truth with too many people, Colette got the brunt of my bad moods. At first, she tried to be supportive, but it couldn't have been easy being around me. She left me a couple of months after the surgery, and her parting words were harsh. I know it was just a bit of tough love, but it hurt."

"Tough love or not, it sounds like it wasn't what you needed to hear."

"I don't know. Good or bad, her words wounded me and it's been hard to shake them. My brain does this thing now where it reminds me of my failings, and it does it in her voice sometimes. Despite the fact that I've created a new life and a new career, one I really love, that voice creeps into my head when I least expect it and reminds me of what I could have been. What I *should* have been."

"Oh, Noah."

"Anyway, I just remembered that when that spirit appeared to me in the school basement, it said the same things. That I'm a failure. And it made me think of what happened with Colette, and I just thought you should know what you're dealing with. My headspace isn't always a happy one. Sometimes, I still go to those dark places and they can be hard to shake." Noah let go of her hand. "Those voices tell me I'm not good enough for you, that you couldn't possibly see anything of value in me. This is me, giving you an out, if you want one."

"Listen to me." She laid her hands on his cheeks. "I don't want an out. I'm all in, okay?"

"Really?" The weight on his chest lessened by a few degrees.

"I think you're amazing. You're strong and sexy and so supportive of others. I know it must have hurt to lose your opera career, but like you told Ava, you're not defined by your ability to sing. You're so much more than that."

"It was my whole identity, Susannah. It's so hard to let it go, even now."

"I hear you, but I still think you're selling yourself short. I look at you, and all I see is beauty and goodness."

The very things she represented to him. "Thanks. Maybe your voice will finally be the one to replace the others."

"To be honest, and I'm trying hard to be honest with myself these days, I've been so worried that you won't see anything worthwhile in me. If I've kept you at a distance, it was just out of self-preservation. I've been hearing voices in my head for years too, and they've never been kind."

Her eyes welled up and his did too. Her tears tore his heart out. "Come here." Noah pulled her down to the mattress and wrapped her in a bear hug. He kissed the length of her gorgeous neck, one of his favorite places in the world, trying to soak up her fading lily-of-the-valley perfume. "I'm sorry. Now, tell me who I need to kill."

Her chest moved with a quiet laugh. "You sound like Edwina."

"I knew I liked your sisters."

"They like you too." Susannah traced his eyebrows with a gentle finger. "But I like you more."

He loved her. He fucking loved her. He'd told her of his secret shame, and she hadn't bolted. Instead, she gazed at him as if he were a superhero.

He wanted to be her hero.

As that desire took root in his heart, some of his shame melted away. He knew it wouldn't disappear overnight, but Susannah made him hope for a time when it didn't overwhelm him. "I think you're amazing too, and I want you to tell me about those voices."

"I guess you should know what you're getting into as well." She sighed. "As a kid, I was told I was highly sensitive. It's actually a thing. I feel too much. I take things too hard. It confused and upset a lot of people, so I had to hide my feelings. I learned early on that I couldn't be myself around anyone other than my sisters. So, I haven't been myself for a long time."

"That pisses me off. I want you to know that you can always be yourself around me. I'm interested in the real you, whatever that entails. You shouldn't have to hide behind a mask."

"I'm afraid, Noah. I'm scared that if I show you the real me, the messy me, you won't want to stay."

"Okay, I'm just going to call it. That's impossible. I'm literally obsessed with you."

She laughed and curled into him a little more.

"Besides, I happen to think sensitivity is awesome. The world needs more of it. Whenever those voices come to you, remember there are people out there who think you're incredible. *I* think you're incredible. I can't get you out of my head. You're all I see. Even when I'm having my worst nightmares, you help me dream of better things, my Susannah Sunshine."

"Noah." She closed her eyes and kissed his neck.

He hardened at her touch, thrilled he could still get it up after what they'd endured. He smoothed a hand over her hip, toward her breast.

Her forehead creased in concern. "Are you sure? I know tonight was rough."

"If you don't want to…"

"No, I do. I want you."

"Then, I'm sure." Noah claimed her lips and rolled her onto him so that she straddled his hips. His cock strained against her. They needed to get rid of their last layers of clothing right away. He yanked at her shirt, pulling it free from her waistband, and slid his hands up her back. Her skin was so soft, so smooth. He moved his hands up toward her breasts. Her nipples stiffened under his touch. He rolled them between his fingers, trying to see how hard he could make them. Every time he made a pass of her nipples, she groaned. Writhing atop him, she closed her eyes and put her hands on top of his.

"That's it. Show me how you like it."

Susannah stopped moving and looked at him. "That's what's amazing about you. You've always known what I like. You understand me."

"I want to know more. I want to know everything."

For a second, Noah expected her to retreat as she always had whenever things smacked of commitment.

But she didn't. Instead, there was a sweet vulnerability in her gaze, one that said she was ready to share it all. He knew she was scared to hand over her heart, but she was doing it anyway. She was placing her trust in him, and he would never betray it. He would cradle her heart in his hands and treat it like the precious cargo that it was.

He was ready to worship her. Hell, he would debase himself just to keep her nearby.

She arched her back, thrusting her breasts against his hands. "Please, Noah."

"I like how you say my name."

"Noah." She licked her lips. "Please."

Such beautiful nipples. So full and soft. He had to taste them. Noah leaned back on his elbow and guided one breast to his mouth. He teased the stiff peak, letting her feel his teeth.

"Yes." She hissed out the word.

"That's it, beautiful. Tell me how you feel." He moved to her other breast, licking there for encouragement.

"I want you inside me." She was rocking so hard on top of him that she had to be close.

Not good. He didn't want her to be close. He hadn't even gotten her panties off yet. "Slow down, love."

Her eyes widened at the word.

Had it slipped out? Yeah.

Was he worried? No. But this wasn't the way to tell her. He would tell her the way she deserved to be told, not in the midst of a frantic grope.

And yet, Noah knew this was more than that. Their connection had grown stronger. It didn't flutter in the wind anymore, always on the verge of floating away. He could grasp it now. It had become tangible, potent.

It was something he would never take for granted.

As someone who may or may not have been slightly possessed that evening, he was suddenly eager to grab onto every ounce of pleasure that life offered. He would hold on to it, and he wouldn't let it go.

More than anything, he wanted to share that pleasure with Susannah, to drive her to the brink of delirium.

But for that, he needed her to be naked and splayed out in front of him. He released her nipple and grinned up at her. "As much as I love your panties, they have to go." He urged her off him, sat on the bed and made her stand between his spread legs. "Take them off."

"Take them off."

Susannah nodded, too overcome to speak. There was something different about Noah tonight. He'd always exuded confidence, but it seemed to spring from a different well now. It ran deeper.

Maybe it was the fact that a vengeful spirit had jumped him and locked him in his office. Maybe it was because he'd shared his fears with her, and she'd shown him compassion instead of contempt.

Then again, maybe it was because of the word he'd uttered moments ago, the one that still hung in the room around them.

Love.

Was it possible he loved her? A shiver of excitement coursed throughout her body.

Don't get ahead of yourself. Just live in the moment.

In this moment, she really wanted to be naked.

So she slipped out of her panties, moving slowly and with deliberation, letting him enjoy the leisurely striptease.

Her breasts were at the level of his face, and he took time to draw each one into his mouth, slowly sucking. She squirmed in her spot, needing him between her legs, but he held her in place. Noah kissed her as if he had all the time in the world. He kissed her ribcage, grazing his lips back and forth as he traced each bone. As he paid homage to each inch of skin, he gripped her ass cheeks, squeezing and plumping them.

And he was trying to hold her orgasm back? Each pass of his tongue brought her closer to the edge. At this point, a few well-placed touches would set her off.

This orgasm would incinerate her, she just knew it. As much as she welcomed it, she almost feared it.

"Lie down."

Susannah lay back and awaited further instructions. She admired his chest, itching to play with the hair there. He was drop-dead gorgeous, but it wasn't his body that stopped her in her tracks. It was the warmth of his smile and the hunger in his gaze.

How could Colette think he was anything other than perfect, even when he was feeling sad?

I'd take you at your worst. Noah's words had been replaying over and over in Susannah's mind, filling her with wonder each time.

She would take him at his worst and be thankful to have him. She wanted to be her best for him.

She...loved him.

A euphoric warmth fanned out from her chest, making her feel as if she could fly.

Susannah would tell Noah she loved him, whether he was a famous opera singer or not. She would just have to find the right moment.

Noah reached for one of her legs and rubbed her foot.

"Oh God." She groaned in rapture. "You might not want to start that, or I won't let you stop."

He chuckled. "That wouldn't be a problem. I'll give you foot rubs whenever you want."

If he kept this up, she might ask him to marry her.

Her sisters would never let her live that down.

The glorious massage carried over to her other foot, and it felt so good that Susannah almost fell asleep.

"Tired?"

"No, just very cozy."

"Good. I want you to be comfortable with me." His dark eyes glittered with a hint of danger.

Okay, maybe he didn't want her to get too comfortable.

Noah knelt before her. "I'm going to lick your pussy now, Susannah. I'm going to lick it until you beg me to stop, but I won't. I'm just warning you."

She gripped the sheets.

He spread her thighs, swiping his thumbs along her wet seam, teasing them into her entrance. Just that one touch caused her body temperature to skyrocket.

The next touch made her melt. Noah insinuated his tongue between her lips, slowly tasting her as if refamiliarizing himself with the territory. He hummed and moaned, clearly savoring her as much as she did him. He stayed away from her clit, in a way that told her he was determined to keep her on the edge of madness. Before long, she was twitching under him, desperate for release.

But he didn't give it to her.

"Noah, please." It seemed her entire vocabulary this evening consisted of only those two words. He'd stolen her ability to string any other phrases together.

To appease her just a little, he flicked his tongue over her clit.

Susannah bucked on the bed.

"Mmm, so good." He dipped his wicked tongue into her folds once again, teasing her. When he slid a finger inside her, she prayed he would finally take mercy on her and let her come. She squirmed, nudging closer to his hand.

He laughed and pulled away, nibbling her thigh.

Susannah was so wet she had to be soaking his sheets, but Noah seemed unconcerned as he feasted on her skin. Unfortunately, he kept avoiding the area where she needed him most. She just wanted to grab his head and plaster his mouth to her clit until he finished the job.

She also wanted this, though. As much as his slow adoration drove her to the brink, she was also happy to luxuriate in his touch.

She trusted Noah, with this and with everything else. She knew he had her interests and desires at heart.

She stopped squirming and begging and allowed herself to simply feel. Her heart raced. Her body softened. Everything inside her opened in acceptance. Susannah could almost swear a shimmery string ran between them now, one that linked them in every way that mattered, one that couldn't be severed by outside forces.

Was this what it was like to give oneself completely to another being? To feel strong and vulnerable at the same time?

"Are you okay?" Noah tilted his head. "You've gotten quiet."

She reached down and touched his face. *So handsome.* "I've never been better."

His lips compressed. "I want you to come now."

As his lips found her clit, Susannah closed her eyes and dug her fingernails into his shoulders. It took no time at all for the wave to crest. It had been building all along, but it now pounded the shore with a ferocity that threw her off her feet. "Yes! That's it. Yes, Noah."

He sucked until her whimpers died away and her arms tumbled from his shoulders. Her legs, so weak and useless, fell open. Her body continued to convulse as he drew out the longest orgasm of her life. As the spasms softened, he gentled his touch, but didn't pull away. Noah continued to drink from her, to soak her in, until a new energy seized her.

She reached up to push him away, to let him know she'd had enough, but at the same time she didn't want him to stop. Somehow, the fingers that should have been nudging him only ended up tangling in his curls. Where she should have pleaded with him to stop, she ended up murmuring, "More. God, Noah, yes!"

His breath was coming hard. She could feel it on her skin. This was nonsense. There was no way she could come again so quickly. Noah continued to surprise her, and her shock erupted in frenzied cries.

Noah latched on to her clit and sucked hard. Everything in her world fell away and she shot into the sky. Susannah saw the moon and the stars, and had never known such beauty. Her limbs danced of their own accord, and she was powerless to stop them. All she knew was Noah, his incredible mouth and the coursing of her blood through her veins.

He was magical.

When her body calmed this time, he let it. His lips swollen and gloriously wet, he climbed up over her and kissed her on the mouth. He tasted of her. Her lips curled into a satisfied grin, even as he drew out the kiss.

"Good?" His voice was soft and deep.

"Unbelievable." She shook her head in awe.

He smoothed a hand over her stomach and between her legs, and she jerked. "Need a break before I fuck you?"

Despite the fact that every muscle in her body seemed to have liquefied, his hand felt so good and Susannah couldn't resist lifting her hips to meet it. She probably wouldn't come again because her nerve endings were already shot, but she still wanted to feel him inside her. "I don't want a break. I want you."

Noah made a noise that could only be described as a growl. It was feral and low and covetous, and it made her heart thrill. He slid off the bed and quickly ditched his boxer briefs, revealing an erection that was so stiff, it had to be painful.

She wanted to ease his pain.

She lifted a finger, which was about all she could do. "Need some help with that?"

He reached into his bedside table and retrieved a condom. His hands shaking, he ripped the package open and rolled it on. Noah then raked his gaze over her, his nostrils flaring. "On your knees."

Yes! She loved it when he got aggressive in bed.

Somehow, she forced her arms and legs into action, and got on all fours.

Noah nudged her opening. "Are you ready for me, sweetness? Are you ready to be fucked hard?"

Susannah moaned.

He slapped her ass, making it sting. "Say the words."

"Fuck me. Hard."

His first thrust forced all the air from her lungs. The second one was so beautifully brutal that she mustered a cry. Noah dug his fingers into her skin, holding her firm. He pounded her until she forgot her own name, moving with efficiency and speed. She was sure it would all be over in seconds.

But then, to her disbelief and amazement, Noah slowed his pace. He was still stiff inside her, so she knew he hadn't come yet. He proceeded to slide in and out of her, building up a new, languid rhythm.

Was he honestly trying to make her come again?

He groaned behind her. She had no idea how he was keeping this up, but he did. And as he moved, a curious tingle shot through her. She began to throb in all the right places. Her nipples tightened and her stomach coiled.

It was happening again, and it was sublime.

Noah eased in and out, whispering her name. With one hand, he sought her clit and caressed the engorged little bud. "That's it, beautiful. My Susannah. My ray of sun."

She was helpless in his arms. Between his expert thrusts and his clever fingers, she came apart again, awash in wonder. This time, he was right there with her. When she shuddered, he gripped her hard and trembled against her.

He kissed the shell of her ear. "You're mine."

"And you're mine."

He held her for a moment then went to the washroom to tidy up. Susannah lay flat on the bed, spent.

When he returned, he sat at the edge of the bed. He pulled her toward him, making her sit between his legs. They faced his dresser and the mirror above it. Staring at her reflection, he caressed one of her breasts. His other hand dipped between her legs, toying with her most sensitive part.

Greedy girl that she was, she wriggled in delight.

"What do you see, Susannah?"

She shuddered to describe it. Her face and chest were flushed. Her hair was all over the place. Her makeup was smudged, the mascara trailing under her eyes. She was an utter mess.

But there was a certain beauty in that disarray. "Freedom."

"This is how I always want you," he murmured, his gaze penetrating as deftly as his fingers. "Open. Honest. Free. Don't ever hide, not from me. Can you do that?"

"Yes."

"Good. You're perfect." He nipped her shoulder, sliding his hand away.

Her entire body groaned at the loss.

He chuckled, the sound dark and dangerous. "Hungry for more?"

"Maybe in a little while."

"I'll be ready."

She took her turn in the washroom. When she returned, the covers were drawn back and a naked Noah lay under them.

He held out his arm. "Come here."

She had never been so ravenous for an embrace. She fell right into it and didn't move.

Noah stroked his fingers through her hair. It was so lovely, *he* was so lovely, and she'd never felt more treasured. Exhausted and full of bliss, Susannah began to drift off.

Just as she slipped into sleep, a warm breath landed on her forehead. It was a kiss, followed by a few whispered words.

She wasn't sure, but she thought she heard "*I love you.*"

Maybe she'd misheard him. God only knew all her other senses were playing havoc with her tonight. Why should she trust her hearing?

Still, it was incredible to believe he might have murmured those words. Either way, it sent her off to sleep with a smile.

Chapter Twenty

The Toronto Conservatory of Music's first board meetings were held to approve its bylaws, set tuition fees and confirm faculty appointments. Of course, Victor Asch had the board's confidence, and any of his recommendations were accepted readily. One of those recommendations was a young piano teacher by the name of Terence Ambrose.

Ambrose was the son of the renowned music publisher William Ambrose. His mother Matilda had passed away immediately after giving birth, a tragic circumstance that left Ambrose alone with a flustered, overbearing father. Ambrose Sr. turned to drink in an attempt to ease his grief.

A child prodigy, Terence excelled at music, but didn't do well in school. He was dismissed from one secondary school for being "incompetent," and from another because he was so focused on music that he failed his other courses. His early years were a source of frustration, and his father expressed his displeasure on what Ambrose called a "constant" basis. Where Terence struggled, William interpreted it as defiance. Unwilling or unable to deal with his son's struggles, William remained convinced that Terence was not only lazy, but irresponsible, and it wasn't unusual for him to lash out in violence.

Despite this, Ambrose finished his schooling and went on to study music at a conservatory in Vienna. While in Vienna, he often wrote to his cousin Albert. In those letters, he documented his relief at no longer being under the sway of "Father's fists."

"He would have made of me another Mozart," wrote Terence, "but I can't think of anything I'd have liked less. I want to teach. I'm meant to be a teacher."

When he returned to Toronto, he offered music lessons to earn a living. His father, displeased with his choice of career, cut ties with his son.

When Victor Asch met Terence Ambrose, the young men had an instant camaraderie. Asch later commented that he too knew what it was like to live under the shadow of a demanding father.

Ambrose went on to have a good career at the Toronto Conservatory of Music, albeit a short one. He was remembered by his students for his smiling face and his eccentricities. He had a habit of walking the school corridors, his hands outstretched as if playing an invisible piano. He referred to all his students as "dear boy" or "dear girl," and seemed determined to impart the kind of nurturing his father had never shown him.

Tradition of Excellence: A History of the Toronto Conservatory of Music by Maureen Peterson.

By the time the night of the school gala rolled around, Noah could barely remember the days leading up to it. There had been so much work and the school had been a hive of activity as decorations went up and students rehearsed for the event.

Although the gala was meant to be a mixer, a chance for Noah and members of his team to impress on their patrons the need for continued support, there would also be some live music. He'd selected a few of the students to do some well-loved pieces. They would stroll periodically among the guests, singing snatches of Italian love songs, like one might see on a street in Rome.

He and the women of DPI had had to put aside the paranormal investigation for the time being, at least until the end of the gala. However, Adelaide had popped in earlier and had done some sort of prayer to "cleanse the space" before the event. It wouldn't be a permanent fix, according to her, but it would hopefully buy them an evening of relative peace and quiet.

Noah could live with that for now.

In truth, it had been eerily quiet since the last vigil, when all the spirits of the Asch had seemed determined to show themselves. Of course, the Darke sisters would still be around to keep an eye on the situation at the gala, in case any creepy-crawlies decided to make an appearance. However, he wanted everyone to be able to enjoy the evening, and he was crossing his fingers it all went off without a hitch.

Noah had brought his tux with him to work that morning. As it got closer to go-time, he changed into it in his office. Half an hour before the event was set to begin, his assistant gave him the heads-up that they were going to open the doors. He made his way down the hall. A small team of students were set up inside the front doors, where Melba Flanagan used to sit, ready to greet the attendees and give them name tags. They all wore suits and dresses. Noah stopped to thank them for their work. "You're all looking spiffy tonight."

"Spiffy?" Zaid Basri cackled and stroked his lapels. "Dean Bellamy, my look isn't spiffy. This suit is fresh."

"Consider me schooled. Hey, did you get any feedback from the audition at the National Arts Center?"

"I haven't heard anything officially yet, but they seemed to like me. They let me finish the aria. That's good, right?"

"Excellent." Noah shook his hand. "If they didn't like you, they would have cut you off mid-breath, trust me. Jim Atkinson is still in charge there, I believe. I'll give him a call on your behalf."

Zaid's mouth fell open. "You wouldn't mind? I mean, I wanted to ask, but..."

"It's my pleasure."

"Aw man, thanks, Dean Bellamy. You're the best."

"No sweat. I'll just tell him you're real spiffy." Noah winked, stuck his hands in his pants pockets, and sauntered away.

Behind him, Zaid groaned over the sound of the other students' laughter.

He headed downstairs toward the school theater. The gala would take place in the spacious lobby, where there was plenty of room for guests to wander. Right now, the event team was in full swing, putting final touches in place. There were flowers, fairy lights and candles everywhere. Tall circular tables had been set up throughout the lobby, so that guests could chat and set their drinks down. Caterers were standing by with finger foods, and the lobby smelled of skewered meat and savory pastry. A bartender was set up in the corner of the room, giving the glasses a last polish. To welcome the guests, a small band played softly in the background. There was even a small space for dancing, should anyone feel inclined.

Noah's phone buzzed.

Susannah: Hey, we're here!

Noah: Be right there!

Noah bounded toward the stairs, then slowed his pace because he knew he probably resembled a dog in heat.

He couldn't help it. He was dying to see her. It made no sense considering he'd seen her just a few hours earlier, but there it was. He couldn't get enough of her.

Although they'd both been busy that week, they'd carved out moments to be together. Susannah had been going back and forth between the library at the Asch and the larger reference library down the street, but she popped into Noah's office often. They'd grabbed a few lunches together, as well as some dinners that turned into overnight stays. If it had been anyone else, Noah would have been glad of a break, but his feelings for Susannah had embedded themselves so deeply into his skin that even a night apart seemed like an eternity.

Still, he was conscious of not wanting to scare her away with too much, too soon.

He reached the main floor and took a second to collect himself. As he walked toward the entrance, he noticed that a few other guests had started to arrive as well. Susannah and her sisters stood before Zaid's table and were putting sticky nametags on their chests. Once she was appropriately labeled, Susannah turned, spotted him and smiled.

Fuck, she was gorgeous.

She was wearing a copper-colored gown that draped over her figure. He had no idea what style of dress it was, but it knocked the air right out of his lungs. There were long slits in the sleeves, so her beautiful arms were visible. It tightened just under her breasts, where a crystal pendant shone, and fell gracefully to the floor. She looked like a column of burnished, edible silk.

Her long hair was pinned up on one side, tumbling into curls on the other. Tiny, sparkly earrings ornamented her ears, and she clutched a small glittery handbag. As for her face, he wasn't sure what kind of makeup witchery she'd conjured, but she was the most ravishing thing he'd ever seen.

"Susannah." Noah reached for her hands, if only to steady his own. He leaned in and kissed her close to her ear. "You're exquisite."

"Thank you. I may have done a bit of impulse shopping for this occasion."

"You have very good impulses."

She smiled. "You're looking hot, Noah. I knew you rocked a suit, but this tux?" She gave him the okay sign. "Is it a rental?"

"No, it's mine."

She waggled her eyebrows. "Nice. So, I'll see it again some time?"

Once again, he put his mouth close to her ear. "You can see it anytime you want."

She made an adorable little hum of approval.

Oh yeah. He would throw his tux on once a week if it meant he got to hear that sound again.

Adelaide cleared her throat in dramatic fashion. "And a good evening to you, Dean Bellamy."

Burning from the neck up, Noah extricated himself from Susannah, but he kept a grip on her hand. "Addy, you look very nice. You too, Ed. No combat boots for either of you tonight."

Adelaide lifted the hem of her forest green gown, revealing matching green sneakers. "Susannah's comfy in stilettos, but personally, I think high heels are an instrument of the devil."

"The sneakers are very you." Noah grinned.

"This is quite the event." Edwina was attired in a simple black velvet gown that had a slit up the side. "I smell food down the hall, so I'm going to go to that place. See you kids later." She grabbed Adelaide's arm and dragged her toward the theater.

He lingered behind with Susannah. He couldn't stop looking at her and ran a hand up her arm where the fabric revealed her skin. "What do you call this kind of dress?"

"Oh, this isn't just a dress. This is a gown of copper charmeuse silk with peek-a-boo sleeves and a bit of ruching at the breast."

"I really like your ruching."

"Do you?"

"You look like a movie star," said Noah. "That color is beautiful on you. You should never take this dress off."

She blushed. "Never?"

"Well, not until I say so."

She ran her hands over the silk at her thighs, and he wished he could do the same. "I probably paid far too much for it."

"No way. It's worth every cent."

"Noah."

"I mean it. I am going to be extremely distracted all night long."

"Don't say that. You have a lot of schmoozing to do."

Just like that, another group of guests entered the school, including Blake and his husband, Nando. They waved, and so did a couple of other people.

Noah groaned softly, but loudly enough that Susannah would know the only thing he could think of right now was peeling that incredible dress off her. "We should go say hello."

"Just one quick thing. I located a couple of digitized editions of books that are no longer available in print, and I have a hunch about our ghost. I think we've had the wrong idea about Terence Ambrose."

"Interesting. Well, then you may be pleased to learn that I've invited someone here tonight who might be able to tell us more about him."

"Really?" She gasped.

"Actually, it's somebody who's really important to me. I'd like to introduce you to her. It would mean a lot to me. Would that be okay?"

At another time, Susannah would probably have hesitated, but she didn't this evening. Her face warmed with what looked like happy curiosity. "If it's someone who's important to you, then I'd love to meet her."

"Awesome." Noah's chest swelled with excitement. He grabbed her hand and led her over to where Blake and Nando were standing. "Let the schmoozing commence."

* * * *

"So then, the conductor said, 'Giuseppe, honey, you couldn't hold that note if it jumped right into your arms!'" Blake's voice rang out in their section of the lobby, periodically drowned out by the laughter. He'd been regaling their group for the last half hour with his opera outtakes and squabbles among certain cast members.

Susannah was sure he was embellishing a bit for effect, but it made for some good storytelling.

She glanced at Noah every so often to see how he was handling all the tales from the opera world. It warmed her heart to see him laughing along with everyone else.

There was a different sort of energy in him this evening. He was, in short, happy. To see him in his element gladdened her as well. All evening long, he'd introduced her to some of the people who patronized the school and there had been some great conversations. She had yet to meet the mystery person he'd mentioned at the start of the evening, but he'd assured her that she would be joining them later.

In the meantime, Noah kept a close eye on his students. There was a core group of them at the event. Some of them were volunteering and others performed the odd aria or duet. Whenever Noah saw any of his students hovering awkwardly on the outskirts of the room, he would hurry over and introduce them to someone else.

Susannah watched him from a distance as he did the same for Zaid. The young man had just finished strolling about the lobby while performing an amazing rendition of a Puccini aria. But once he finished, he seemed flustered by the applause, and retreated into a corner. Noah went over to congratulate him and steered him toward a group of patrons who were thrilled to shower heaps of praise on the young singer.

Noah returned to where Susannah was standing. She grabbed his arm, stroking its length. "You're such a good dad to your students."

"You know what it's like when you're at that age. Events like this can be intimidating. When I was getting started, I sang with a small ensemble that regularly did performances at private parties in some fancy houses. Those folks supported the group financially and we were expected to get out there and mingle. I came from humble stock. I knew nothing about that world and it was really hard for me to interact with high profile people. So, if I can help my students meet a few key patrons now, I hope it'll help them later."

"Well, that woman just gave Zaid her business card, so I think a connection has been established."

Noah smiled proudly at the young man.

"Tell me about your parents," said Susannah.

"They both just retired but my dad was a trucker and my mom was a third-grade teacher."

"They must be very proud of you."

He met her gaze, and a chord of understanding passed between them because of all he'd shared with her. "Yeah. They always have been, no matter what." A server approached them with a tray of avocado bruschetta bites, and he took one and popped it into his mouth. "How about your folks?"

"My dad's a teacher too. Math, in his case. Mom's an accountant."

"Wow, that's a lot of left-brain activity between the two of them."

"Hmm. I have no doubt the world of numbers was a comfort to them when their daughters started engaging with the dead."

He laid his hand on her lower back, softly stroking through the charmeuse silk. "I can't even imagine what some of the conversations must have been like in your house. Actually, I take that back. I feel like I have an inkling now."

"Oh, it could be intense, but it helped that we were all on board. I mean, my grandmother could do what Addy does, so my mom is familiar with the world of spirits. And my dad, well, he was forced to get used to it quickly. He always used to say to Addy, 'Just don't tell me if anyone's standing right behind me.' I think, in some ways, he prefers to stay in the dark." She remembered the look her dad used to get whenever Adelaide talked to Maria. It was part amusement and part stifled horror.

"I totally get that." Noah faced forward, watching the crowd for a moment. He then grabbed Susannah's hand and played with her newly polished fingertips, seemingly lost in thought.

Despite the fact that they were surrounded by lots of chatty people, strolling singers and music, Susannah felt comfortable in her own little world with Noah. She loved the way he stroked her hands, slowly caressing the length of each finger. She regarded his handsome profile, certain she could spend hours concentrating on each dot of stubble or the creases near his eyes and never grow bored. The more time she spent with him, the more she was certain she had no interest in seeing anyone else.

Noah was it for her. She knew that now.

As he had said before, something was happening between them, and it was wondrous and even a little scary. When he was around, she had heart palpitations and the sweats. It was a small miracle that she hadn't perspired through her expensive charmeuse gown.

There were moments when it seemed like too much to handle, but the emotions were more joyous than terrifying now. In celebration of that fact, she decided to reveal another one. "Noah, I've been having such a good time with you tonight. I'm really happy to be here with you."

He turned to her and kissed her hand, grazing his lips against her knuckles. "I'm honored to be here with you." He drew close and kissed the tender spot on the outside of her left eye. Susannah closed her eyes and soaked in his scent and the soft press of his lips. "Come home with me tonight. Unless, of course, you're getting sick of me."

"I could never get sick of you."

"I'm glad to hear it." He pulled away and glanced at something over her shoulder. His face broke into a big smile. "She's here. Ready to meet the person I mentioned?"

"Of course."

Susannah turned and was surprised to see a tiny elderly lady standing a few feet away, leaning on a younger man's arm. She couldn't have been any taller than five feet and she wore a sequined blue dress and matching silk flats. Enormous eyeglasses amplified her brown eyes, making them appear huge. Susannah guessed the woman was at least eighty-five years old.

When the woman saw Noah coming, she smiled with great affection and held out her free arm. "There's my boy."

Noah leaned over and gently hugged the elderly lady. "Edna, it's so good to see you. You look stunning."

Edna dismissed his compliment with a soft laugh. "You were always a charmer." She turned to the man on her arm. "You know my grandson, Bill. He was kind enough to be my date tonight."

"Of course." Noah shook the man's hand. "Nice to see you again, Bill."

"You too, Noah. The school's looking great tonight."

"Thanks, but I can't take any credit. The student committee did all the decorations." Noah grabbed Susannah's hand. "Susannah, I'd like you to meet Edna Peabody and her grandson, Bill. Edna was my favorite teacher here at the Asch, and I love her to pieces. She taught me everything I know."

"It's a pleasure to meet you both." For some reason, Susannah's emotions kicked into high gear as she shook Edna's wrinkled hand. Maybe it was because she was another connection to Noah and to the part of himself that he'd lost.

Bill craned his neck toward the drinks table. "Would you all excuse me for a moment? I'm under strict instructions to get my grandmother a glass of wine. Granny, you're okay if I leave you with Noah and Susannah?"

She winked at her grandson. "Oh yes, but make it a big one."

Bill left to fetch the wine. Noah brought Edna over to a nearby grouping of chairs and helped her get comfortable. He and Susannah sat next to her.

"Edna had an amazing career in opera," explained Noah. "She sang all over the world before she became a teacher."

"Fascinating." It was hard to imagine the tiny lady belting out tunes on a stage, but Susannah guessed Edna hadn't always been so frail. "Did you have a favorite role?"

"My absolute favorite was Mozart's Queen of the Night. It was so much fun to play a villain." Edna giggled.

Susannah met Noah's gaze and smiled. She already loved Edna. "That's a powerhouse role. You were a coloratura soprano?"

"Once upon a time. What about you, dear? It sounds like you know about classical music. Are you a singer too?"

"No, I'm a historian and a paranormal investigator."

Edna's eyes widened. "And you called my work fascinating? I think you take the cake." She looked between Susannah and Noah. "And how long have you been...friends?"

"We're more than friends," Susannah said. "We're together."

Edna clapped her hands together. "Oh! How wonderful." She leaned in. "He's a very good person, you know."

"Yes. I've discovered that."

Noah blushed.

"He's always been kind to me," said Edna. "He visits me all the time and sends beautiful flowers on my birthday. You should see the bouquets. Some of them have been bigger than me."

Susannah's eyes misted at the thought of Noah looking in on his old teacher. "Sounds like Noah. Was he a good student?"

"The very best. Always respectful and so talented. Just a pleasure to have in class. You must understand, by the time I met him, I was already close to retirement, but I put it off for a few years so I could continue teaching him. I taught him for a couple of classes, but we also did quite a few private lessons together. Once I heard Noah sing for the first time, I knew I wanted to be able to nurture and coach him. He was a rare one, even then."

Noah exhaled a long breath. "The two of you are going to give me a big head if you keep this up. Edna, we both know the reason you put off your retirement was because the school refused to let you go."

Edna just laughed it off.

They exchanged pleasantries for a few minutes. When Noah told Edna that Susannah was researching the history of the Asch Institute, Edna looked on in interest. She tapped Susannah's hand. "Yes. Noah did mention that you might have some questions for me. I have a long history here at the school, and I've met many of the teachers and students over the years. I'm happy to help in any way I can."

Susannah met Noah's gaze and a shiver of excitement traveled along the exposed skin of her arms. Books were great, but there was nothing better than a firsthand account. "I'm most interested in a couple of people. One of them is Melba Flanagan."

"Edna," said Noah, "I remember you telling me once that your singing teacher knew Melba Flanagan quite well. Is that right?"

"Yes, indeed. In fact, because of my teacher, I got to meet Melba a few times myself."

They both stared at her in shock.

"But she retired in 1936," said Susannah.

"Yes. I met her much later. She wasn't working at the school any longer, but she still came to school functions long after she'd retired," explained Edna. "Of course, I was very young at the time and Melba was an old lady by then. She was a lovely woman, always so interested in what the students were doing."

"I've been reading a lot about that first generation of faculty here at the Asch," Susannah said. "I've been trying to find out a bit more about a teacher named Terence Ambrose, but he died young and not much has been written about him."

"Terence Ambrose." Edna mulled over the name. "Oh, yes. I heard a few stories about him. My own teacher, Sally Arden, taught voice here for many years. Ambrose was before her time, of course, but she got to know Melba quite well toward the end of her life. Melba must have known she was dying, and I think she found comfort in talking about the old days with someone who understood. Sally was the sort who appreciated a good chinwag, so she listened. Much later, she shared some of those stories with me."

"Could you tell us more about the nature of the relationship between Melba and Terence Ambrose?" Not wanting to upset Edna, Susannah stopped short of telling her that Melba and Ambrose were currently haunting the school.

"I don't normally like to tell tales about the dead, but I don't suppose it would hurt anyone really. They're all long gone now." Edna folded her hands in her lap and leaned forward, her eyes shining with interest. "Melba and Terence Ambrose were madly in love with each other. From what I understand, it was quite the passionate affair. It wasn't common knowledge, of course. Melba insisted they keep it under wraps because she didn't want to compromise her role at the Asch. Unfortunately, Terence ended up dying young, and I guess she didn't see a point in telling anyone about their relationship after that. But when she was near the end, I suppose she changed her mind, and she told Sally all about it."

Susannah was reminded of Melba's final words. *Please help him.* "I've read every page of Melba's memoirs. She never said a word about being in love with Terence, or anyone else for that matter."

Edna's smile was laden with sadness. "Melba wasn't the sort of person to kiss and tell, dear. I've read her memoirs too, and it's there, if you read between the lines. She never married, you know. Some said she was too dedicated to her job to tie herself down, but Sally always used to say that Melba was still mourning the young man. She lived to a good old age too. That's a long time to be alone, missing the only person you've ever loved."

Susannah reached for Noah's hand and squeezed it. They had to help Melba. They had to free her.

That meant, as much as it terrified Susannah, that they might need to help Terence Ambrose too. What if he hadn't meant to terrorize the music students all these years? What if he really had been the kind, eccentric teacher depicted in her sources, and he'd merely been trying to communicate? If Melba had seen something good in him, that goodness had to endure somehow.

His words lit up her brain, as if in garish neon. *"How I've missed you, dear one. Shall we play?"*

Susannah swallowed hard.

Okay, Terence. We'll play.

Chapter Twenty-One

I don't like to think about the year 1895. It was the year my dear friend and colleague Terence Ambrose passed away.

He was too good for this world, and far too good for the likes of some others.

I can't recall much about the happenings at the school that year, although I came to work every day and did what was needed of me. Dr. Asch was kind, at least, and somehow we muddled through together.

Oh, dear reader, I can say with total honesty that of all my years on this earth, none left such an indelible impression on me as 1895. It was, in short, the worst of years.

Life and Times: A Memoir by Melba Flanagan.
Registrar, Toronto Conservatory of Music, 1886-1936

Susannah was quiet and distracted as they entered Noah's condo late that night. It filled him with an intense need to lighten her load and make her feel better. He could swear he spent whole hours of his days now just thinking of ways to entertain and amuse her, ways to make her smile.

They still had their gala duds on, but she'd packed a small bag, clearly anticipating a night at his place. Just the sight of that bag had made him giddy because he was at a point where he didn't want to spend an evening without her.

He turned on the lights in the living room and the kitchen, then hit the power switch on his sound system. The last thing he'd been listening to at home was a compilation of some vintage crooner love songs, so he turned it on now for background music. Despite his love of classical music and opera, he'd also always had a soft spot for singers like Nat King Cole, Mel Tormé and Rosemary Clooney. It was probably because his grandfather used to sing their songs a lot. Anytime Noah went to visit his grandparents, he'd hear his grandpa puttering in the yard, belting those old tunes.

Susannah had only brought a silky wrap to wear over her gown, and he'd given her his tux jacket to wear a couple of hours ago, so she wouldn't be cold. He helped her out of the jacket now, bringing it to his nose for a second because it smelled a bit like her lily-of-the-valley perfume. Grinning, he hung it on the back of a chair.

They sat and she opened up her overnight bag, pulling out the copy of Melba's memoirs. She flipped to a page and pointed it out to him. "Look at this part. It's the only time Melba refers to Terence's death in the entire book. When I first read it, it just seemed like one friend simply paying respects to another, but now I see so much more. *'I don't like to think about the year 1895. It was the year my dear friend and colleague Terence Ambrose passed away. It was, in short, the worst of years.'* Edna was right. I should have read between the lines. Melba loved Terence."

"I don't blame you for not jumping to that conclusion. Why would you? I would think you spend most of your time trying not to make assumptions when you're researching. Isn't it more important to always rely on facts in your business?"

"Facts. Hmm." She played with a silver ring on her finger. "Something told me I was on the wrong path for a while. Maybe I need to trust my instincts more. Did I tell you that Addy thinks I might be an empath?"

"An empath, huh? How do you feel about that?"

"I'm not sure yet, but it does make sense. I've been fighting my sensitivity most of my life, trying to be tough, but I think it's time to stop fighting. Addy thinks that it might even help me in our investigations if I learn to open myself up to the emotions of others in a healthy way. I've been reading about how to do that."

"If I can support you in any way, tell me. I want to be there for you."

"Thanks. I'd like that."

Every time she opened up to him a little more, Noah felt a rush of thrilling energy. "So what are your instincts telling you now about our investigation?"

She looked him right in the eye. "I believe Terence's spirit has caused some of the activity, but I don't think it was done out of malice. I think he's just been trying to reach out. My instincts tell me his father is behind the more insidious activity."

"William, right. Remember what the ghost said to Ava? *'I'm disappointed in you, Terence.'*"

"Exactly. And I keep coming back to that EVP. *'Are you happy, Father?'* If Terence is capable of communicating in an intelligent way, of interacting with the living, then he must be capable of interacting with the dead too. That means William's here. Terence had a terrible relationship with his father. William abused him and his addiction to alcohol is documented. Terence never got his approval, not even in death. I've studied reports of hauntings for years. At their core, there's always some sort of overriding emotion, whether it be love, regret, guilt or a need for revenge. If those types of feelings can survive beyond death, why not the toxic Ambrose family dynamic? I think that's what's poisoning the school."

Noah shook his head, amazed. "You're saying William might still be browbeating Terence in the afterlife?"

"Maybe, on some level, Terence is still seeking his father's approval. William might still be withholding it. If there's one thing I've learned in working with Addy, it's this. The dead don't always find perspective and peace once they've passed over. If they were awful people in life, sometimes they end up being awful people in death too."

"What do we do? Are you saying we should be staging some sort of family intervention for a couple of dead guys?"

"I don't know, but my gut is telling me that William has somehow anchored his son to this place."

Noah shook his head. "You think he trapped him here somehow?"

"Not literally, of course, but they both seem stuck in this unending cycle of volatility. I can see how it might trigger a haunting. It would certainly explain the feelings of oppressiveness around the Asch. When I took lessons here, I struggled with the sense that I just wasn't good enough. Luca felt the same way, and now Ava's dealing with it. You experienced it too. That's the exact message that William gave to Terence again and again."

"Do you honestly believe we can fix it?"

"I'm hopeful. As far as I'm concerned, the priority is to help your students feel safe and proud of their work. I don't want them to leave here feeling like Terence did, like I did. If we can help any benevolent spirits move on to a place of peace as well, I would like to do that."

"And William?"

"If my hunch about William Ambrose is right, and he is here, hopefully we'll move him on too."

"What if he refuses to leave the school?"

She sat up straight, her jaw tight. "We won't give him a choice."

"Remind me to never get on your bad side, Susannah Sunshine."

She relaxed and smiled. "In the interests of transparency, I should probably tell you that I absolutely love that nickname."

"Good."

She shivered and a series of intriguing goosebumps arose on the exposed skin of her arms.

"Are you cold?"

"A little."

Noah stood and held out his hand. "Here. Let me warm you up."

She took his hand and rose to her feet.

Noah pulled her into his arms and buried his face in her fragrant hair. He closed his eyes, breathing her in, loving the feel of her body under the silk gown. Doris Day was now singing in the background. The song, *Too Marvelous for Words*, had a slow, gentle rhythm and they started to sway.

Doris had barely sung two lines before Noah realized he wouldn't have stopped their slow dance for the world.

He knew the investigation was worrying Susannah. It was worrying him too, but he found he was able to shake off his own anxiety to some extent. Her concerns, on the other hand? They weighed him down. They'd become a thing to be vanquished. He wouldn't stop trying to make it all better for her.

She rested a hand on his chest and gazed up at him. "I love these old songs. They're so romantic."

"Yeah. My grandfather used to sing a lot of these to my grandmother."

"Was he a singer?"

"No, he just loved music and he loved her."

"That's sweet."

"My grandma always used to insist that I got my talent from him. We didn't have any other musicians in the family, so I guess she was right."

Susannah gazed at him, her face full of interest and something more, something that tugged at Noah's heart in a way he'd never felt before. For a moment, neither of them spoke, caught up in Doris Day's voice and the gorgeous accompaniment.

But then, her voice cracking with emotion, Susannah spoke. "Noah, I watched a recording of you and Luca singing together."

Thwack. Her comment smacked him hard in the chest, knocking all the breath out of his lungs. He wasn't mad at her for looking up one of his performances. If anything, he figured early on she might have done so. Susannah was one hell of a researcher. It stood to reason she would have researched him.

But there was still a part of him that couldn't deal with Susannah comparing who he was today with who he used to be. He was terrified to look less than what he'd been before.

"Ah."

"It was indescribably beautiful."

He wasn't sure how to respond. It should have been a simple 'thank you,' but that wasn't what his brain spit out. "I'm not that person anymore."

"I know, but the man I see before me now is still indescribably beautiful."

Noah searched her eyes, expecting to see a hint of pity, but there was none. It made him want to believe her. It made him want to allow her deep into his heart, into the place no one else saw.

She rested her head on his chest, and they continued moving in time to the music. His brain spun as he searched for a way to explain how much she meant to him.

Just then, the track changed and Mel Tormé began to sing, *P.S. I Love You.*

It was one of Noah's favorite pieces of all time, and it seemed wrong to dismiss the opportunity to show her, instead of just telling her.

Knowing Mel would back him up, Noah took a deep breath and began to sing. It was the first time in years that he'd even tried. His voice was quiet and ragged in places, nowhere near the robust sound he used to be able to produce, but because the song had a simple melody it wasn't as horrifying as it could have been. Noah put his heart into those tentative first notes, sustaining them as best as he could.

Her intake of breath was sharp. Before she could turn her astonished gaze upon him, he buried his fingers in her hair, a silent plea for her to keep her head on his chest. He hoped she'd understand that he couldn't do this while she watched — at least, not yet. But he could be brave as long as she remained in his arms.

She was quiet and just kept swaying with him.

Although it had been so long, and it was painful to hear himself, Noah didn't stop. He sang every note of the song, even the higher ones that he couldn't quite reach as well anymore. Somehow, as they held each other, his condo living room became a church, and Susannah became his religion. He wanted to pay homage to her in the only way he knew how. As rough and untrained as his voice now sounded, he prayed she'd still find some beauty in it.

When the piece was over, they didn't let go of each other. However, Noah took a breath for courage and removed his hand from her head.

When she looked up at him, there were tears in her eyes. These tears, however, didn't upset him. They gave him hope.

"Susannah," he whispered. "I love you."

"Noah…"

"It's okay. You don't have to say anything," he babbled, more nervous than he'd ever been. "I know we're probably not in the same place. I just needed you to know."

"Noah," she said a bit more forcefully, laughing through her tears. "I love you too."

His chest expanded with happiness. "Really?"

She slid her hands up to cup both his cheeks and kissed his nose, then his mouth. "Absolutely." Then she kissed him again, but this time her pretty lips parted and their tongues met.

Noah closed his eyes, awash in sensation, and angled his head so he could claim every sweet corner of her mouth.

Susannah Darke loved him.

Him. Noah Bellamy, of the battered voice and the bruised heart. She'd seen past his wounds, finding something precious underneath. He might never fully understand exactly what she saw in him, but there was no way in hell he would ever take it for granted.

With that in mind, he went over to his sound system. He turned off the music and turned out the lights. Then Noah, his heart much less bruised than it had been in recent days, scooped Susannah into his arms and carried her into his bedroom.

Chapter Twenty-Two

Ambrose & Co., one of Canada's first publishers of classical music, shuttered its offices last month. Founded by William Ambrose in 1874, the company made its name by publishing the parlor music and art songs that were so popular during the Victorian era. Later, they expanded their repertoire and began to publish and promote works by Canadian composers.

Although he had a head for business, William Ambrose was no musician. Despite possessing a tremendous appreciation for it, his talents did not extend in that direction. His son Terence, on the other hand, was a gifted pianist from a young age. An examination of William's accounts reveals numerous payments made to piano teachers, but not all of them were for his son. William struggled to learn the piano for much of his adult life. He later admitted he did not understand "how to make the notes travel from the brain to the fingers," and he remained disappointed in himself.

He did, however, find great success in publishing the works of others, but there is a shadow that looms over his legacy.

Ambrose, a harsh disciplinarian at the best of times, also suffered from alcoholism, a condition that worsened after the premature death of his wife Matilda. She died giving birth to their only child, Terence.

According to family letters, Terence was the one to feel the brunt of his father's temper on a regular basis. William never forgave his son for Matilda's demise. Terence claimed that, when William was in his cups, he would openly blame him for "killing his mother."

He also pressured the boy to perform, something Terence never enjoyed. When Terence defied him, William would punish him by locking him in a closet. He made the boy practice piano for hours at a time, keeping him from his friends. Terence later admitted he'd grown up friendless as a result.

Despite this clear pattern of abuse, Terence did eventually excel. He procured a teaching position at the famed Toronto Conservatory of Music. He is regarded as having been a good teacher. Dr. Victor Asch, the conservatory's director, called him "exceptionally gifted and compassionate. He is a gentle soul who inspires his students to climb to great heights."

As Terence settled in at the Toronto Conservatory of Music, he distanced himself from his resentful father and moved past his troubling youth. Sadly, Terence would not reach his thirty-third birthday, dying of fever in 1895.

His father did not attend the funeral.

Victor Asch went to see William Ambrose several months later, in the hopes of soliciting his help to establish a scholarship in Terence's name. Ambrose turned him away.

According to family, he never spoke his son's name out loud again.

William Ambrose died a year later, almost twelve months from the day that his son had died.

Talent or Tyrant: The troubling legacy of William Ambrose by Frank Fisher.
Forte Magazine, June 1975

Susannah returned alone to the Asch Institute the next night. She walked up the front stairs with the whir of the Toronto traffic at her back, and only the light from her cell phone before her. She keyed in the code Noah had given her and unlocked the front door.

Inside, the school was robed in darkness, but hints of light pooled on the floor underneath some of the windows. With the festive atmosphere of the gala still fresh in her memory, the hallways now seemed cold and empty in comparison. The changing weather didn't help. The fall shadows had lengthened, a harbinger of the upcoming winter.

At the same time, Susannah knew the vibe had nothing to do with the time of year.

It was the Asch. The old building was expecting her.

She should have been afraid to come here at night on her own. It made perfect sense to be afraid under the circumstances, but she wasn't. After all, this school had once been her happy place and she was determined to reclaim it.

William Ambrose had oppressed it for far too long.

There was no longer any question in Susannah's mind, or anyone else's, that the dark entity was William Ambrose. Her most recent research seemed to confirm it. More importantly, her gut told her so. She'd made a conscious decision to trust it.

They couldn't allow William to continue exerting such a negative influence on the student body. They needed to make him understand the impact of his actions. Wanting to test her abilities as an empath, Susannah had volunteered herself for the task. She would try to appeal to him on an emotional level and hopefully discover whether or not any humanity still dwelled in the intimidating shadow man from her memories.

She wasn't completely unarmed for the occasion. Around her neck sat Adelaide's necklace, the one with the heart pendant from their grandmother. When Adelaide had taken it off, Susannah had been shocked.

"Are you sure?" she'd asked Addy. "You never take Gran's necklace off."

"I can live without it. It's not as if the pendant gives me special powers. It just reminds me of her, and of those who came before us. It tells me I'm not alone and reminds me of my own strength. You're strong too. Don't ever forget that."

Susannah touched the pendant now, as she walked through the dark hallways toward the staircase that led to the theater.

She'd wanted a reckoning. Tonight, she would get it. She felt it in every bone and sinew. Although she'd entered the Asch Institute alone, she wasn't the only one walking through the corridors. The spirits watched. She might not be able to see them like Adelaide and Edwina could, but as she opened her heart, she sensed them.

As she descended the stairs toward the theater, everything seemed darker and closer. The light couldn't creep into the basement the way it did upstairs. A bit of perspiration beaded on Susannah's upper lip. The temptation to turn back was strong, but she avoided it. After all, she had another secret weapon with her.

Noah's love.

Since they'd both admitted their feelings last night, she'd been floating on a cloud. She'd never been so happy. In fact, she wasn't sure she'd ever dared to be so happy. It brightened her soul and that light now illuminated the corridors of the Asch, perhaps not literally, but in a way that was just as potent.

Noah loved her and she loved him.

Her body hadn't been dashed on the rocks after all.

That was why Susannah was able to enter the blackened theater. It was what propelled her legs to carry her up the stairs to the stage. It helped her sit at the beautiful grand piano and lift the fallboard to expose the keys. She set her cell phone down on the bench and turned on the LED piano light.

Noah had arranged some sheet music for her in advance. She glanced at it now and her heart swelled.

Beethoven's Piano Sonata No. 14 in C-sharp Minor, Opus 27, No. 2. The Moonlight Sonata.

The last time she'd tickled the ivories she'd been ten years old. She hadn't touched a piano since then, had barely allowed herself to think about one. The last time she had played, she'd been learning the Moonlight Sonata for the purposes of an exam. In fact, she'd been on the verge of memorizing it and she'd been so proud.

Would her hands still remember how to play?

She touched the sheet music. It was so clean and pristine, so unlike the copy she'd used as a kid. She could just about visualize her old sheet music — torn at the edges from so much handling, with a circular brown stain in the upper corner from that time she'd set a wet can of cola on it.

C-sharp minor. It had been her favorite key because of the haunting piece. Even without caressing the keys, she could hear the sonorous first note, a breathtaking G-sharp.

Susannah bit her bottom lip to keep it from trembling and called into the empty theater. "Terence Ambrose, this is for you."

She placed her hands on the keys. Then, after so many years away from the instrument she cherished, Susannah began to play. The first few chords were a bit shaky, but they still brought tears to her eyes because they felt like coming home. She'd worked so hard on this piece. Her teacher Ms. Hickey had praised her efforts, saying her playing was so mature for her years. Susannah had heard her talking to her mom after one lesson, and she'd said, "That girl plays like she's been on this earth before. I don't know any other ten-year-old kids who perform with such sensitivity and nuance."

Susannah hadn't understood what nuance meant. All she'd known then was that she lit up any time she touched the piano.

With each new chord, each exquisite hint of dissonance, tears fell over her cheeks. As the music reached one of its dramatic crescendos, a sob broke from her chest. No torture had ever been so sweet.

Just then, the energy shifted in the great room. She couldn't see anything unusual, but it made her uneasy. It was as if the theater itself had grown a pair of eyes.

Something bad was here. The room practically pulsed with its vile breath.

All at once, the sheet music flew off the piano, floating to the ground the same way it had when Ava had been singing.

But Susannah didn't stop playing. Her muscle memory had taken over and she wasn't intimidated by William's tricks.

She wasn't afraid of him anymore. Now that she understood his story, she knew he was just a bully, and she'd faced worse bullies in her time. Possessed by a need to bring all of this to an end, she finished her piece, allowing the final chords to die out before removing her hands from the keys.

William might not know it yet, but this was his last night at the Asch Institute of Opera. She wouldn't leave until he was gone.

She braced herself for the ominous shadow figure, but what she heard instead was a gentle voice. "That was beautiful, my dear one. Thank you."

Icy air hit her cheek, but not once did she feel the urge to run. There was no need to run from Terence.

It was only as his gauzy figure materialized at her side, capped off by the kind eyes and the freckled face from the old photo, that Susannah truly understood he'd never meant to scare her all those years ago. He'd simply longed for a connection with the students that he'd loved. Those attempts at connection had been unsettling, but the frightening phenomena had come from another source.

Her heart beating with the intensity of a drumroll, she turned to face him. He had a quiet sort of handsomeness, with soft features and a boyish smile, and she could see why Melba had been attracted to him.

"You did well, Susannah. I'm proud of you."

"Not bad, considering I haven't played in over twenty years, huh?"

"Has it been that long? I have no sense of time." There was a tightness about his mouth. "I'm sorry to hear you gave it up."

"You understand why, don't you?"

He focused his troubled gaze on the keyboard. "Play something else for me, my dear."

"Terence, no. I need you to listen to me. We need to talk about what's happening here at the school. I know you loved your job at the conservatory, but the students today are traumatized. I don't think you would want that. Ava can't even come to class right now."

His shoulders drooped as he let out an enormous sigh. "Ava."

"She's afraid."

"I only wanted to help her."

"I know, but your father tried to hurt her. He locked her in a basement room, just like he locked you in that closet. He isolated her from her friends, as he did to you. And he told her she'd end up like Luca, a young man who died here."

The spirit man dug his hands through his hair until it stuck up in places. A low growl began deep in his chest. As he turned and began to pace, it made the stage floor shake under her feet. "Nothing I did was ever good enough for him. He hated me for my very existence. At the same time, he wanted me to become another Mozart, another Beethoven. But all I ever wanted to do was to teach. I got such joy out of seeing my students succeed. That bitter, twisted old man was never happy, and he'll never leave me alone." Terence's features began to waffle and fade.

"Please," Susannah implored. "Don't go. I need you to understand he has no power over you."

He shook his head, despondent. "I'll be stuck here with him forever."

"No. You are not stuck, Terence. You can go anytime you want."

"But I have to stay for the students…"

"They'll be fine, I promise. You were a great teacher and now you can rest in peace."

"I don't know." He backed away.

Susannah touched Addy's pendant, silently praying for a way to show him he wasn't bound to the Asch. Then it hit her. "If you go to the light, Melba will go with you. I'm sure of it."

"Melba?"

"She's here, Terence. She's always been here, walking these halls since the day she died, trying to find a way back to you. I know you loved her. Wouldn't you like to see her again? Wouldn't you like to give her peace?"

When he sighed, the melancholy noise filled the theater. "Melba. She was the greatest thing in my life."

Susannah closed her eyes for a quick second, calling out to Melba. *Terence needs you. Please come.* When she opened her eyes again, she was relieved to see him still there.

Once again, the energy in the room shifted. There was a new heaviness that signaled another presence. Susannah gripped the piano bench, hoping Terence's dad wouldn't make an appearance instead. Not yet, anyway.

However, there was nothing eerie about this energy. In fact, it was accompanied by the scent of roses.

Yes! Susannah wasn't sure if this experiment with the spirit world would cure the school of all its ills, but if she could help Terence and Melba finally reunite, she'd still consider it a win.

Melba appeared on the stage and her wistful gaze landed on Terence. She was less diaphanous than the last time Susannah saw her. This time, Susannah could make out the weave of her gray jacket and the finer threads in the lace at her throat. There was a slight flush to her cheeks and Susannah could hear each one of her unsteady breaths. Perhaps Terence's appearance was giving her strength.

"My love," she said. She floated toward Terence and gripped his hands. "How you've suffered."

"Melba?" Terence bit back a sob. "You're here? How is it possible? I never saw you, never felt you around me."

"I've always been here, my darling, but he kept you from me."

He hung his head. "I'm so sorry. I wouldn't have wanted this existence for you."

She offered him a smile. "It doesn't matter anymore. We're together now."

They embraced. When they moved apart, Terence turned to Susannah. "If we leave, he'll still be here."

"I know, but we'll be ready for him."

"I know that, in his heart, he didn't mean to hurt me. It was just always easier for him to express anger than love."

"I promise that if we can help him, we will," Susannah said.

Melba laid a hand on Susannah's shoulder, sending shivers up and down her arm. "Tell Noah I'm proud of him. He's good for this school. I want him to always remember that."

Susannah nodded. "I'll tell him."

Melba reached for Terence's hand and they began to fade. "You'll help Dr. Asch too?"

"I swear it."

"Thank you," she replied. On a final waft of rose, they disappeared.

For a moment, all was still in the theater. And yet, Susannah knew her task wasn't done. However, for this next part, she would have help.

Even still, when the creaky footsteps sounded up on the catwalk, fear gripped her body like a titan's hand squeezing her ribs.

William Ambrose appeared as the shadow figure, his eyes blazing. When he spoke, it shook the rafters. "You took my son from me."

Susannah stared him down. "Don't you dare pin this on me. You pushed him away."

The shadow alighted, floating off the catwalk toward the stage, landing behind Susannah.

She whipped around on the piano bench and stood to face him. Nausea hit her, more tangible than a slap in the face, but she held her ground.

Ambrose emerged from the shadows that robed him, materializing as the sour man from the old photo. As his form became more substantial, he aimed his vile energy at Susannah. Once again, he tried to wear her down, doing his best to make her feel small and insignificant.

However, she wasn't the little girl in the pigtails anymore.

"You're a bully, William, and I'm not afraid of bullies. You demean others because it makes you feel strong, but I know your truth. You're weak, and you always have been. Only a weak man would hit his son."

Ambrose moved closer to her, his lip curled, emanating nothing less than antipathy.

"You don't belong here. There's nothing for you at the Asch Institute and it's time for you to leave. You're dead, do you hear me? You're dead and you need to go. Even Terence has left. You're all by yourself now."

He angled his head, mocking her. "You're all by yourself as well. You have no power, Susannah Darke, and you can't make me leave."

Susannah clenched her fists at her sides, grappling with a fresh wave of hostility. "That's the thing, William. I'm not actually alone."

From the wings of the stage, Noah, Adelaide, Edwina and Blake emerged. They rushed forward, holding hands, encircling Ambrose. Noah grabbed Susannah's hand, bringing her into the circle, and Blake took her other hand.

With Ambrose closed in, Adelaide spoke. "William Ambrose, you no longer belong on this plane. You are no longer welcome at this school. It is time for you to move on from this place."

"No!" The spirit man covered his ears and shouted. "Stop it! I won't go."

Adelaide repeated her demand, but Ambrose fell to his knees and dug his fingernails into the wooden stage floor. As he clawed the wood, marks appeared.

"Dude, you're not making this any easier for yourself. Just go," Edwina said.

Ambrose continued to howl and protest.

Susannah was shocked. They'd dealt with stubborn spirits, but this guy took the cake. He'd destroy the theater before they got him out of there.

They needed to try another tactic.

As much as Susannah hated the idea of opening herself up to Ambrose's emotions, she allowed them to wash over her in a foul wave. She had the urge to dry heave as she tasted his anger and his resentment. But there was something else there too, something he'd never allowed anyone to see in life. "He's afraid to go. He's terrified of what awaits him."

Ambrose stopped squirming and met her gaze.

Adelaide sighed. "It isn't Judgment Day that awaits you, William, but you will need to face your son again. You'll need to take responsibility for how you treated him in life."

"I was only trying to guide him. The boy had talent, real talent! I would have done anything to possess what he had, but he wasted it."

"Terence didn't want to perform. He loved teaching," said Susannah. "He loved this school, but you turned it into a place of fear."

Ambrose hung his head in his hands. "My son."

Adelaide began again. "William Ambrose, I demand that you leave this school and the lands around it. You will no longer make any attempts to communicate with anyone connected to this place. I hereby release you from this plane, in the name of all that is goodness and light, and I pray that you will find peace and understanding in the realm beyond. Go now."

Ambrose struggled for a moment, but he quickly started to fade. As soon as that transition began, he looked into the distance, toward something they couldn't see, and gasped. All at once, he grew calm, his face filled with wonder. "I see now, and I'm sorry. I'm sorry, Terence!"

William Ambrose, and every ounce of bad energy that he'd brought to the school, disappeared. Susannah felt it, even without hearing Adelaide say the words yet. Her nausea lifted, her head felt light and her heart was glad.

Suddenly, there was a tapping upstage, the distinct and excited tap of dress shoes and a cane.

They all turned. Even though nothing was visible, the jaunty noise moved into the wings then faded away.

Adelaide smiled. "That was Dr. Asch. He's gone now too."

They broke their circle. Noah hugged Susannah. "You were awesome." He reached under the back of her shirt and gently pulled off the microphone that

Edwina had taped to her earlier. They'd set up a small command center in one of the rooms just inside the stage door and had been listening to the entire exchange in case anything went wrong.

As Susannah had stated, she really wasn't alone at all.

Noah shook his head. "Your playing was incredible, Susannah."

"Maybe you could set me up with one of the teachers here at the school," she said. "I think I'd like to start taking lessons again."

"I can arrange that." He smiled and she once again wondered how one smile could make everything right with the world.

"Come on," said Edwina. "We need to sage the school, getting into every room and closet. Considering the size of this place, we'll be here for the next hour."

Blake elbowed Noah. "Oh, and you'll need to get someone to sand this floor. Those claw marks are fucking creepy. We don't need any reminders of what went on tonight."

As they gathered up their things, Susannah glanced around the theater. She felt good about clearing the school of the spirit people, but something was still off.

When she caught Noah standing by himself, sighing, she realized what it was.

They'd heard from all the spirit people except for Luca.

Susannah's brief moment of triumph turned into one of sorrow.

She'd wanted to give Noah closure, but she'd failed.

Chapter Twenty-Three

"I'd like to thank everyone who's taken some time to join us today." Noah winced as microphone feedback screeched through the Asch foyer. The student who was helping him with the mic rushed over and adjusted its position. "Thanks, Jude. See? No ghosts, just the sound system."

He appreciated the fact that a few students chuckled at that one. Sometimes his jokes elicited nothing more than tumbleweed. As Zaid Basri often reminded him, "It's because you tell dad jokes."

Feeble attempt at humor notwithstanding, he was happy to see so many staff and students crammed into the foyer. Of course, it wasn't every day that they commemorated someone at the Asch Institute. However, in this case, it was long overdue, and it was the reason Noah now stood just inside the entrance, right where Melba Flanagan used to have her desk.

It had been about a week since the spirits of the Asch had gone into the light. Since then, everything had been relatively quiet. The Darke sisters had returned a couple of times since then, so Adelaide could take the temperature of the place. According to her, the ghosts had indeed moved on. Noah was relieved to hear it. In truth, the entire building had a lighter feel about it. Students didn't seem to be looking over their shoulders anymore. No one had been locked in the practice rooms. The hallway conversations tended to be about assignments, performances and who was hooking up with whom. The Asch was a regular school again.

Susannah and her sisters were in attendance for today's event. Susannah smiled at Noah from her spot near the stairs, which gave him the courage to go off-script. He folded up the paper on which he'd written out some notes and tucked it into his jacket pocket.

"We hear a lot about Dr. Victor Asch around here, and rightly so. He was the one who got this place going, and look where we are today. When our students graduate, they are prepared to take on roles with any opera company in the world. But Dr. Asch wasn't alone in making this school the exceptional center for learning that it is. He had a great deal of help, and most of it came from one woman."

Noah moved closer to the wall, where a large plaque had been hung, one that was currently covered in a black cloth. He tugged at the cloth, unveiling the tribute to Melba Flanagan. It was a nice piece, if he said so himself. Her photo was embedded in the plaque, and it bore her name, her title and her dates at the bottom.

"Not everyone here will have heard of Melba Flanagan," he continued, "but her influence is still felt today. Melba handled everything from registrations to exams to running the library. I can't even conceive of how much work that would have been, even at a time when the school was much smaller. Melba worked here for an unimaginable fifty years. She was a witness to some tremendous changes and she navigated the school through them. In addition, she helped Dr. Asch through the most difficult period of his life, all while dealing with her own challenges and heartaches."

He glanced over at Susannah, his heart full. "Thanks to some invaluable help from investigators Susannah, Edwina and Adelaide Darke, I've recently had the opportunity to learn a lot more about Melba. I would encourage you all to read her memoirs and to learn more about this amazing woman. We keep a copy right here in our library. And the next time you enter the Asch Institute and give Dr. Asch's knuckles a swipe, wave hello to Melba as well." Noah turned to the plaque. "Wherever you are, Melba, I hope you can see this. Thank you."

When the applause broke out, it took Noah aback, but in a good way. Even better was seeing several students go up to the plaque to read its details.

Susannah and her sisters joined him. She slipped her arm through his and gave him a kiss on the cheek. "That was lovely and I'm sure Melba saw."

"Thanks, Sunshine."

Noah, Susannah and her sisters stopped to talk to a few of the students and staff. Word about the investigation had naturally spread within the school community and people had questions. He couldn't say he blamed them.

As the Darkes chatted, Noah wandered down the hallway toward his office. He stopped in front of Luca's memorial photo and looked upon his old friend's face.

His dreams had stopped the night they cleared the school of its ghosts. It was a good development, but Noah was still uneasy. He'd really been hoping he might hear from Luca one last time, just so he'd know he was okay.

But, unlike the other spirits, Luca had been silent.

In a way, that bothered Noah even more than the nightmares. At least the dreams had been a method of communication. The hush that had fallen over his sleeps had left him with even more questions.

Was Luca still bound to this place? And if so, was it Noah's fault?

Was he still here because Noah hadn't done enough to save his friend?

He had a feeling that question would bother him for the rest of his life.

It had been on his mind since the evening at the theater. As a result, Noah just couldn't seem to perk up. The cloud that used to hang over the Asch Institute had shifted, settling over him instead. His worries burned in his chest. They made his food taste bad and soured his pleasures.

Even his moments with Susannah had been impacted. He wanted so much to have her in his life, to be planning a future with her, but some days he could barely see past the fog in his brain.

He'd confessed his concerns to Susannah one morning upon waking. "I need to know Luca's okay. I was hoping for a sign."

She'd run her fingers through his hair. "Unfortunately, we don't always get them."

Maybe Noah just needed to move on and trust his friend wasn't trapped in some strange dimension.

Someone tapped him on the shoulder. "Dean Bellamy?"

He turned. "Ava. How's it going?"

She grinned, her eyes no longer haunted. "I'm great."

Ava had returned to school a few days earlier. She'd been nervous that first day back, but Noah had checked in on her several times. Susannah had remained in touch with her as well, just in case. It turned out their vigilance had been unwarranted. Ava had said that the moment she'd walked through the front doors, she'd known everything had changed for the better.

"Everything still quiet?" asked Noah.

"Yeah. It's been awesome. I haven't heard any voices. I don't feel like I'm being watched anymore. I've been hanging out with my friends a lot more and I just feel normal again."

"I'm happy to hear it. I mean that."

"I wanted to thank you again for everything you did. You and Susannah…you gave me my life back. I wish I could repay you."

"Ava, that's not necessary. Just keep doing the things you love. That's all I need from you."

"I will. Thanks, Dean Bellamy. See you in class on Tuesday?"

"You bet."

She hurried down the hall, where a group of her friends was gathered. Their happy chatter trailing behind them, they exited the building.

Noah turned back to Luca's photo. "I know you probably can't talk to me like Ava did, but just give me one little clue. Anything. Please."

But Luca, unchanged by age and circumstance, just kept smiling.

* * * *

Several nights later, Noah awoke in a panic, his body drenched in sweat.

He must have shouted, because Susannah stirred next to him. She switched on the bedside table light and sat up, caressing his shoulder. "Hey, are you okay? You cried out."

She looked adorable wearing one of his T-shirts, her long hair all over the place, but he hated that he'd caused her concern. "Must have been a dream. I'm sorry."

"Want to talk about it?"

"It's three in the morning."

"I don't mind."

"I just..." All of a sudden, Noah couldn't even remember what the dream was about, just that it had shaken him up.

Bits and pieces started to fall back into place. He'd been at a rock concert at an outdoor stadium. *Yeah, that's it. The Sam Roberts Band, back in the day.* The music had been awesome and the place had been packed. Noah had gone to the concession stand to buy a drink, but when he'd returned, he couldn't find his seat so he started wandering up and down the aisles. The more he'd looked, the more his pulse had raced in confusion. He'd been there with someone. Had they left without him?

But then a friendly voice had called out. *"Hey, buddy. I'm right over here. I wouldn't leave you."*

Noah had known that voice, yet when he'd turned around, the stadium had gone dark. The band had disappeared and the music had faded away.

Noah had woken up feeling sick and disappointed.

"I think the dream was about Luca."

Susannah's face crumpled. "Not the nightmare again."

"No." He was quick to assure her. "At least, not the same kind of nightmare, anyway. He was *there*, Susannah, in my dream. I could hear his voice, but when I turned around, he was gone."

She rubbed his back, caressing his muscles. "I'm so sorry I wasn't able to get you the closure you needed."

"I don't know. I think he might have been trying to give me that closure himself. He wasn't screaming, like in the other dreams. He sounded, well, like he was having fun. I think that must have been why I cried out. Once I realized it was him, I didn't want the dream to end."

"Of course." Susannah sighed. "Try to rest now." She reached for the light.

"I'm just going to grab a drink of water." He leaned over and kissed her. "I'm sorry I woke you. Go to bed. I'll be right back."

She nodded and lay back down.

Clad only in his boxer briefs, Noah threw back the covers and padded out of the bedroom toward the kitchen. He didn't turn on the overhead light, just the smaller light above his kitchen sink. He grabbed a glass from the cupboard, filled it with cold water and swallowed it back in a few big gulps.

"You could have thrown a robe on or something, dude. Those briefs don't leave much to the imagination."

Noah spun around, straining his eyes in the semi-darkness, and almost dropped his glass.

A slight figure emerged from the shadows, his curls falling into his smiling eyes. "Hi, Noah."

"Luca? Is it really you?"

"In the flesh." He rolled his eyes. "You know what I mean."

All the grief and guilt that he'd carried for twenty years burst from him in a chest-shaking sob. "I'm sorry."

"No, no, no." Luca moved closer. "You need to stop that. I'm not here for your apology."

"But…"

"Noah, listen to me. You couldn't have done anything to help me that day. Okay? I need you to believe that. It was just my time to go. I really did have a bad heart. I've been trying to tell you for a while now, but the situation at the school was making it hard to communicate. That Ambrose douchebag really messed with my flow."

In spite of himself, Noah laughed. "Then you're okay?"

Luca smiled. "I swear to you, I'm more than okay."

Susannah crept into the room, wearing his shirt and a pair of his PJ pants. "Noah? Who's with you?" When she saw Luca, her mouth fell open and her eyes grew as round as saucers. "Ohmigod."

Luca's smile widened. "Looks like you're okay too, Noah." He winked at Susannah.

Noah was laughing like a madman now. "You are *not* flirting with my girlfriend, dude."

Suddenly serious, Luca approached him. "Remember what I said. No more blame, no more wondering."

"Okay."

"And by the way, I've been listening in on some of your internal dialogue over the years. Noah, you have never been a failure. You're doing what you're supposed to be doing. You were always a good friend to me and you're a hero to the students at the Asch, and I never want to hear you feeling sorry for yourself again. You got that?"

"I got it. Thank you." He reached for Susannah's hand, wiping his tears with the other hand. "I miss you, Luca."

"I miss you too, but we'll see each other again."

Noah pointed at Luca's Sam Roberts Band T-shirt. "Maybe you could get yourself a new shirt by then?"

Luca gasped and held out the edges of the shirt. "And get rid of this baby? Never. Now, go get some rest, old man. I need to pay Blake a little visit too." With another cheeky grin, Luca disappeared.

Susannah faced him, her own face wet with tears. "Closure?"

Noah nodded and brought her into his arms. "Yeah."

Chapter Twenty-Four

Susannah knocked on Noah's office door and popped her head around the corner. "Can I come in?" She held up a bag from his favorite lunch place. "I bring sustenance."

He smiled and waved her in, his eyes bright with hunger. "You're the best, you know that?"

She set the bag on his desk and opened it. "So you keep telling me."

"I'm not going to stop, you know."

"You have my permission to continue." She pulled a wrapped submarine sandwich from out of the bag and presented it to him. "Turkey and avocado club for you. Egg salad for me."

"Thanks, Susannah. It's been so busy I barely have time to breathe." He bit off a large piece of sandwich, chewing and groaning. "This is so good."

"Good. And you just keep on breathing, okay? I need you to stick around for a while."

They ate while catching up on each other's mornings. The Asch Institute was getting ready to put on its latest operatic production and Noah had taken the helm as the director, so he'd been pulling a lot of late nights over the past few weeks. Susannah had understood. If anything, she'd had some time during those evenings to delve back into her piano lessons. Noah had helped her connect with one of the teachers at his school, and Susannah was having a blast rediscovering her love for music. On evenings when she didn't have a lesson, she usually joined Noah at the Asch so she could watch the opera rehearsals. Ava Choi was performing the role of Iphigénie in *Iphigénie en Tauride* by Gluck, and she was doing an amazing job. It was so good to hear her enjoying herself while singing again.

Susannah's relationship with Noah was thriving, and they were both in much better places mentally. No longer burdened by guilt, he'd really begun to flourish and was taking the Asch in exciting new directions. Susannah's work was keeping her busy too. Knee-deep in research once again — her favorite state of being — she was in the midst of outlining a book of ghost stories from Canadian history. It was a daunting prospect, but she was eager to see how it would all unfold.

Thanks to a lot of invaluable help from Edwina and Adelaide, she'd also learned a lot more on how to manage her emotions as an empath. She was no longer overwhelmed by the feelings that coursed through her. If anything, she'd come to regard her sensitivity as a sort of early warning system.

Adelaide had been really helpful in giving her pointers on how to deal with her empathy without getting drained, and she'd been reading a lot of articles that echoed those suggestions. Susannah had been practicing mindfulness lately, as well as a whole lot of self-compassion. She'd been doing her best to incorporate some outdoor time into her schedule, even just a ten-minute walk here and there, because it helped her relax. She'd also been discussing her challenges with her therapist, learning how to set boundaries that worked for her but still enabled her to have a full social life.

She still had walls, and probably always would, but she'd welcomed Noah through the gate and had shown him around. It turned out he liked hanging around with her inside her borders.

There was a knock on his office door. He called out for the person to enter.

Zaid Basri stood just outside Noah's office, hopping with excitement. "Hey, Dean Bellamy." He looked back and forth between him and Susannah. "Sorry to disturb you."

"It's fine. What's up?"

Zaid took two steps toward them. "I just had to let you know. The National Arts Center called. They want me to sing for them in September."

Noah dropped his sandwich and bounded out of his chair. He pumped Zaid's hand. "Ah, congrats, Zaid! That's the best news I've heard in a long time."

"It's a small part. I'll be in the chorus for now, but it's a paying opera gig."

"I'm really happy for you. You've worked hard for this and it's well deserved. And the chorus is nothing to sneer at. You watch. Before long, you'll have your pick of the roles."

Susannah clapped her hands together. "Congratulations, Zaid. I think this calls for a road trip in September. Right, Noah?"

"You couldn't keep us away."

"Thanks for everything. I can't believe my time at the Asch is almost done," said Zaid. "It's been so quiet lately. Do you ever miss the ghosts?"

"No," said Noah and Susannah in unison. They laughed.

Zaid chuckled. "Yeah, I guess you're right. Anyway, I have to get to class, but I wanted you to be the first to know. If it hadn't been for your support, Dean Bellamy, I wouldn't have even auditioned."

"Congratulations." Noah fist-bumped Zaid. "I'm proud of you."

Zaid thanked him again and exited the office.

Susannah stood and walked around the desk to embrace Noah. "Luca and Melba both had it right, you know. This school is lucky to have you." She dropped a kiss on his mouth. "And so am I."

"I'm the lucky one, Susannah Sunshine. I love you more than anything."

"I love you too."

They kissed and Susannah knew without a doubt that she had found her happy place again. Only this time, it wasn't encapsulated by the music-filled corridors of the Asch Institute. She hadn't found it among the keys of her new piano.

It was here, with the man she loved.

And she knew she would have it for the rest of her life.

Want to see more from this author?
Here's a taster for you to enjoy!

Darke Paranormal Investigations: Darke Homecoming
Rosanna Leo

Coming Winter 2023

Excerpt

It wasn't unusual for Adelaide Darke to encounter handsome men in the cemetery, but nine times out of ten, those men were dead.

This handsome dude, on the other hand, was definitely alive.

She sat on her favorite bench in the Necropolis, the one that perched in the shade of an overgrown willow tree, and tried not to appear too obvious as she ogled him. She held up her book, a dog-eared and worn copy of a behind-the-scenes guide to the making of *Star Wars*, and discreetly cast her eye toward him.

The man led a small group of people toward one of the graves, about twenty feet away from where Adelaide sat. He was tall, white and slim, with angular features, ones that were somewhat softened by his tousled sandy hair. It was a warm summer's day and he was dressed for the weather in shorts, sneakers and a gray T-shirt. Adelaide peered at the familiar logo on the shirt, an illustration of Edward Gorey's *The Gashlycrumb Tinies*.

She had the same shirt. They clearly shared the same dark sense of humor.

The view just got better and better.

The man gestured toward the grave, a red stone obelisk, and spoke to the people in his group. "This is the monument for Thornton and Lucie Blackburn. Enslaved in Kentucky, the Blackburns escaped in 1831 and headed to Michigan. They lived there until being recaptured and arrested two years later. While they were in prison, visitors were allowed, and Lucie was able to escape after switching her clothes with those of another woman. Thornton, on the other hand, was shackled and heavily guarded. The day before he was set to be returned to Kentucky, the Black community rose up in protest, an event now known as the Blackburn Riots. A crowd of about four hundred men stormed the jail and Thornton escaped. The couple reunited and settled in Toronto in 1834, and Thornton went to work at Osgoode Hall, which houses the law society and now a law school. Thornton was a waiter there, and in his travels, he realized that the city had need of a taxi service, so he ordered blueprints for a cab from Montreal and created one. By 1837, his taxi business was established. It was called 'The City' and consisted of a horse and carriage. The business grew over the years, giving the Blackburns resources to assist other enslaved people with their escapes. They remained active in the community and with anti-slavery activities, and helped to build Little Trinity Church. When Thornton died in 1890, his estate encompassed eighteen-thousand dollars and six properties in Toronto. Lucie passed away five years later. In 1985, the remains of their home were discovered under a local school. After an archaeological dig, a plaque was erected to commemorate this amazing couple. They were deemed 'Persons of National Historic Significance' in 1999." He gestured for the group to follow him. "Now, let's head over to the grave of Ned Hanlan, Canada's famed professional rower."

He must be the new tour guide at the Necropolis. The previous tour guide, Nancy, had told Adelaide someone would be replacing her.

Because Adelaide hung out at the cemetery a lot, probably more than her sisters thought was healthy, she'd gotten to know Nancy. When the guide had mentioned she was retiring, Adelaide had assumed her replacement would be...similar.

"Another old lady, you mean?"

"Ssh, Maria. Not now."

She must have said the words louder than she thought because the hot tour guide glanced in her direction, a curious expression on his face. He then led his group toward the Hanlan grave.

Great. Yet another person who thought she was a weirdo for talking to herself when she wasn't actually talking to herself.

Maria had been with Adelaide for as long as she could remember. Adelaide's recollection of her early years was remarkably vivid, including the first time Maria had materialized. Addy had been in her crib, happily gurgling away, when all of a sudden, a little girl had entered the room. She'd smiled at Addy and held out her hand, saying they would be best friends forever, that she would take care of her. Even at such a tender age, Adelaide had experienced a surreal calmness and a sense that everything was right.

They'd been inseparable ever since. Maria had guided her through tough situations and had helped her through her most difficult paranormal investigations. With her sisters, Edwina and Susannah, Adelaide ran Darke Paranormal Investigations, and they'd made a name for themselves by clearing their clients' homes and businesses of unwanted spirit people.

So, basically, she and Maria were a package deal. As much as she was at peace with her strange reality, she still couldn't help feeling like an outsider sometimes.

"He's attractive. Definitely has that 'I-was-a-goth-in-high-school' vibe," Maria teased. *"Just your type."*

Adelaide frowned and shoved her book back into her tote bag. She pulled out a green apple and angrily nibbled it.

"What? You know I'm right. Don't you have that exact same shirt?"

"Irrelevant," Adelaide mumbled behind her apple.

Curious about the new guide, she got up from the bench and followed his group discreetly, pretending to read a couple of the headstones. Of course, she didn't really need to read any of them to learn about the occupants of the graves. All she needed to do was close her eyes and concentrate on the person, or touch the monuments, and images would flood her brain.

It was a lot to take at times, but Adelaide had learned how to filter the information and the messages from the dead.

It didn't mean they didn't sneak up on her sometimes.

The tour guide hit a few of the other graves that Nancy had included on her tour. George Brown, a Father of Confederation. William Lyon Mackenzie, rebel and Toronto's first mayor. John Ross Robertson, historian and founder of the *Toronto Telegram*. Kay Christie, one of only two Canadian nurses to have been taken prisoner in World War II.

Every so often, the guide's gaze strayed toward Adelaide.

She hung back, conscious of the fact that she wasn't a paying customer. She didn't want him to think she was trying to get the tour for free.

He approached another grave and turned to it, a wistful expression on his face. "I think, of all the monuments here at the Necropolis, this one means the most to me. It's not flashy, like some of the others. It's not dedicated to a famous person. The headstone is simple, made out of a plain, gray marble. What fascinates me most is the inscription. 'Sarah Byrne, died Nov. 24, 1860. Aged 28 years. Sheltered and safe from sorrow.'"

He paused, never lifting his gaze from the headstone. "I've had the opportunity to do some research on Sarah Byrne. She was an Irish immigrant, one of the many who escaped Ireland during the Great Famine. Birth records tell us that Sarah and her husband Aiden had five children, all of whom died before the age of three. Although she didn't have to deal with famine here in Toronto, her life would not have been an easy one. Sarah's family lived in a worker's cottage at the north end of the cemetery, on Amelia Street. For people like the Byrnes, there was plenty of hardship and poverty, and residents of this area were constantly battling the cold, malnutrition and disease. During the time Sarah was alive, Irish Catholic immigrants lived on the edge of society and formed the greater part of the urban poor. My own ancestors came here on the 'coffin ships' from Ireland, ships that were so rife with overcrowding and sickness that many of those passengers never made it."

His voice cracked. "'Sheltered and safe from sorrow.' Only twenty-eight years old. I hope she is safe now. Well, we've got a couple more stops. Watch your step on the tree root as you follow me around the bend."

Moved by the guy's words and the emotion in his voice, Adelaide approached Sarah Byrne's burial place. She'd never really noticed this grave before on her previous cemetery jaunts. It looked like so many of the other headstones. Still, the poignant inscription definitely made one pause.

Out of habit, she touched the marble stone, curious to learn something more about the woman resting under it. A terrible wave of sadness washed over Adelaide, distressing her to her core. It was an overwhelming, clawing sensation and it dug its nails into her being.

"*Be careful*," warned Maria.

All at once, Adelaide's gaze was drawn to some movement at the far end of the cemetery. A spirit woman glided between the monuments, her face turned toward the tour group. Her Victorian garb was torn and dirty and her brown hair hung loose around her shoulders. Pale in the face, paler than anyone ever should be, her eyes were lit with a frightening sort of focus. She walked right in front of Adelaide without sparing her even a glance.

Strange. They always come right to me.

Instead, she headed toward the tour guide. All her attention was concentrated on him.

As the man continued his talk, leading his group to several other graves, the spirit woman followed. She snaked between the tourists, even passing through a few of them, her unsettling gaze never faltering. At one point, she extended a hand toward the guide, as if trying to latch onto him.

"That might be a problem," Maria said.

Immediately on edge, Adelaide put up her mental wards. Over the years, she'd learned how to protect herself from invasive spirits. In general, they swarmed her once they sensed her light, but she was able to erect a sort of barrier when the attention from the dead became a bit too much.

But this woman didn't even seem interested in her.

Without trying to connect directly with the dead woman, Adelaide tried to glean as much information as she could about her.

All she saw was harrowing anguish.

"Who is she, Maria?"

"She is darkness."

Maria could be cryptic sometimes.

The guy finished up his tour and thanked the others for joining him. A few people lingered to ask him questions, but most of them scattered quickly, obviously having had enough of cemeteries. Adelaide understood. Places like the Necropolis oozed creepy, gothic atmosphere.

As it happened, Adelaide was quite comfortable among creepy, gothic things. She understood dead people.

Living people, though? They were the ones who sometimes freaked her out.

"You have to tell him," Maria urged.

"And say what, exactly? 'A dead woman has taken a shine to you?'" Normally, Adelaide didn't have an issue with approaching strangers with messages from the dead, but this guy intimidated her with his tousled hair, chiselled jaw and superior taste in T-shirts.

"Tell him. If she lingers, he's not safe."

"Okay, okay. Just let me do it in my own way. No outbursts, please."

The guy said goodbye to the last tourist and headed over. His generous mouth curled with what looked like a shy sort of interest. He was completely oblivious to the gruesome specter following him.

Adelaide's face heated.

"Sorry to bother you," he said. "I couldn't help but notice that you seemed interested in the tour. We run them every second Saturday."

"Oh, I know. I knew Nancy, the previous guide."

"So, you're a…regular, here at the cemetery?"

And here we go. Cue judgment in three…two…

"Because I love it here," he interjected. "So much history in one place and it's really beautiful. You can see why Victorian people made coming to the Necropolis a bit of an event. They'd come to pay their respects to dead loved ones and then hang out for a few hours, having picnics and catching up with family."

Hmm. He really was a nerd, just like her. "Yeah, right. And, um, yes. I guess you could say I'm a regular." As a psychic medium, Adelaide needed lots of time in the fresh air, to break up the moments spent in the presence of the deceased. Aside from her work with Darke Paranormal Investigations, she was a professional medium and did a lot of readings. All that spiritual energy could be draining. "I live nearby and I come for a lot of walks here."

The whole time they spoke, the spirit woman hovered near him, drinking him in.

As much as it put Adelaide on guard, she could understand the fascination. Up close, he was definitely cute. He had amber brown eyes and the cheekbones of a soap opera actor. There was something lovely about the way he was smiling at her, but Adelaide knew that smile would disappear the moment he figured out she was a weird girl with an interest in dead things.

She was definitely interested in the dead thing clinging to him.

He held out his hand. "I'm Will Moran."

"Adelaide Darke." She waited a nanosecond before grasping his hand. Touching others could sometimes be problematic for people like her because it tended to release the hounds, so to speak. Sure enough, as she slid her fingers against his, a barrage of other spirits appeared behind him, wanting to pass on messages. Adelaide tuned in for a few seconds, in case anyone had pressing concerns, but they were mostly just trying to share their love. She released his hand and silently held his dead relatives at bay. She couldn't afford to become invested in his family backstory, not while he had another, darker entity attached.

The spirit woman gazed at him like she wanted to make him her next meal.

Somewhere in the background, Maria began to cough. That was her way of warning the living that shit was about to go down. Adelaide quickly covered her mouth and pretended to be the one coughing.

"You okay?" asked Will.

Begging Maria to settle down, Adelaide held up a finger. "Sorry about that. Seasonal allergies." Once she was convinced Maria would behave, she resumed the conversation. "So, are you a full-time tour guide?"

"No, that's just a fun side hustle." He pulled a face, obviously aware that not everyone would consider that fun. "I work for the City of Toronto Museums. We're opening a new museum right here in Cabbagetown, in one of the old worker's cottages on Amelia Street. I'm the lucky guy who gets to curate it."

"Amelia Street. Where Sarah Byrne lived."

"You really were listening." His voice rose in delight. "And yeah. Believe it or not, that's exactly where I'm working. The City was able to acquire the Byrne house when it went up for sale, so that'll be the museum's home. That's what first led me down the Sarah Byrne rabbit hole."

"Interesting." Adelaide tried once again to extract information from the dead woman, but she refused to engage. "It must be fascinating to be a curator."

He leaned in conspiratorially. "Well, I think so, but I'm kind of geeky that way. And how about you, Adelaide?"

Gosh, her name sounded nice in his mouth. *Hello*, she reminded herself. *There's a dead woman hanging off his every word, just as much as you are.* "Addy's fine."

"Addy, then." He grinned, then nibbled his bottom lip.

Is he flirting? I think he's flirting. It hadn't happened in a while, so she wasn't sure.

"*He's totally flirting*," added Maria.

"So, what do you do, Addy?"

She hesitated with how much to reveal. After a number of tragically bad dates recently, she'd grown hesitant talking about her career. Hell, her vocation.

On one date, when she'd mentioned she was a medium and paranormal investigator, the dude had accused her of flat-out lying. Another date had teased her to the point of annoyance. A third one had actually tried to argue that there was no such thing as ghosts. She had no time for those people. Besides, he'd shut up pretty quickly when Adelaide listed off by name all the spirits flitting around him.

Of course, it wasn't as if Will Moran had asked her out on a date. She'd likely never see him again. For that reason, she decided to put it all out there and amuse herself with his reaction. "I'm a psychic medium. I do readings and I investigate haunted locations."

Wait for it....

In a second, he'd avert his gaze. He'd make some limp excuse about needing to be somewhere, anywhere but there. He'd head for the freaking hills.

Only he didn't. Will angled his head and narrowed his eyes, without even a twitch in his smile. "And you called my work interesting?"

"I run a paranormal investigation group with my sisters. I literally see the dead all around us."

"Is that right?"

"Yup."

"Look, I don't want to take advantage, but do you mind me asking if you see any dead around me?"

For the first time since she'd appeared, the spirit woman looked directly at Adelaide, her pale eyes full of a cold awareness. She brought a finger to her lips and said, "*Sshhh.*" She then drifted away, disappearing within steps. Immediately, the atmosphere around them lightened.

Thank goodness.

"Nope, no dead around you." Adelaide cleared her throat. "Sorry. That's not quite accurate. When we shook hands, I saw your grandmother, an uncle and a great-grandfather. They all want you to know they're proud of you."

"Really?"

"Yeah. Their names were Nell, Jake and Francis."

Will's mouth popped open.

"You did ask. I'm just passing it on."

"No, that's fine. It's awesome, actually. Thank you."

Her own lips parted on a surprised breath. She was unaccustomed to responses that weren't dripping in scepticism and disdain.

"I was really close to my grandmother. You've made my day, Addy Darke." Will chuckled. It was a deep and heady sound, one that sent pleasant shivers up and down her arms.

She could grow addicted to that sound.

"You know, my colleagues insist that the museum site is haunted."

"I wouldn't be surprised. An old worker's cottage would be full of history. Have you had any experiences there?"

"There's a distinct...energy about the place. We'll sometimes arrive in the morning and discover that things have moved around. It's been interesting but it's never been bad enough to scare me away from my work." He checked his cell phone. "I have to leave for an appointment, but could I...call you some time?"

"Sure, but we have a bit of a waiting list for our services."

"Ah. I'm sure you do." He dragged a hand through his hair. "But I wasn't actually thinking of that. I was hoping maybe we could grab a coffee sometime because I think you're really interesting and I like talking to you." His voice rose at the end of the statement, as if he wasn't sure he should have admitted it.

"Oh." It didn't even occur to her that he was asking her out. *Dweeb.* "Sure. Coffee's cool."

"Great." Will asked her to put her number in his phone, then gave her his. "I'll give you a call in a couple of days."

Adelaide stared at the new number in her contacts, knowing she'd likely have to erase it soon. Will Moran would likely never call, not after he'd had a chance to reconsider it. "Looking forward to it."

"All right. Talk to you soon, Addy." He waved and walked away, looking once over his shoulder to give her another cheeky grin.

Her knees wobbled a little.

That smile should be outlawed.

Adelaide waited a few minutes, then followed Will out of the cemetery, passing under the decorative Gothic Revival entryway. When she got to the intersection of Winchester and Sumach Streets, she glanced out of habit toward the Witch House, the property that had so fascinated her as a child.

Just like all those years ago, the little blonde girl waved at her from the top window, unravaged by time.

Adelaide had passed the house often in her travels over the years, and had always seen the girl. Day or night, summer or winter, the child was always there and she always acknowledged her.

Her heart tugging, Adelaide waved back. Why was she stuck there? She would give just about anything to get inside that house so she could help the girl move on. She'd even knocked on the door a couple of times through the years, but the previous owners hadn't wanted to let a stranger in.

A sign in the front yard of the house caught her attention. She drew nearer. It was a real estate sign.

The Witch House was for sale, and there was an open house coming up soon.

Adelaide glanced toward the top window. The girl smiled, then faded away.

Her skin prickling in excitement, Addy pulled out her cell phone and messaged her sisters.

About the Author

Rosanna Leo writes contemporary and paranormal romance. She is the First Place Winner of the 2018 Northern Hearts Contest (Contemporary Romance) for *A Good Man.*

From Toronto, Canada, Rosanna occupies a house in the suburbs with her husband and their two sons, and spends most of her time being tolerated by their cat Sweetie. When not writing, Rosanna works for her local library, where she is busy laying the groundwork to become a library ghost one day.

Rosanna loves to hear from readers. You can find her contact information, website details and author profile page at https://www.totallybound.com

Home of Erotic Romance

Sign up for our newsletter and find out about all our romance book releases, eBook sales and promotions, sneak peeks and FREE romance books!